Community Sale near
Huguenot St.
New Paltz, NY 10/17/98

PENGUIN CRIME FICTION

SARATOGA HAUNTING

Stephen Dobyns is a professor of English at Syracuse University who also teaches in the MFA program at Warren Wilson College. He is the author of fifteen novels and eight volumes of poetry. *Saratoga Haunting* is his seventh Charlie Bradshaw mystery.

SARATOGA HAUNTING

Stephen Dobyns

PENGUIN BOOKS

PENGUIN BOOKS
Published by the Penguin Group
Penguin Books USA Inc., 375 Hudson Street, New York, New York 10014, U.S.A.
Penguin Books Ltd, 27 Wrights Lane, London W8 5TZ, England
Penguin Books Australia Ltd, Ringwood, Victoria, Australia
Penguin Books Canada Ltd, 10 Alcorn Avenue, Toronto, Ontario, Canada M4V 3B2
Penguin Books (N.Z.) Ltd, 182–190 Wairau Road, Auckland 10, New Zealand

Penguin Books Ltd, Registered Offices: Harmondsworth, Middlesex, England

First published in the United States of America by Viking Penguin,
a division of Penguin Books USA Inc., 1993
Published in Penguin Books 1994

1 3 5 7 9 10 8 6 4 2

PUBLISHER'S NOTE
This is a work of fiction. Names, characters, places, and incidents either are the product of the author's imagination or are used fictitiously, and any resemblance to actual persons, living or dead, events, or locales is entirely coincidental.

THE LIBRARY OF CONGRESS HAS CATALOGUED THE HARDCOVER AS FOLLOWS:
Dobyns, Stephen.
Saratoga haunting/Stephen Dobyns.
p. cm.
ISBN 0-670-84581-7 (hc.)
ISBN 0 14 01.7162 2 (pbk.)
I. Title.
PS3554.O2S255 1993
813′.54—dc20 92–50750

Printed in the United States of America
Set in Times Roman

For John Skoyles and Maria Flook

Heu, cadit in quemquam tantum scelus?
("Alas, who would dream of such a crime?")

Virgil, *Eclogue IX*

SARATOGA HAUNTING

1

The word *bucolic* derives from the Greek word for herdsman with the first syllable referring to the oxen that the herdsman is tending. Traditionally a bucolic setting includes shepherds, farmlands, lush foliage. But even the bucolic can suffer the pangs of modernization and in the present instance the ox has been replaced by a bright yellow backhoe, the herdsman by the backhoe operator. It was a warm Tuesday morning in Saratoga Springs in early November and the hinged bucket of the machine dipped and lifted a mouthful of dirt and rotten wood which it appeared to munch thoughtfully before turning and unloading its contents into the back of a blue dump truck.

The backhoe operator's name was Eddie Gillespie and he was half asleep, having spent much of the night pacing the floor with a colicky baby. In addition he felt stunned by the hairpin turns through which life had whisked him. Not many months before his late nights had been agreeably spent in discos and nightclubs, card games and pool halls: the respectable occupations of a young man about town. He picked up what little money he needed as a bartender or stable guard, even as an assistant private detective. But then one of the party girls with whom Eddie passed his time had turned out to be a party girl with a hidden purpose and before he even felt himself in danger, Eddie had been wearing a powder-blue tuxedo and escorting his bride down the aisle of the Pacified Jesus Methodist Church. "You're over thirty," Irene had told him, "you've got to look out for your future." And now Eddie was the father of a three-week-old squawling daughter by the name of Angelina and he couldn't look the baby in the face without thinking: How the fuck did this happen?

In bucolic poetry, the herdsman who caught a glimpse of a nymph was changed into a tree or flower. These days the nymph transforms the man about town into a herdsman, although in the 1990s to be a herdsman tending a giant yellow ruminant provides a steady income with health and retirement benefits. The sun was warm and heated the yellow metal, which made the beast appear content. Over his ears Eddie wore yellow noise suppressors like stereo headphones that reduced the roar of the backhoe to a digestive rumble. The noise suppressors squashed down Eddie's skillfully tousled black hair, the perfection of which being the single art form that quickened his pulse. Eddie had stripped off his jean jacket and wore khaki pants and a white T-shirt depicting a ballerina from the New York City Ballet performing an arabesque (a gift from his wife). Although it had snowed on Halloween, these first days in November were mild and even a few dandelions had been coaxed into blooming.

Nonetheless bad weather was coming. There were storms in Minnesota and tales of cars being stranded on Interstate 80 in Iowa. The probability of many more warm days was slight and Eddie's job this morning was one that should have been completed the previous week: clearing the land where Jacko's Pool Hall had once stood before the ground froze so that construction of the new library could begin in the spring.

Those who took pleasure in sentimentally exaggerating the mythos of Saratoga Springs and its rapscallion past had found something appropriate in the fact that the public library owned a pool hall. "Only in Saratoga Springs," they liked to say, thinking more of the old casinos and racetracks than of pool halls. But it amused them to think of the librarians hanging out at Jacko's, after putting the books to sleep, and betting who could sink the eight ball on the break. Actually the library had no interest in the pool hall itself and only wanted the ground on which it stood and which would eventually be the home of a newer and grander library, although probably not as pretty as the old one located on a corner of Congress Park. The lot was situated in a treeless hollow back behind Caffè Lena and bounded to the east and west by Henry and Putnam streets. At one time there had been a livery stable on the site, although for as long as Eddie Gillespie could remember (which wasn't very long) it had been the pool hall, which in fact had been built using part of the old livery stable and which was why Jacko's had a dirt cellar and was freezing in winter.

Eddie Gillespie had learned to shoot eight ball at Jacko's. He had won money on the cigarette-scarred green tables and had lost even more. He'd been drunk, he'd been in fights, he had sworn brotherhood and sworn revenge, he planned car thefts and seductions, he had puked in the men's room—all at Jacko's. And now he was removing the last bits and pieces and making the ground ready for books. Even this amazed him, and as he manipulated the controls of the yellow backhoe (which he called Homer without intending a literary reference), it seemed he could feel remnants of his old drinking and gambling self, his old devil-may-care car-thieving self, his Don Juan and committed-bachelor self, gathered in the warm Indian-summer air around him. And as that rakish self had been at last obliterated by marriage and fatherhood, so was Eddie Gillespie obliterating the final traces of the spot where some of his most disreputable behavior had been enacted or planned. He was patting down the ground as if smoothing the dirt on his own grave. But he wasn't simply burying himself, because after all he had begun a new life: wife, child, reputable employment, even a little house; rather, it seemed as if he were taking over somebody else's life, a life that didn't resemble Eddie's but which was like his father's—a serious wage earner with a belly full of ulcers who had always made Eddie Gillespie grind his teeth. Eddie had been sidetracked into his old man's life and with it came his father's oft-repeated warning: "You wait 'til you're my age!"

Jesus, thought Eddie, nothing's going to be interesting ever again. It wasn't that Eddie didn't love his wife and daughter but he felt he had been tricked into becoming another person, as if he had put on a Halloween mask and couldn't get it off again. It was glued to his face. Nothing fun anymore, nothing dangerous. No more private detective stuff, no more carrying a gun. No more late nights, no more fast lane. No excitement, ever!

As these thoughts assailed him and he felt increasingly sorry for himself, Eddie became aware of somebody shouting but, it seemed, from very far away. Near the dump truck he saw the driver, Louie Paloma, bright red in the face, waving his arms as if attempting to fly. Eddie snatched off the noise suppressors and over the roar of the backhoe he could hear Paloma shouting, "Stop Homer, stop Homer!"

Eddie flicked off the key and the machine sputtered to a stop. Then he looked toward the hinged bucket, following Louie Paloma's pointed finger. There, stuck on the bucket's rusted middle tooth was a skull, a human skull. It was tilted slightly to the left and seemed to stare rather jauntily at Eddie. And, after all this thought about the death of his own past life, the death in fact of his youth, even the death of Jacko's Pool Hall, it occurred to Eddie, certainly irrationally and only for the briefest of moments, that the skull presently attempting to stare him down from its wobbly perch was most probably his own.

2

"What the fuck's a seven-letter word beginning with 'e' for a bucolic poem?" asked Victor Plotz.

Charlie Bradshaw looked up from his section of the Albany *Union Leader* and tilted his head so he could see Victor through the top part of his bifocals. "What kind of poem?" It was Wednesday morning and they were sitting in Charlie's office on Phila Street in downtown Saratoga Springs. Sunlight slanted through the window and warmed the back of Charlie's neck. He had never liked crossword puzzles. They unpleasantly recalled the intelligence tests that so filled him with anxiety during his grade-school years: glum results and baffled teachers.

"A bucolic poem, it's probably a poem about Halloween. Don't you have a dictionary around here?"

Charlie began to ask why a detective's office should need a dictionary but then he thought that the Pinkertons probably had hundreds of dictionaries. "No, not recently," he said. "Why is it a Halloween poem?"

"You know, Boo! as in Boo-colic." The windows of Victor's lime-green Mercedes 190 had been badly soaped on Halloween and the subject was still near to his heart.

Charlie felt unwilling to accept this definition but neither was he prepared to argue. Victor had been his friend for nearly seventeen years and Charlie knew that once having linked the word *bucolic* to Halloween, Victor would vigorously defend it without the least need of proof. "Stands to reason," he would say. Or: "It makes common sense. What're you, against common sense?"

"Call the library," suggested Charlie, "you got a phone there."

Since July Victor had been carrying a cellular phone at all hours of the day and night as if his life would be meaningless without it. First he had used it at the track to be in constant, although spurious, contact with touts and bookies and to bandy about the names of famous trainers ("Say, Wayne, what about Wonder's Delight in the third?"), which thoroughly unnerved anyone standing within thirty feet. This seemed Victor's only purpose. It being his belief that a sleeping dog is a useless dog: meaning he liked to rouse them roughly from tranquillity. And recently Charlie had accused Victor of getting Eddie Gillespie and other friends to telephone him in public places (restaurants, bars, movie theaters) for a buck a call so that Victor could shout out: "Buy at two hundred!" or "Sell at three hundred!" Or even: "Has the Japanese market closed yet?"

"What the fuck do libraries know about Halloween?" asked Victor, returning to his crossword puzzle and chewing the eraser of one of Charlie's pencils. Victor was a man in his early sixties, although for some years he had frozen his age at fifty-nine. Charlie knew that Victor was almost exactly ten years older and now he felt a kind of dismay that he was creeping up on him. Recently Victor had even been threatening to get a face-lift and Charlie considered with aversion the possibility that Victor might be transformed into a younger friend, although when Victor mentioned the face-lift, Eddie Gillespie had remarked that that kind of elevation would require the use of his backhoe. Already Victor had begun tinting his hair, changing it from a light gray to a darker gray: the hair itself stuck out in all directions as if to caution young children not to stick their fingers in light sockets. Victor called it a Jewish Afro. "It's what Moses brought back from Egypt," he explained.

Victor apologized for these changes in his appearance, saying they were not due to vanity, but to the requirements of his new occupation as stockbroker, which was how he described his dealings with a number of gullible older women who had entrusted him to invest their money. "I gotta transform myself into glittering 3-D," he would say: "dapper, dynamic and dependable." How many clients he had lured into his ventures varied with each telling. How much he knew about the stock market also varied, as did his successes, his hopes for the future, his plans to buy a condo in Palm Beach. There was the flesh-and-blood Victor and there was the mythic Victor and between these two phenomena existed a constantly shifting space. Although as Victor said, "Hey, Charlie, I'm driving the Mercedes and you're driving the Mazda 323. You figure it out."

Beyond his new career as a stockbroker, Victor had also acquired some rental property: two duplexes which he rented to Skidmore students during the year and to racing fans during the five weeks of racing, which brought him more money than all the rest of the year combined. In fact, Victor had a variety of money-making schemes, while Charlie limped along as a private detective and on the money his mother paid him for taking care of the Bentley, Mabel Bradshaw's Victorian hotel in downtown Saratoga, which was closed from Labor Day to Memorial Day while she spent the winter months in Vence: a small perched village on the French Riviera.

All that Charlie could say in favor of his own semi-impoverished state was that it was exclusively his own and that's the way he wanted it. A stint in the army followed by twenty years as a Saratoga policeman had filled him chock-full of other people's orders. Better to be half broke by himself than flush while working for someone else. Of course Victor seemed to do all right but it wouldn't have surprised Charlie in the least if someday the FBI came bursting through the door and led Victor off to jail. What Charlie liked was a life without interference and he wasn't one hundred percent sure that Victor had that.

Charlie turned back to the paper. November was a slow time in the detective trade, he told himself, although the same had been true of October and September. He had some insurance cases, a couple of surveillance cases which he had farmed out, several missing persons and a woman who kept getting threatening letters that Charlie suspected she was mailing to herself. Charlie liked to think that his expanded leisure time gave him the opportunity of painting his small house out on Saratoga Lake, of developing a serious swimming regimen, which meant losing another pound or two, and of seeing more of Janey Burris, the woman whose face drifted across his consciousness like a robin across a blue sky perhaps one hundred times a day.

But despite these pleasures there were bills to be paid and Charlie knew he was barely scraping by. He sighed and glanced over at the poster of Jesse James that was Scotch-taped to the wall. Once he had thought that he liked Jesse James because he was a symbol of the romantic outlaw life, then he thought he liked him because Jesse seemed a symbol of American expansionism and unlimited frontiers. Now he thought he liked Jesse James because Jesse had been without existential dilemmas: no doubt, no hesitation, no scratching his head and wondering what it all meant, no loneliness, no vaguely looking out the window, no uncertainty as to what to do next. Action—that was Jesse James: a soul like a karate chop. And certainly it was significant that his one aesthetic moment—standing on a chair and straightening a picture—had been the moment when Bob Ford put a bullet in the back of his head.

"If you were a *real* pal," said Victor, giving the paper a reproachful shake, "you'd get a dictionary. I know lotsa people who've got dictionaries and I could do the crossword with them a heck of a lot easier, but no, I hang out with you because I like you best, even though it fucks up my crossword."

But Charlie wasn't listening. He had noticed a vaguely familiar name at the back of the paper, and then, thinking about it, he was chagrined to realize that the name belonged to someone who had at one time filled his thoughts. "They let Virgil Darcy out of prison!" he said. "They paroled him."

"Who the heck's Virgil Darcy?" asked Victor, feeling it unlikely that any human being could compete with the elusive meaning of the word *bucolic.*

"A kid I arrested about twenty years ago. I'd known him a long time."

"Well he ain't a kid any longer," said Victor, giving the paper another shake. Then, after a moment, "What did you arrest him for?"

"He was the driver for a bank holdup in Albany and a guard got killed. The two guys that did the holdup never got caught. Virgil claimed he hadn't known they were going to rob the bank and had no idea where they had escaped to. He must be in his early forties now."

Looking again at the short news article, Charlie saw that Virgil's age was forty-three. It mentioned the robbery of the Marine Midland Bank and that the other two robbers, Joey Damasco and Frank Bonita, were still at large. About two hundred thousand dollars had been stolen and the bank was still offering a ten-thousand-dollar reward for its recovery. The robbers had planned the holdup so meticulously that no one believed Virgil's protestations of innocence, although later Charlie felt that Virgil had been telling the truth, even that Frank Bonita might have been getting even with Virgil for some quarrel or stolen girlfriend or imagined insult by convincing Virgil to drive the car. And it had also occurred to Charlie that Bonita had at some point gotten rid of his partner Joey Damasco, taken the money and gone off to start a new life under an assumed name, although Charlie had no evidence of this. But Bonita was cagey, intelligent and as cold as a snake—wiping out his old life and starting a new one would have meant little to him. At least this is what Charlie had thought for years, but now he wondered what evidence he had ever had for that.

As for Virgil Darcy, Charlie guessed he had first met him in the early sixties, about the time when Charlie had been promoted from patrolman to plainclothesman. Virgil was twelve years old and had been picked up for shoplifting at the Grand Union. The store manager said it was the third time he had been caught—each time he had been stealing candy: gumdrops and Hershey's Kisses. Charlie had been touched by the idea of a clumsy shoplifter with a sweet tooth. Virgil Darcy had light-blond hair of the kind that invariably gets a kid nicknamed Whitey, but Virgil didn't want a nickname. He said his name was Virgil and didn't want it fooled with. And Charlie liked that too, that the kid seemed to have some sense of himself, despite a lousy home environment with a missing father, too many younger siblings, a mother who had to hold down a waitressing job and a grandmother who was too old and tired to care. In fact, it was a common story, except that Virgil was proud of the name Virgil and had a sweet tooth. The name made him different and when other kids made fun of him for it, Virgil would fight, even though he was small for his age and got beaten.

"Twenty years is a long time in the slammer," said Victor. "How'd you happen to arrest him if the robbery was in Albany?"

"He lived here, or at least his mother did. When the call came over the radio about the robbery there was a description of the driver and it said he was a young man with nearly white hair. Virgil had hair like that and I sort of knew it was him. Not just because of the hair but because of the guys he'd been hanging out with. One of them, Frank Bonita, had been up for armed robbery before. Anyway, I went by Virgil's mother's house. It was clear something was wrong, although they said they hadn't seen him. Virgil had had a part-time job at a marina out at the lake. I drove out there and found him hiding in an old boathouse. Actually I had to talk him into giving himself up. Then at the trial they thought he was holding back and protecting his friends so they threw the book at him, giving him life for the killing of the guard, plus twenty years for the bank robbery. Virgil kept saying I had betrayed him. In fact, he said he'd kill me."

"Kill you? How was he goin to do that?"

"I don't know, it was just talk. But for a couple of years he wrote me and threatened he was going to do it, and he told other people as well. We'd been pretty close and I'd helped him get a couple of jobs and kept him from getting kicked out of high school. My arresting him wiped out all of that. Later I thought I'd made a mistake, that I should have just stayed out of it. Someone else would have collared him eventually. I sure wasn't doing him a favor."

"Maybe he still wants to kill you," suggested Victor.

"After twenty years in jail? I doubt it."

"You take it pretty calmly. He might be driving toward Saratoga right now."

"Why? So he can go back in the slammer again? I've felt bad about this for twenty years and what amazes me is that I'd nearly forgotten about it. I mean, when I saw his name here in the paper, I hardly recognized it."

"I don't know, Charlie. Here you betrayed a friendship—he probably wants to nail your skin to a tree." Victor grinned affably, showing his neatly capped teeth.

Charlie knew that he was being teased but he didn't feel happy with the subject. The courts had tried to make an example of Virgil and Charlie set him up for it. Before the trial, he had talked to the prosecutor in Virgil's favor but it never made any difference. Charlie was just a small-town cop, even though by that time he had been made sergeant. Now he considered getting hold of Virgil's parole officer to see if there was anything he could do to help the kid. And again he thought: He's not a kid anymore.

"You going over to Forest Gardens this afternoon?" asked Charlie, trying to change the subject. A friend of theirs was dying, an old gambler by the name of Maximum Tubbs. He had fallen and broken his leg, then, in the hospital, it had turned out that he had bone cancer. Now the cancer was in his lungs and he was in a hospice. Almost every day Charlie and Victor visited him. Tubbs had been gambling in Saratoga for over sixty years and had winning money on Jim Dandy, the 100–1 shot that whipped Triple Crown winner Gallant Fox in the 1930 Travers Stakes.

More important, Tubbs had known Charlie's father, a passionate gambler who had shot himself when Charlie was four years old. The small amount that Charlie knew about his father came from Maximum Tubbs, because his mother disliked talking about him, referring to her former husband as "water over the dam." For Charlie all that remained of his father was a bristly cheek, a loud laugh and cigar smoke. Then a memory of the house being full of policemen when his father locked himself in the bathroom and put a bullet in his head.

"I was planning on going," said Victor. "You still got his money in the safe or have you spent it?"

"Of course I haven't spent it," said Charlie crossly. The previous week Maximum Tubbs had given Charlie an envelope with fifteen thousand dollars, saying that no more than two thousand should be used for the funeral and the rest should be spent on his wake, which, he insisted, had to be fun.

"You want me to try and double it for you?" suggested Victor. "I got some great stocks."

"No thanks. The whole subject depresses me."

"Maybe I should stick around here, Charlie, in case this Virgil guy shows up and tries to carve you up with a butcher knife. You're gettin old, you need someone to look out for you."

Charlie turned back to the paper, again tilting his head so he could see through the bottom part of his glasses. "Give me a break," he said. Charlie's bifocals were new and he hated them.

3

Around one o'clock, after Charlie had finished swimming his two thousand yards at the YMCA, he walked up Broadway to police headquarters, which was situated behind city hall. Chief Peterson had called in the late morning saying he wanted to see him, then he had given a mysterious laugh. Perhaps *mysterious* wasn't quite the right word, thought Charlie. It was more enigmatically superior, although Charlie couldn't imagine what his ex-boss had to feel superior about.

Even though it was the second week in November, the weather felt like spring: a warm southern breeze, cloudless sky and Charlie had even spotted some robins in Congress Park where two workmen with portable wind machines were piling up leaves: a form of leaf removal that Charlie mildly thought of as cheating. Charlie had taken off his gray sport coat and had it draped over one shoulder. His thinning hair was still damp from the shower and occasionally he caught a whiff of chlorine from his skin.

As Charlie strolled up Broadway, he thought how he had been walking along this same street for about fifty years. When he had been much younger, Broadway had been lined with huge elms—all gone now—and there had been the gigantic hotels: the Grand Union and the United States, although both had been nearly broke.

The hotels had been torn down long ago and ugliness had been put up in their place: a strip mall and fast-food joints. Now, in an economic turnaround, the mall was to be demolished and another huge hotel would be built. But even the shops had changed: banks had become bars and then had become gift shops, restaurants had appeared and disappeared, one clothing store had replaced another. Maybe half a dozen stores out of a hundred were the same. And always the changes had been toward the fancier, the more expensive. No more army surplus and work clothes, no more cheap lunch counters. Even in fifteen years Charlie had seen an almost complete turnover and one of the few remaining stores was the boutique owned by his ex-wife and her sister, although even the term *boutique* now seemed old-fashioned. Certainly it wasn't a term for the nineties.

Charlie and Marge had gone through an acrimonious divorce in 1976. Marge hadn't cared two hoots for him (of this Charlie was certain), but she had felt it was an affront to her dignity that he should ask for a divorce when she was the one with all the complaints. Although unsympathetic to the man, she had liked his job title—sergeant in the Youth and Community Relations Bureau—and she had liked being connected to his three successful cousins: men of importance within the community.

Charlie and Marge had no children and led separate lives. He hated living with someone who treated him as a biological blunder, whose jaw tightened whenever he walked into the room, who couldn't address him without snapping out her words. And he had hated working for a chief of police who berated him for not being sufficiently militaristic, for letting human emotions (Were there any other kind? thought Charlie) get mixed up with his job performance and who liked to act as if Charlie were feebleminded ("Charlie, anyone knows that two plus two is four"). Then one day Charlie quit his job as a cop, moved out to the lake and said, No. No marriage, no respectable job, no being a good cousin anymore. He was tired of living a life that other people wanted, which didn't mean he wanted a life very different. For some years he had worked as chief of security for a local stable. After that he had become a private detective, and, for a short time, the hotel detective in the Bentley, his mother's hotel.

For a large portion of his life Charlie had felt guilty at being the sort of person who hated working for other people. Now he didn't let it bother him. Likewise, for at least a dozen years, he had avoided walking down Broadway for fear of meeting his ex-wife or her sister. He had hated their cold critical stares, their pushy silences. Now they meant nothing to him. In fact, to his mind, they were the ones who had become impoverished: bony, dried-out women with powerful permanents who brandished lipstick-smeared cigarettes in the way gunslingers once brandished six-guns. Likewise, for years Charlie had avoided his three successful cousins. He had hated their disapproval, their attempts to find him a respectable job (janitor at the high school, clerk in a hardware store, even a policeman again), their superiority. Now he couldn't imagine being bothered by them: shallow, pitiless men who lost sleep worrying about their neckties and whether they would be elected to some post in the Elks, Lions, Kiwanis, etc. Charlie was astonished that it had taken so long to say: Those things don't matter to me. And it also astonished him that here he was in his fifties and he was just getting to a point where he felt moderately comfortable with himself. At this rate, he thought, by the time I'm seventy I'll at last be ready to begin my life. How ironic, as if he had taken a wrong turn during adolescence and it had taken thirty years to get free.

As he walked, Charlie occasionally caught a glimpse of himself in a store window: his white short-sleeved shirt and striped necktie, his graying hair standing up despite his best efforts to make it lie flat, and bifocals in thin tortoiseshell frames. He was five feet eight inches, had a slight belly, and recently he had come to understand that he had spent most of his fifty-four years trying to be invisible: the anonymous figure at the edge of a crowd, the face that can never be quite recalled. Now he understood that was impossible: his eyes were too blue and his stare was too focused. He had a watchful quality which made him more noticeable than he would have ever imagined.

As for the glasses, Charlie had had them a week and had been tempted to destroy them a thousand times. At first they had made the ground seem closer so he was constantly tripping. Then he was always trying to read through the distance part or see people through the reading part. Even walking down the street, he was aware of cars, trees, shops, people moving back and forth between a fuzzy blur and clarity. The bifocals were for Charlie his clearest sense of aging. Ten years earlier they would have mortified him. Now they were simply an irritation.

These changes in Charlie, new ways of seeing himself and a forgetting of the old ways, were mostly due to his relationship with Janey Burris. It wasn't that she had transformed him, but the fact that she liked him and continued to like him made him feel different about himself. In fact, he would even propose marriage if he didn't think it somehow silly, that at fifty-four the role of groom was unsuitable, and perhaps he was also afraid she would turn him down. But Janey also had three daughters ranging from ten to fourteen years old and Charlie, although he loved them, had no wish to live with them, had no wish to leave his small house on Saratoga Lake where in the early morning he could sometimes see herons and how the layer of reddening mist over the water seemed to squeeze his heart. And recently there had been flocks of Canadian geese and all night he could hear them honking on the other side of the lake.

Chief Harvey L. Peterson, Commissioner of Public Safety, had been Charlie's boss for ten of his twenty years as a policeman. During his prime Peterson had been a loud, healthy man who seemed packed to the earlobes with roast beef. He was tall and liked to stand on tiptoe to make himself taller. He filled his three-piece blue suits like air fills a balloon and the passion of his life were several generations of Irish setters that brought him a variety of ribbons, bronze statues and plaques praising him for improving the quality of the breed. Peterson was a man without modesty, subtlety or tact, and a few soft-spoken words from him would be a roar from anybody else. Although he imagined himself a staunch Republican, he would have been most at home in a military government. "Uniforms for everybody!" was his covert motto. For years he had treated Charlie with mockery and condescension, while being secretly aggravated by his successes.

But that had been the old Peterson. Now he was in his early sixties with high cholesterol, high blood pressure, angina and the prospect of a quadruple heart bypass in the near future, as soon, in fact, as he could get up the courage. What Peterson had these days was a sense of fragility and it made him quieter. Even seeing his old boss, Charlie was struck by the changes. It wasn't so much that Peterson seemed thinner but that he had shrunk in relation to his clothes. They hung on him. And his hands were nervous and his eyes never settled on anything for long and sometimes he seemed to have trouble catching his breath. He sat at his large desk and watched Charlie enter his office without moving his head. Peterson had a faint smile as if he was looking forward to something. His eyes were bloodshot and he stared from under his thick gray brows in a way that showed the white beneath the brown irises. Charlie knew that just because Peterson was quieter didn't mean that Peterson liked him any better. To Charlie's mind, the fact that Peterson had become quieter only meant that he was sneakier.

"You're looking fit, Charlie," said Peterson, leaning back in his swivel chair.

Charlie considered a response but it seemed that all the possible ones pointed to the differences between them: Charlie's health, Peterson's illnesses. "Thanks," said Charlie, shaking Peterson's hand, "you look all right yourself.'

Peterson raised an eyebrow in recognition of Charlie's polite deceit. "Slowing down a little. You remember when you used to work for me, what was it, about ten years?"

"Until 1975," said Charlie, lowering himself into a chair and holding his gray backpack on his lap.

"You had a lot of different cases, didn't you?"

"Like anybody, I guess." Charlie wondered if Peterson had asked him to come over out of nostalgia. But Peterson looked too sly for nostalgia.

"You remember Grace Mulholland?" Peterson smiled slightly.

Charlie found something familiar and unfamiliar about the name. He thought of the thousands of names that had crossed his desk and how few he remembered. "Tell me something about her."

"She worked for an insurance company in town and disappeared in 1974. There was a lot of money missing."

"Several hundred thousand," said Charlie, suddenly recollecting. "She left the country."

"Some people thought that," said Peterson, again with his little smile.

"But wasn't there a note she sent to her niece from Mexico saying not to worry?"

"Some of us never believed that note, Charlie." Peterson kept rubbing the backs of his hands that lay on the green blotter as if trying to remove the small brown spots.

Had Peterson doubted the note? Charlie couldn't remember. The insurance agency had been a big one and Mulholland had put in a number of false claims: a burned house, several car wrecks, all with supporting photographs and documentation. She had been in her early thirties, a mousy woman who no one had ever paid any attention to. No boyfriends, no excitement, a boring job. So she had embezzled over two hundred thousand, had gotten false papers and had lit out for Mexico or Costa Rica or Panama.

"But it seemed obvious," said Charlie. "Remember? We found all those travel brochures. She's probably on a beach in Costa Rica right now."

Peterson leaned back and knitted his fingers across his belly. Tilting his head to the right, he smiled with one side of his mouth. It was a gesture that brought back the past. This was Peterson at his most superior. ''You talked to your friend Eddie Gillespie recently?''

''No, he's been working and his kid keeps him up at night. Poor guy's all worn out. What's going on?''

''Your pal Eddie found Grace Mulholland yesterday morning. Or at least he found her skeleton. Somebody bashed in her skull and buried her under Jacko's Pool Hall. And Charlie, there was no money with her. Just a pair of earrings.''

4

Charlie no longer drank much beer except during the hottest days of summer, because it made him feel bloated. But there was something about this warm November weather that gave him a thirst, and so before driving over to see Janey Burris he picked up a six-pack of Rolling Rock. He had missed lunch and he hoped she would give him a sandwich in exchange for a couple of beers. He even cracked one open as he started his red Mazda and he took pleasure from drinking furtively from the can and watching out for cops, just as when he had been a teenager. Normally he was perfectly law-abiding, but spending any time with Chief Peterson always made Charlie want to behave in ways that he shouldn't.

Mostly his mind was full of Grace Mulholland, as he tried to recall the case which had occupied so much of his time eighteen years earlier. He had never met her. At best he might have seen her about town—after all, she had grown up in Saratoga—but years ago studying her photograph Charlie had felt certain that he had never laid eyes on her. She was four years younger than Charlie and had gone to St. Peter's, the Catholic high school. When she disappeared, Charlie had spent a long time staring at her picture trying to imagine what her serious face had concealed. And he had seen the picture again in Peterson's office: it showed her standing on a front porch with a forced little smile patiently waiting for the picture-taking to be over. Her face had a self-consciousness that had touched Charlie, as if she were the sort of person who could never forget herself, who was always watching her own behavior and finding it wanting.

Grace Mulholland had been a small woman, about five feet three inches, slightly plump with short curly brown hair that was almost no color at all. She wore colorless glasses, had a round little face and liked to wear long-sleeved flowery dresses that buttoned to her neck. Sometimes the dresses had a little lace at the throat and wrist. A few years after graduating from high school Grace Mulholland had taken a position with a large insurance agency in Saratoga. She lived with her widowed mother and had a married older brother who was an electrician. Her father had been killed in the South Pacific.

When Grace was thirty, her mother had died. Grace continued to live by herself in a small house which she rented from her brother. She had appeared to be one of those people who are remarkable in their unremarkableness, although Charlie kept thinking about her self-consciousness, as if she had never really trusted herself to life. She attended St. Peter's Roman Catholic church and belonged to a book club. More important in Charlie's eyes, she had belonged to a group called the Travel Bugs which met every two weeks at the library, during which time someone would give a talk, with slides, about a recent trip. Grace Mulholland herself never went anywhere except Great Sacandaga Lake where her brother had a cottage, but she subscribed to travel magazines and *National Geographic* and had several coffee-table books full of beautiful pictures of faraway places: Rio, Seville, Costa Rica.

Her crime had been quite simple. First she insured a nonexistent automobile and then the car was reported destroyed in a fire. Photographs were submitted, documents were forged and the insurance company paid up. Two other nonexistent cars were insured and destroyed, and finally a house was insured—a house that never existed—and after a while the house burned to the ground. Some insurance companies are quick to investigate a claim, others aren't. Somewhat unhappily the insurance company sent in the check and a week later Grace Mulholland disappeared. This was in April 1974. Shortly after her disappearance, the insurance company contacted the agency with further questions about the burned house and Mulholland's fraud was revealed. There was no doubt about her guilt. The papers were in her handwriting as were the forged signatures on the checks. The big question was what had happened to her.

In her house were several recently purchased books about Latin American countries. Additionally, there was a small pamphlet on how to acquire false papers. The method of choice was to study old newspapers for obituary notices detailing the deaths of children or young people who were about one's own age, then write off for a dead person's birth certificate and use the birth certificate to acquire a passport. It seemed obvious, at least to Charlie, that Grace Mulholland had left Saratoga to start a new life, even though no one had seen her go, nor was she remembered at the bus station, train station or the Albany airport. Her car had been left in her driveway. On the other hand, Grace Mulholland's niece had looked through the house and she said that clothes and suitcases were missing.

And after two months or so the niece received a typed note from Mexico which said very little and was in fact unsigned but which indicated that Grace was happy and safe. Even though she had stolen over two hundred thousand dollars, her crime had not struck people as particularly villainous. After all, stealing from an insurance company wasn't exactly like stealing from a living, breathing human being, or at least that was the general argument. Anyway, to Charlie's mind, the note from Mexico seemed to put the whole business out of his jurisdiction.

Only two people disagreed with him on the subject of Grace's disappearance. The first was the niece who argued that Grace was so pathologically shy that she was physically incapable of going off to start a new life. She might dream of other places, but the truth was she had hardly been out of Saratoga. The other disagreement came from an investigator hired by the insurance company. He argued that everything looked too neat. If Grace Mulholland had really fled to South America, then why had she left these books and papers lying around which suggested that she had fled to South America? The submission of the false claims with supporting data had been done flawlessly, then why this apparent sloppiness with the papers and books unless someone wanted to make it *seem* as if she had fled to South America?

However, when the note arrived from Mexico, the insurance company had accepted Charlie's report, even though their own investigator remained skeptical. And all that time Grace Mulholland's body had been lying in a shallow grave under Jacko's Pool Hall which was about a block from where she had lived. She had not gone anyplace. Instead, someone had bashed in her skull.

Janey Burris lived in a three-story Victorian house a few blocks east of the Amtrak Station. For years her house had teetered between the ramshackle and dilapidated but recently Janey had been letting rooms to two male Skidmore students who had agreed to paint the house in exchange for rent. After several weeks, however, there had come a disagreement over how much their work was worth and they had stopped painting with the job unfinished. Consequently half of the house was bright yellow with a pretty brown trim, and the other half was peeling gray. Charlie wasn't sure if the house reminded him of before-and-after fat people's ads or was an enactment of schizophrenia.

Charlie parked in the driveway, then walked across the grass to the front steps, kicking his feet through the leaves and taking pleasure in the sound. He had left his coat in the car and he carried the remainder of the six-pack under his arm. It was after two o'clock and already the sun was low in the west. Janey's fourteen-year-old daughter, Emma, was on the front porch being charmed by a ragged adolescent who gave Charlie a come-and-get-me-copper stare. Charlie winked at Emma and was tempted to tell the youngster that his fly was unzipped but he restrained himself. Where do these ideas come from? he asked himself.

Janey was in the kitchen reading the *Saratogian* and eating chocolate. "Your friend Eddie Gillespie found himself a head," she said getting up to give Charlie a kiss. Janey was wearing her white nurse's uniform. She was a thin, athletic woman in her mid-forties with short black hair that she cut in bits and pieces—much in the way that the young men were painting her house—so that it stuck out in various places and one side was shorter than another. It was oddly attractive in a punk sort of way and Charlie expected that in Manhattan young women spent big money for what Janey did to herself with a pair of blunt nail scissors. "Eddie Gillespie has all the luck," she added.

Charlie put two Rolling Rocks on the table and stuck the rest in the refrigerator. "Does it give a name to the woman?"

"It doesn't even say it's a woman. Was she an old girlfriend of yours?" Janey pressed the cold can to her forehead, sighed, then cracked open the tab.

Sitting down at the table, Charlie told Janey about his call from Peterson. She leaned forward to listen, nibbling chocolate and sipping beer as if those two tastes complemented each other perfectly.

"Two earrings were found in the dirt next to the skeleton," said Charlie. "Long turquoise-and-silver earrings. She herself hardly ever wore jewelry and wore only the slightest makeup. I've probably been in Jacko's twenty times since 1974. All those years I thought Grace Mulholland was off in Costa Rica leading a happy life, and there she was right under my feet." Charlie found that even more surprising than that he had been wrong about her: the fact her body had been so close.

"I bet some guy gave her those earrings," said Janey. "Probably the murderer himself. She tried them on and he brained her with a brick. Why'd you think she'd gone to Costa Rica?"

So Charlie explained about the travel brochures and books about Latin America and the Travel Bugs. "It seemed clear she'd gone away. There wasn't any evidence of boyfriends or accomplices. To my mind it looked like she'd run off to start a new life. But obviously there was somebody else. Somebody who worked hard to keep his or her existence a secret."

"The man who gave her the fancy earrings," said Janey. Her elbows were on the yellow Formica of the table and she supported her chin in her hands.

"Maybe," said Charlie. Had there really been a man? It was astonishing to think that all his thinking had been wrong. Why had he been so ready to believe that she had gone off to South America? Even as he thought that, Charlie had a sense of déjà vu. Who else had gone off to start a new life? Then he recalled his conversation that morning about Virgil Darcy being paroled from prison. The two men who robbed the Marine Midland in Albany had never been caught and Charlie had suggested that they had fled the country. Several years separated the bank robbery and Grace Mulholland's disappearance. Even so, Charlie wondered why he had been so ready with that explanation. And were there others? Had he been tempted to explain every disappearance in terms of someone's desire to start a new life?

"Do you mind if I make myself a sandwich?" asked Charlie. "I'm starved." And he wondered if he was truly hungry or if he was only trying to combat his sense of failure with food.

"There's tuna fish. Do you want me to make it?"

"I can do it." Charlie opened the refrigerator. A bowl of tuna salad was on the second shelf surrounded by several half-empty bottles of red pop.

"Are you going to do anything about Grace Mulholland?" asked Janey, getting Charlie two slices of white bread.

"I'm not a policeman anymore, thank goodness. Peterson will look into it. But I keep thinking there must be other reasons why I thought she'd gone off. Maybe I'll look into the files again. I must have written up notes and a regular report."

"The person who killed her probably feels pretty smug," said Janey crossly. "I bet he got her to fall in love with him and then got her to file those false claims. He probably told her they could run away together."

Charlie was surprised at Janey's anger. "But maybe it was someone in her family. You can't immediately assume it was some bad man who took advantage of her tender feelings."

"Perhaps," said Janey, "but somebody killed her and stuck her body under the pool hall and whoever did it has never been caught. Also the person tried to trick you into thinking that this woman had run away to South America and you bought it hook, line and sinker. Don't you feel bad about that?"

Charlie grinned. "I make lots of mistakes."

Janey threw a piece of chocolate at him which bounced off his upraised arm. "You're not doing anything now except drinking beer and eating my food. Does she still have a family here? I guess there'll have to be a funeral."

"I don't know," said Charlie. "I hadn't thought about it." The body had been no more than a skeleton, but there had been shreds of clothing, a watch, a locket with a picture of her mother and the earrings. The police had been fairly certain as to the skeleton's identity and dental records had confirmed it.

From another room Charlie could hear the ringing of the phone, then the slam of the screen door as Emma ran to answer it.

"Charlie," she called, disappointed, "it's a man for you. Some reporter."

"Tell him I just left," said Charlie getting to his feet. Then he sat down again and took a bite of his tuna sandwich. He guessed that someone wanted to ask him about Grace Mulholland and it surprised him that people knew where he was to be found. He didn't like it. He had a sense of the world slowly turning its attention to the discovery of the skeleton. And who would the world find accountable? Charlie hated talking to reporters. They always misquoted him. Through the reading part of his bifocals, he saw Janey's blurred expression of concern. Then he tilted his head so he could see her better.

5

Maximum Tubbs lay on his back with a sheet pulled up to his unshaven chin and glared at Charlie. "Certainly, I'm going to die, Charlie. Eighty-seven years old and full of cancer and you think I'm going to get better? Stop trying to cheer me up." His voice was a hoarse whisper.

Charlie had merely said that Tubbs looked pretty good, which was an untruth, but it seemed better than saying he looked worse than the day before, which was in fact the case. Tubbs was thin without an ounce of fat and his eyes had sunk deep into his narrow skull. Hidden by the sheet, the lines of his body suggested an assemblage of sticks. For as long as Charlie had known him, Tubbs had had thick gray hair, but chemotherapy had made his head resemble the bald skull of a baby bird. It was shortly after seven o'clock Wednesday evening. The window was open and a warm breeze made the curtains tremble.

"To my mind I'm getting out just in time," said Tubbs. "Did you hear about that writer who swiped my name, called his book *Maximum Bob*—the vultures are gnawing at me before the meat's even had a chance to turn cold."

"Maybe it was just a coincidence," suggested Charlie. He stood at the foot of the bed and realized he was squeezing the metal bar until his knuckles had turned white.

"What coincidence? These guys visit Saratoga and they've heard of me. How quaint, they think. A little flavor of the old days, they think. So they swipe my name. Means nothing to them, but it happens to be mine."

Tubbs stared at the ceiling when he talked as if he were not strong enough to turn his head toward Charlie. A television attached to the wall was showing footage of Boris Yeltsin giving a speech, although the sound was off. Yeltsin appeared to have all the hair that Maximum Tubbs had lost. Wrinkling his brow, Tubbs looked serious for a moment, then he said, "Take this, will you, Charlie?" He fumbled under the sheet and came out with a blue plastic bedpan, which trembled in his hand. Charlie put it on a chair. "Nothin decorous about death," said Tubbs. "Nothin polite, nothin phony. That's what I like about it. Death calls a spade a spade." Tubbs wore gray silk monogrammed pajamas, having refused the more conventional pajamas that the staff at Forest Gardens had offered him.

"Did Victor come and see you?" asked Charlie.

"Yeah. He said that Eddie Gillespie found himself a head under Jacko's Pool Hall. What was he doing crawling around the basement of the pool hall?"

"They ripped down the building," said Charlie. "That's where they're going to build the new library."

"Ripped down Jacko's?" said Tubbs, as if they had ripped down city hall. "I'm getting out just in time. Junking a bunch of good pool tables for a bunch a crummy books, what will they think of ripping down next? The track? I spent a good piece of my life at Jacko's. They know who the head belongs to?"

And so Charlie told Maximum Tubbs about Grace Mulholland and how she had submitted the false claims at the insurance agency and disappeared with the money. He had wanted to tell the story all along but hadn't wanted to tire the old man, and he was relieved to settle on a subject other than his friend's impending death or the extravagant party he was planning for his wake, which seemed the only other subjects available and which filled the room with their dismal presence. "And then she sent her niece this note from Mexico," concluded Charlie, "and everyone figured that Grace was all right."

"The murderer must have sent it," said Tubbs, still staring at the ceiling. "Somebody must have been putting pressure on him. You goin to reopen the case?"

"I'm not a cop anymore."

"But you messed up."

Charlie found it distracting to have Maximum Tubbs talk to him without looking at him. "I ran that investigation as hard as I ever did anything. If there was evidence suggesting murder, I'm sure I'd have found it. I mean, this went on for months."

"Until the murderer sent that note," said Tubbs.

"Maybe." Now that the skeleton had been found, it was impossible to think that Grace Mulholland had fled to Costa Rica or wherever, but back in 1974 nearly everyone had been certain that she had gone off to start a new life. Hadn't Peterson thought that as well and hadn't Peterson urged him to close the case and get on to other business?

"Think of shooting pool with that woman lying beneath our feet," said Tubbs in his raspy whisper. "I wonder who knocked her off? I betcha we know who he is. Probably even shook his hand. I was seventy years old back then, a mere child."

It occurred to Charlie that in 1974 his mother was a waitress at the Spa City Diner and now she was a wealthy woman living in the south of France. She had been half owner of a winning racehorse named Ever Ready which she and a friend had claimed for five thousand dollars and then retrained so that it wouldn't panic in the gate. Then she had increased her winnings at Atlantic City. And who had he been back in 1974? A cop, a husband, a Little League assistant coach, Charlie could hardly remember. "I don't remember you back then," he said.

"We moved in different circles, Charlie. You were a copper and I was the guy you arrested."

"I didn't arrest you often, did I?"

"Enough. You knew where people gambled and sometimes you'd break up a game. You'd have even arrested your old man. Isn't that a shame? Your old man was one of the most passionate gamblers I've ever known and the kid's a cop. See what I mean? The younger generation always sticks a knife into the older."

"I can't even remember myself back then," said Charlie.

"You were a miserable cuss. I remember your old man once stole a car so we wouldn't miss a crap game up at Lake George. Something big came up and he acted decisively—that was one of the things I liked about him. You would of just thrown his ass in jail."

"I was doing my job."

"That wasn't a job, it was just an excuse for living. You let your job make all your decisions."

What Charlie remembered about that time was long hours, lots of anxiety and feeling bad about himself. "I always thought I was a pretty good cop," he said.

"Maybe so, but you didn't make it as a human being."

"You remember a kid named Virgil Darcy who used to hang around a lot, the one who was sent up for being the driver in a bank holdup in Albany?"

"Sure, a little white-haired kid. I used to send him out for coffee when we had an all-night game."

"He was let out of prison the other day."

"You arrested him too, right?"

"A guard had been killed . . ."

"You did a lot for that kid. He was a shoplifter, right? If it hadn't been for you, he'd have been convicted a couple of times, gotten off with a warning, then gotten off with probation or maybe he would have gone to some reformatory for eighteen months for petty theft. Instead, you save him from all that and he catches a big one and is sent up for life. Let's consider the possibility that you didn't do so much for him after all."

Charlie began to get angry and then stopped himself. How do

you get angry at someone who is dying? Tubbs was just speaking his mind. "You make me sound like a monster."

"You were just a tight-assed cop with good intentions," said Tubbs. "Sometimes they can be worse than monsters."

Charlie felt bad about Virgil Darcy but it was hard to feel too miserable about something that happened twenty years ago. That time was long gone and he was a different person. He felt great regret and even embarrassment but little guilt. He looked down at Tubbs and was about to mention that Virgil had wanted to kill him, but then he saw the old man was asleep. His chest rose and fell, how slowly it moved. A clear plastic oxygen tube was inserted into each of his nostrils. Soon—maybe even in a few days—Tubbs would be dead. Then who would be left to tell Charlie about his past? It would be like part of his own mind being cut away. People said, "He's eighty-seven, he's had a long life." But Charlie thought that no life was truly long enough and after a while they all seemed short. And look at Grace Mulholland, she would have been around fifty were she still alive. Over the years Charlie had imagined her with a little gift shop in San José, maybe even married.

On the TV several men were sitting around a table. It was "The MacNeil/Lehrer Newshour" and Jim Lehrer was talking. He had the dark eyes of a woodland animal and exuded a mixture of stillness and wisdom. Charlie sometimes watched the show, mostly because he hated the advertisements which were the major networks' only reason for being. He kept wondering about Grace Mulholland and what he should do. Who could advise him? Maximum Tubbs had his dying, Victor had his jokes, Peterson had his spite, Janey Burris had her concern. Charlie remembered from his German during his years in the army that *Lehrer* meant teacher. As he watched Jim Lehrer silently discussing some vital issue, Charlie wished he could call him up and ask his opinion.

Several hours later Charlie paid a visit to his mother's hotel on Broadway. It was past nine o'clock and the warm southern wind had gotten stronger, filling the Bentley with noises as if the old hotel were muttering and complaining to itself. Charlie was wandering through the building making sure that everything was closed tight: no leaks, no open windows, no prowlers. The electricity had been shut off but he had a powerful flashlight. Downstairs in the bar, he heard a noise in the darkness: the sound of something small being knocked over. Charlie turned his flashlight so that its beam moved slowly across the darkened lounge, making the Art Deco chrome and white tile twinkle. He guessed it was a mouse; he hoped it wasn't a rat. Maybe it was only the wind.

For a while Charlie had been paying Eddie Gillespie to check the building, but Eddie kept making excuses, saying he had to feed the baby or that he had been up all night with the baby or that the baby had colic. It seemed to Charlie that Eddie had been more dependable as a car thief. Now that he was a father with a respectable job, his reliability was shot to hell. But more likely Eddie felt nervous walking through the darkened hotel. Even during the day he hadn't liked it and once he had told Charlie that he was certain someone was hiding nearby. "Sometimes it seems there's a guy keeping just a couple of rooms ahead of me," he had said. "Or maybe it's a dame."

Charlie normally didn't mind the dark and the unexplained noises. But the wind this night crowded the old building with creakings and bangings and Charlie found himself thinking about spectral presences waiting behind half-closed doors. He stopped by the stairs. Through the windows of the lobby he could see the lights of cars passing on Broadway. Even the streetlights were swaying in the wind, and shadows swung across the etched glass on the double front door. A shutter banged upstairs and Charlie jumped. Then he took hold of himself, telling himself that he didn't believe in ghosts. It occurred to Charlie that the ghost he had in mind was Grace Mulholland, as if her spirit were crossing the dark lobby just behind him. But it wasn't her spirit, it was all the thoughts of her that filled Charlie's head, making him feel that her spirit was actually present.

Charlie also felt unsettled because he had had a slight quarrel with Janey Burris who had wanted him to come back to her house when he was finished at the hotel, whereas he wanted to go out to his cottage on the lake. He wanted to be by himself and think, and he wanted to hear the noise of the waves whipped up by the wind. No matter how much he loved Janey Burris, Charlie wanted to sit by himself, drink a little whiskey in private and brood about Grace Mulholland. Janey had accepted this but she hadn't liked it and Charlie realized that part of her hated his house on the lake. Perhaps *hated* was too strong a word, but certainly she resented it. She disliked his love of privacy. "Charlie, how can we have fun if you want to be by yourself all the time?" she had asked. And he would say that it was difficult to read at her house or that her daughters' music disturbed him, but what he missed most was the silence of his house at the lake.

When Charlie had stopped by his office before coming up to the hotel his answering machine had contained several messages from reporters who wanted to talk about Grace Mulholland. One reporter from the *Saratogian* referred to the case as Charlie's "goof-up." The term made Charlie bristle and he hadn't returned any of their calls. The afternoon paper had identified the bones as belonging to Grace Mulholland who had embezzled $233,000 when working for the Grand View Insurance Agency in 1974. Her brother and niece had been interviewed. Both had been "shocked and horrified." The brother was described as a retired electrician who lived on Great Sacandaga Lake. The niece was identified as Joan Chaffee whose husband owned Chaffee Toyota in Saratoga Springs. Charlie had been surprised to see that Joan Chaffee was forty years old. When he had last spoken to her she had been a senior at Union College in Schenectady.

Up on the third floor of the Bentley, Charlie found a window that had blown open and he shut it. Then he listened. All the other creakings and stirrings seemed to have explainable causes. There was a half-moon. Scattered clouds were racing across the sky. From somewhere a church bell began to ring. Charlie returned to the hall. As he paused to listen again he felt something brush against his ankle. He stumbled back and swung the light around. It was a gray cat that sometimes got in through the basement. The cat began to wind in and out of Charlie's legs. He bent down to scratch its ears. "You're no ghost," he said. "Or maybe you're a reincarnated spirit." He grinned at the idea. "Let's go down and find some cat food," he told the cat.

As Charlie descended the stairs, he thought again of the person who had killed Grace Mulholland. Presumably this person had then made off with the $233,000. What had he done with the money, or had it been a woman? Had Grace ever had a boyfriend? Charlie didn't think so. Although there had been men in her office, Grace had little contact with them. And there must have been men in her book club and in the Travel Bugs as well. She was shy with everyone but especially men. But was that entirely true? Charlie couldn't remember. But he had no recollection of a boyfriend, no friend of either sex, just mild acquaintances who felt slightly sorry for her. The person she had been closest to was her niece who often came home from Schenectady on weekends to see her family and to use their washing machine.

Reaching the first floor, Charlie went back to the dark kitchen. The gray cat remained at his heels. A week earlier Charlie had bought a box of dry cat food which claimed to have a chicken flavor that Charlie had been unable to detect when he had tentatively nibbled a hen-shaped tidbit. He poured some into a bowl and set it on the floor. After a moment came the crunching sound of the cat eating. Charlie sighed. Even without actually deciding to do it, he knew he would have to go over to the police station in the morning and look through his old files. Grace Mulholland had gotten herself stuck in Charlie's head and he wouldn't have any peace until he knew whether he had actually made a mistake. Was she really his goof-up? Had there been evidence that he had missed? And who was he back in 1974? Maximum Tubbs had described him as a "miserable cuss." Perhaps his reluctance to dig into his old files was not because of what he might find out about Grace Mulholland, but what he might learn about himself.

6

The next morning when the sun came up Charlie was sitting at the end of his small dock that jutted out into Saratoga Lake. The water noisily lapped at the pilings and the wind was blowing strong. Branches had blown down in the night, and leaves and twigs spotted the surface of the water. Farther out there were whitecaps. Charlie let his legs dangle over the end of the dock as he sipped coffee from a blue mug that had ''Charlie'' printed on it in large white letters. Janey Burris's daughters had given it to him for his birthday in April. He liked drinking from it but the mug also made him feel slightly foolish so he only used it when he was alone. From somewhere across the water Charlie could hear the honking of geese but it was still too dark to make them out. Most of the other cottages that he could see were closed up for the season. This was the time of year that Charlie liked best: nice weather, no people. ''Don't you sometimes get lonely out there?'' Janey's oldest daughter would ask. And Charlie would be surprised by her question, hardly understanding it.

Charlie had awoken that morning not thinking about Grace Mulholland but of Bob Ford who had shot Jesse James in the back of the head on April 3, 1882, in St. Joseph, Missouri. Jesse had taken the name Thomas Howard and was living with his wife, Zee, and their two children in a little white house on Lafayette Street. Ford and his brother Charlie had belonged to the James gang for about two years, although they had done little more than brag. Bob Ford was a small man, 135 pounds, twenty-two years old with a baby face who liked to be photographed holding a gigantic Colt .45 revolver. He said afterward that he had only meant to arrest Jesse so that he could claim the ten-thousand-dollar reward being offered by Governor Crittenden, then Jesse could later escape from jail. But Jesse had refused to be arrested. He drew his gun and Ford claimed he was forced to shoot. He said it was a lie that he had shot Jesse in the back of the head and if Jesse's body hadn't been snatched away so quickly, he could have proved he was telling the truth. Ford and his brother had immediately surrendered to the police. They were tried for murder, convicted and then pardoned by the governor. Bob Ford kept saying, "If I thought I'd have had to kill Jesse, I'd never have done it." But nobody believed him. There were too many witnesses who swore that Jesse had taken off his guns and had been shot in the back of the head while standing on a chair. After a while Ford began to say, "I know what I done and what's going to come of it." He said this again and again.

It was that phrase which had been on Charlie's mind when he woke up Thursday morning: "I know what I done and what's going to come of it," and the words lingered in his memory like a sharp taste. Charlie assumed the sentence was rattling around in his head because of Grace Mulholland and he was surprised at his own unconscious mind for ambushing him with a sentence that was for him so significant, after all Jesse James was one of his heroes, while Bob Ford, in the words of the song, was that "dirty little coward who shot Mr. Howard." Did Charlie really have such a sense of disaster about Grace Mulholland? "I know what I done and what's going to come of it." Charlie had made mistakes before, even big ones, but there was something particularly upsetting about the body being under the pool hall. Certainly there were times when Charlie had stood directly above it. Of course he hadn't put her there, but it was as if he had left her there, had abandoned her for eighteen years until she had been accidentally dug up by his erstwhile employee Eddie Gillespie.

Charlie finished his coffee and walked back to his house, really a small three-room cottage with a large stone fireplace but it had some space around it, meaning it wasn't jammed up cheek to jowl with a lot of other cottages. He would shave, then drive in to the police station and start reading those old files. The warm wind pushed at his back. The wind, which had been pleasant on Tuesday and Wednesday, now felt abnormal, as if the season were somehow unsettled. The screen door slammed behind him. The phone was ringing but he ignored it.

Seven other people had worked with Grace Mulholland in the Grand View Insurance Agency: three men and four women. Grace had been office manager and, apart from keeping the accounts, she had been the conduit between the insurance agents (the men) and the secretaries (the women). All seven had liked Grace but none had been especially friendly with her. Two of the secretaries had found her a "little superior." The insurance agent who had been closest to her in age (the other two men had been in their late fifties) had found her "mousy and awfully businesslike."

Charlie sat at a table in an unoccupied office in police headquarters surrounded by files that had the yeasty smell of damp paper. Peterson had made no real objection to Charlie looking at the files, which had already been stacked up on the table as if waiting for his arrival, but Peterson had also wanted Charlie to know that he was doing him a considerable favor by letting him "stick his oar in department business." Charlie had listened without comment. He knew Peterson was shorthanded and was glad to receive help with an embarrassing problem. Peterson's ideal scenario, Charlie understood, would be for Charlie to do the work and let Peterson receive the credit.

"But you don't even have a client, Charlie," Peterson had said. "How can you go investigating anything?"

"I'm not investigating. I just want to look at those old files. After all, I wrote them."

The files consisted mostly of official reports, transcripts of interviews, detailed descriptions of times, dates and places, and Charlie's notes from which the sanitized reports had been written. Charlie was mostly drawn to these notes.

"Frank Augustine might be queer," began his notes about the insurance agent who was closest in age to Grace Mulholland. "He is unmarried. There is no sign of a girlfriend and he has a prissy way of talking. There is no evidence that he had contact with Mulholland outside the office. He claims never to have asked her out and says he had no wish to see her outside of working hours. Possibly Augustine encouraged or lured Mulholland into embezzling the money out of a hatred of women. Then they might have split the money. Maybe he once asked her out and she refused him. Maybe she became for him a bad example of all women and so he found it necessary to punish her. Could she have really embezzled that money without a man to help her?"

These were ideas which Charlie had later abandoned, but rereading this paragraph he was struck by its improbability. What evidence did he have that Augustine was gay? What was a prissy way of talking? And even if he happened to be gay, what evidence did Charlie have that Augustine hated women? And why would Mulholland need a man to help her with the embezzling?

Of one of the secretaries, Charlie had written: "Betsy McGovern is clearly a man-hater. She has nothing good to say about Frank Augustine or the other men in the office and she is divorced. She is forty years old and dresses 'mannishly.' She describes Mulholland as 'superior' and seems to feel that Mulholland's job should have been hers. Her rudeness to me is further evidence of her hostility toward men."

Charlie tried to remember Betsy McGovern but no image came to mind. However, he felt she could have been short-tempered for other reasons than that she hated men. Maybe she hadn't liked how Charlie kept interrupting her work with questions. And was her divorce any evidence that she was a "man-hater"? What did it mean that she dressed "mannishly"?

The two older men in the office Charlie had found "callous and indifferent." Of the other three secretaries, the youngest had said, "If she really ran away with that money, then I'm glad. She seemed to have a terrible life with the agents nagging her and having no friends. Maybe she's happy now, I sure hope so." And after this Charlie had written, "Perhaps the agents should be alerted to her attitude."

To everyone in the office Charlie's younger self had apparently attributed covetousness, sloth, envy, greed, lust and vanity. Gluttony was the only one of the seven deadly sins which he had found missing, or, more likely, it had struck him as unimportant. This secretary disliked that secretary. This agent held a grudge. That agent took excessively long lunch hours. It seemed to Charlie as he read through these notes that his younger self had been more interested in imposing a moral grid on the other employees than in analyzing where they stood in relation to Grace Mulholland. Charlie's reaction to this was not so much surprise as disappointment, as if his younger self had let him down. He tried not to let himself be distracted by what his younger self had been like, yet the notes gave constant evidence of a narrow, unhappy person.

It now seemed clear that Mulholland had had a secret partner of undetermined sex who had killed her. Perhaps Mulholland had had a romantic involvement with this person, perhaps not, although the earrings suggested a romantic involvement. The two older men and two older women in the agency seemed the least likely suspects. Partly their age was against them and partly because they had long and conventional life histories with spouses and children and nothing out of the ordinary, despite their dabbling in the seven deadly sins. The other three, Frank Augustine, Betsy McGovern and Aurora Bailey (the young woman who had hoped that Mulholland was happy), needed to be looked at again, if only to see if any wealth had come into their lives or if they were gamblers who might have wagered and lost the $233,000. In any case, Charlie wrote down all seven names on a separate piece of paper. He needed a list of the people who had known Mulholland and he needed to know where they were today and how their situations had changed.

Having finished with Mulholland's office colleagues, Charlie turned his attention to her family. Here Charlie's younger self had found many potential suspects. Grace's electrician brother, Fred Mulholland, was a potential gambler. His wife, Gladys, was a potential drinker. The daughter, Joan, a student at Union College, was having an "illicit affair" with Burke Chaffee (later her husband). Any might have helped Grace Mulholland in her crime in return for a percentage of the money. Again Charlie was impressed by how quick he had been to think the worst of people. Why had he bothered to use the word "illicit" to modify the daughter's "affair"? Were there licit affairs?

It was also clear that his younger self had no doubt that Grace Mulholland had fled the country, which had turned some questions into leading questions. Had other people thought that Mulholland had left the country before Charlie himself gave them the idea? Again in reading his old notes Charlie was aware of a controlling moral grid. For instance he had discovered that Fred Mulholland occasionally did electrical work for friends who then helped him paint his house or fix his car or helped him with a plumbing job. Charlie's old note to himself had read, "These 'gifts' constitute income. Does he report them on his taxes?" The implication was that if Fred Mulholland fudged on his taxes, then perhaps he would have been morally lax enough to help his sister embezzle $233,000.

Charlie pushed his chair away from the desk. "What a jerk!" he said, meaning himself, or who he had been eighteen years before. What sort of person would be so quick to suspect moral negligence? And instead of investigating the crime, gathering information and analyzing it, hadn't he instead been looking for specific evidence to support his own particular idea—that Grace Mulholland had run away to start a new life—while rejecting or not even considering any evidence to the contrary? Who knew what important information he had overlooked only because it hadn't fitted in with his theory?

It was approaching twelve o'clock and Charlie decided to walk over to the YMCA in order to swim his required laps. He felt so irritated with himself that he had pulled a muscle in his back and he hoped that swimming would relax it. He also wanted to get away from these old notes and what they revealed about himself. Narrow and unhappy, he thought again. What a jerk.

Leaving the building, he found that the day was still warm and the wind was still blowing. Convertibles had their tops down. Skidmore students were dressed in shorts and halter tops. Charlie bought a *Saratogian* and read it as he walked up Broadway. His backpack with his swimming gear hung from his shoulder. On the front page was a new article about Grace Mulholland. Charlie began to read it, then stopped so quickly in front of Bookworks that several people bumped into him. He hardly noticed.

In the article Chief Peterson was quoted as saying that Charles F. Bradshaw had been in charge of the Mulholland case and had quit the police department shortly afterward. The statement suggested that Charlie's departure had something to do with Grace Mulholland; specifically, that he hadn't found her. As a matter of fact, right after the Mulholland case, Peterson had transferred Charlie to the Youth and Community Relations Bureau, a transfer which Charlie had requested. And a full year and a half later Charlie had resigned, feeling by that time that any position in the department was more than he wanted. He had quit because he was sick of Peterson and sick of taking orders from him. And now Peterson was giving him a little something back. "I know what I done," said Charlie to himself, "and what's going to come of it." In a way, he admired Bob Ford's precise sense of cause and effect, as if he had foreseen all the trouble but still thought that the fame of killing

Jesse James was worth the cost. But what had Charlie done? Apparently his younger self had been so concerned with identifying the moral shortcomings of his fellow creatures that he couldn't see past them. It seemed to Charlie that he no longer did that. But what am I like now? he thought. And how did I change?

7

Leroy Skinner's retirement home was a recently built log cabin perched on a ridge between Greenwich and Cambridge, twenty miles east of Saratoga Springs. From Skinner's front porch Charlie could see the Green Mountains to his left and the Adirondacks to his right. Hundreds of miles of hazy November landscape lay before him and it made Charlie's knees tingle, as if he were in danger of falling. Yellow leaves were caught up in the air like confetti, carried aloft by the warm wind. Way off to the south several dozen miniature dairy cows moseyed in single file along a fence line.

Skinner was a gray sack of a man who had spent forty years as an investigator for the New England Regency Insurance Company. He moved as ponderously as an elephant, and as he came out the screen door onto the front porch, bringing Charlie a cup of coffee and a slice of freshly baked apple pie, Charlie had a quick memory of his impatience at the big man's slowness eighteen years before. Skinner had investigated the false claims that Grace Mulholland had submitted to New England Regency and he and Charlie had often been together, or least they had crossed paths.

"So how long have you been living up here?" asked Charlie, taking the coffee and pie and trying to balance both on his lap.

"Six years. I retired on my sixty-fifth birthday. Harriet and I already had this place built and we moved up here from Mechanicville right away. It's great for my planes."

Leroy Skinner's passion was building model airplanes that had wingspans of up to twelve feet. These he would fly in the fields in front of his house. There were also clubs, regional shows and national meets—a huge network of model-plane enthusiasts. When Charlie had known Skinner years before, the insurance investigator had talked incessantly about his model planes until Charlie had begun to have fantasies about sneaking into his garage and smashing them. How, he had wondered, can any self-respecting adult dedicate his life to toy planes?

Skinner lowered himself into a white wicker chair that creaked under his weight. His broad slow face surveyed the landscape and he pursed his lips and moved his jaw as if chewing, although his mouth was empty. Charlie remembered this expression as well—Skinner's cow face, he had called it, as if he were chewing his cud. Skinner was mostly bald and large liver spots—like little replications of Africa, Australia and New Zealand—marked his scalp between the long, colorless fragments of hair. From inside the log cabin came the sound of water running and plates knocking together in the sink as Skinner's wife tended to the last of the lunch dishes. It was three o'clock and Charlie had driven out to Skinner's house after finishing swimming, only having taken the time to stop by his office to make some calls to see where Skinner might be located. Again, on his answering machine, had been messages from reporters.

"It was on the TV about finding her skeleton," Skinner said slowly. He had picked up several glued pieces of wood and was trying to fit a third slender piece to them. "Under a pool hall, is that right? I never played much pool myself, could never shoot straight. How far was that from where she lived?"

"About a block."

"And someone had crawled under the building?"

"There was a cellar with a dirt floor. The police think she was buried there and then something was moved to cover the spot. And the grave was shallow, not much more than two feet."

"Could a woman have done it?"

"Maybe," said Charlie. "Needing to get rid of a dead body probably gives you all kinds of energy."

"I suppose so," said Skinner. He took out a red-handled Swiss Army knife and began carving the end of the stick so it would fit with the others.

Eighteen years ago Skinner had doubted that Mulholland had fled the country. His theory had been that she had a partner and that the partner must have killed her. He and Charlie had disagreed about this, and Charlie remembered thinking that the man was stupid. Probably he had even been rude to him. Now that Skinner had turned out to be correct, he seemingly felt no need to provoke Charlie or to point out that he had been wrong. Charlie appreciated that.

"I was looking through my old files this morning," said Charlie with his mouth full of apple pie.

"Say what?"

Charlie swallowed the pie, then repeated his remark more loudly. "So far I've only gone through the people she worked with and her family."

"You turn up anything?" A hawk was circling above the pasture and Skinner paused in his whittling to watch it, as if the hawk's circles formed the ideal which Skinner was trying to approximate with his model planes.

"It occurred to me," said Charlie, "that my investigating was based on the assumption that she didn't have an accomplice and that she had fled the country."

"I remember that." The hawk dove, then flapped away at a forty-five-degree angle with some small thing in its talons.

"And it also occurred to me," continued Charlie, more uncomfortably, "that if any evidence had turned up pointing to another theory, I might have discounted it. Not on purpose of course. I remember you thought she had a partner. Did you think this other person had been her lover?"

"I don't think I made my mind up about that, although those earrings might have been a gift. It was a long time ago. But I recall feeling certain she must have had someone pushing her along. She herself didn't have much of a motor. Too shy and hesitant."

"Was there anyone you suspected in particular?" Charlie finished the apple pie and set the empty dish on the floor.

"No, I worked pretty much by disqualifying people rather than qualifying them. I had a list of about fifty people who were known to have had contact with this Mulholland woman and then I probably disqualified about forty of them. When that note arrived from Mexico to her niece, the insurance company was glad to accept your theory that she'd flown the coop." As he spoke Skinner fitted the stick to the others and glued it in place.

"How'd you feel about being pulled off the case?"

"I figured I had a nine-to-five job and if New England Regency wanted to switch me to something else, that was their business."

"Did you have notes on your investigation and make reports?"

"Nothin like police reports. But sure I made notes. I didn't keep them though. I mean, I stuck them in a file and after a couple of years I probably chucked them."

Charlie began polishing his glasses with his necktie. "What was I like back then?" He had wanted to ask this question all along but felt hesitant about sticking it into the conversation. "I'd like to know," he added abruptly. "You don't need to worry about hurting my feelings."

"You were a cop," said Skinner turning his large brown eyes in Charlie's direction.

"Is that all?"

"I used to be a cop. I lasted three years in Springfield and then I quit. I couldn't stand it anymore. Mind you, I've known some wonderful cops, but there's an attitude they get. Like everyone is a potential lawbreaker and if someone hasn't done something wrong yet, it's just because they haven't had the guts or the opportunity."

Charlie asked himself if he had known any wonderful cops. Certainly there had been many he had admired. But wonderful?

"And you were kind of a gloomy guy," continued Skinner. "Henpecked, I remember, or so I thought. Your wife kept calling you or you had to call her. It made you preoccupied. Don't get me wrong, there seemed to be plenty of evidence that she'd gone off to some foreign country and maybe there was no evidence at all of another person. But it looked too tidy. For myself, I've never trusted tidiness." Skinner began fitting a piece of red paper on the collection of sticks, which Charlie realized was part of the horizontal tail of a plane.

"What did you think when that note came to her niece from Mexico?"

"More tidiness. I figured somebody thought we were getting close."

"You were getting close."

"Possibly."

"So you think I was transferring a desire to run away from my life onto her?" asked Charlie. "It's like using the world as a mirror: a person always stares out at his own reflection."

"I never really considered it," said Skinner cutting the red paper with the scissors on his Swiss Army knife. "You were gloomy and maybe the idea of a new life was like a big picture in your brain. So here was Grace Mulholland who was missing with a lot of money. To you it was obvious that she had gone off to start a new life. After all, that's what you thought about."

"And what did you think?"

"I've got my planes and I've got grandchildren and I've got a wife I like. There was nothing missing from my life. For you, I guess, something felt missing."

"So what should I do now?" Charlie knew the answer but he wanted to hear what Skinner had to say if only for reassurance.

"You figure it's still your case?"

"I can't get it out of my mind, although I'll need to find a client."

"Who benefited? You got a list of fifty or so people, who's got a pile of money or who's a gambler or who's a drunk? Of course, after all this time the person might be dead, but if he or she isn't dead, then I'd be careful because they're probably scared. I bet they've been worrying about that body turning up for eighteen years and now it's finally happened."

"What do you know about this person?"

"Not much, except that he or she wants to stay hidden. On the other hand, the person must have gone to some trouble to get that letter mailed from Mexico. And the person's a killer, that's the part you can't forget."

Charlie wondered about his ability to deceive himself. Definitely it had been possible for Grace Mulholland to have fled the country, but what made it seem especially probable for Charlie had been his own desire to live differently. Was all analysis so subjective? How distressing. He glanced out at the hills through his glasses, then lowered his head to look over the frames. The view moved from clarity to fuzziness. Could the fuzziness be called subjective vision? And he thought how, before he had bought new glasses, he had accustomed himself to blurry vision and had thought it was the real thing.

"Where do you keep your planes?" asked Charlie.

Skinner jerked his thumb over toward a two-car garage. "Most of them are in there. I got more'n twenty now." He finished gluing the paper onto the tail.

"Can I see them?"

Skinner grinned. "You used to make fun of them. Said they were toys and kids' stuff."

Charlie didn't have any answer for that and he didn't feel like apologizing. "I'd still like to see them," he said.

"Well, let's do it," said Skinner, putting his hands on his knees and pushing himself up.

There were gliders and planes flown by remote control and planes with little gasoline engines. Some were replicas of World War I German fighters, others were racers from the 1930s. They came in all colors and sizes. Charlie and Skinner took one with a small gasoline engine out into the field.

"This is the *Evangeline,*" Skinner said. "I always liked the poem.'' The plane had a four-foot wingspan and was painted yellow and brown to look like a bee. Skinner put it down in the center of a large circle where the grass had been cut, then he began fussing with the motor. Once he had it started, the *Evangeline* went round and round on a long cable, making a high buzzing like the drill of a crazy dentist. After a while, Skinner let Charlie try it and Charlie liked how the plane pulled at his arm as if struggling to get free.

''You ever think of retiring?'' Skinner asked at one point.

Charlie laughed. ''Sometimes it seems as if I'm already retired. No, I like digging into people's lives. I'm too curious to retire.''

''I guess what I like is perfectibility,'' said Skinner, ''and I find it in model airplanes more often than in people.''

''You don't like people?''

''Don't get me wrong. I've known some wonderful people, but these days I just keep my distance, unless they make model planes of course. Watch out you don't dip it too close to the ground.''

8

Physically, Charlie had no sense of being very different from the person he had been in 1974. Of course eighteen years had passed and he had been in his late thirties, still a young man. But now because of his swimming he was probably in better physical shape than he had been back then. His hair was gray, but he was thinner. His joints sometimes ached, but he was stronger. He still looked out the same eyes as ever, and even though those eyes now needed bifocals, the actual experience of looking felt about the same. And certainly he was happier now and felt relatively in control of his life.

But seeing Joan Chaffee brought home to Charlie most clearly that eighteen years had gone by. Back in 1974 Grace Mulholland's niece had been a college senior, a slender black-haired girl, perhaps not beautiful but youthful with all the beauty of youth. Now, although not unattractive, she was forty and had given birth to five children. She looked every bit her age and a little more. Her black hair was no longer glossy and had gray streaks. Her figure was thick. Her round face was puckered about the mouth and lined about the eyes. It wasn't that she looked old, but she looked different; she looked as if a large period of time had passed and Charlie was certain he wouldn't have recognized her had he passed her on the street. He wouldn't even have found her familiar.

Charlie and Joan Chaffee sat in a Victorian gazebo with white latticework sides which occupied a corner of the side lawn of a large house on North Broadway. Charlie guessed that the house had at least twenty rooms. Built of red brick, it had several turrets, a greenhouse and a little iron groom out in front that offered a dwarfish white-gloved hand to take a nonexistent horse. Originally the groom was probably black, but now its face had been painted pink. The lawn was immaculate with the grass freshly cut and the leaves all raked. At the rear was a brick carriage house where the caretaker lived. It was late Thursday afternoon and Charlie had driven into Saratoga after seeing Leroy Skinner. The setting sun gave the yard a yellowish tint: the light being a promise of the colder light of winter. The tops of the pines swayed back and forth in the warm wind.

Joan Chaffee wore jeans and a green chamois cloth shirt. In her lap she held a little brown dog who she had introduced as Rosy. Tufts of brown fur on the dog's head were done up with pink ribbons. The dog was dozing and as Joan Chaffee talked to Charlie, she patted its head with a slow but unfaltering rhythm, rather like the drip of a faucet.

"But aren't the police investigating my aunt's death?" asked Mrs. Chaffee politely. "A policeman by the name of Novack visited me yesterday morning."

"I'd like to investigate it as well," said Charlie and he tried to make his voice sound as pleasant as possible. This was the aspect of being a private detective that he liked least: the need to sell himself. "You see, it was originally my case and I'd like to see it through to the end. And it would make it easier if I had a client." He smiled in a way that made his cheek muscles ache.

"But why should I pay you for what the police are doing for free?"

Charlie felt that he detected a note of irony in Mrs. Chaffee's voice. "You'd only have to give me a dollar, just a token recog nition of my service. That gives me the ability to poke around without anyone objecting. Anyway, I can give it my complete attention and the police have other cases." Charlie wanted to say that the police were also understaffed and overworked but he decided it wasn't true. He had never liked Ron Novack who had been a police sergeant for some years. He was a weight lifter with a nineteen-inch neck who believed that J. Edgar Hoover was the greatest twentieth-century American, with Elvis Presley being second.

"But you were mistaken about my aunt before," said Joan Chaffee, patting the dog's head a little harder.

"That's why I'd like to correct my mistake now." As Charlie spoke, he noticed a middle-aged man in an expensive brown suit walking purposefully toward them across the grass. He guessed it was Mrs. Chaffee's husband: Burke Chaffee, the owner of Chaffee Toyota. The man had a red, puffy face and looked unhappy. Seeing her husband, Mrs. Chaffee began to pat her dog even harder. The dog blinked its eyes and growled.

"What's this guy doing here?" said Chaffee disagreeably. He glanced briefly at Charlie, then looked away as if what he had seen had bruised his eyes. He was a big man and had his fists shoved into the pockets of his suit coat.

His wife smiled at him somewhat nervously. "This is . . ."

"I know who it is: Bradshaw the detective. What's he want?"

"I was asking your wife if she would hire me to look into the death of her aunt," said Charlie as matter-of-factly as possible. He was surprised at the man's animosity. As far as Charlie knew, he had never met him before.

"Get lost," said Chaffee. "What do we need a detective for? Jesus, I thought we were finished with Grace Mulholland!"

"Burke's worried that all this attention will hurt his business," explained Mrs. Chaffee, as she continued to pat her little dog rather roughly.

"You know five reporters have called here?" said Chaffee, raising his voice. "And one of them had the nerve to ask where I got the money to start the dealership. Can you imagine? I wanted to say that I got the money when I murdered my aunt!"

"Burke!" Mrs. Chaffee nervously began pulling the dog's ears. The dog opened its eyes and began to growl again. Charlie wondered if Rosy was ever allowed to walk on its four paws.

"Look, Bradshaw," continued Chaffee, ignoring his wife, "I'm a businessman and I sell a pretty good product. But people also come to Chaffee Toyota because they see me on TV talking about the cars and they think I'm a regular guy. Maybe even honest. You know what it'd do to my business if people thought I got the original capital by knocking off my wife's aunt? I'd have to sue somebody just to clear my name."

Charlie was tempted to ask Chaffee where the money had in fact come from, but instead he tried to smile in an understanding manner. "If you hired me, then maybe I could clear your name."

"You kidding? If people knew I'd hired the guy who messed up before, they'd probably figure I was guilty and had hired you just because you'd never discover I was the one who'd done the murder." Chaffee laughed at his own joke, then scratched the back of his neck and glanced at his wife to see if she had found it funny as well. She hadn't.

Charlie decided that he needed to assert himself before Chaffee completely controlled the terms of their discussion. He abruptly got to his feet, knitting his eyebrows and trying to look mad. Chaffee took a step back. He was about five inches taller than Charlie with the body of an ex–football player who has gone to seed. "Look here, Chaffee, plenty of people thought Grace Mulholland had left the country and the note from Mexico seemed to prove it. As for my successes or failures, I've done pretty well for myself. Whether your wife hires me or not, I plan to find out who killed your aunt. It would just make it easier if I had a client." Charlie was also tempted to say that he owned a Mazda and he was glad he had bought a Mazda and not a Toyota, but he felt he had said enough.

"I don't care what my wife does," said Chaffee softening his voice a little. "If she hires you, that's her business. But I don't want you hanging around here. Guys like you, detectives, you're like parasites, feeding on other people's bad luck."

Charlie was still standing. "Just how did you get the money to start the dealership, Mr. Chaffee?"

Chaffee took three steps toward Charlie and reached out to grab him, then changed his mind, letting his hands fall to his sides. "I know your cousins," he said in the same tone of voice that he might have said: I know the Queen.

Charlie started to say, "So what?" but he kept his mouth shut. It wouldn't have surprised him that Chaffee and his cousins were all Rotarians together. Probably they shared secret passwords and handshakes and gave each other discounts.

"I'll tell you what I'll do," continued Chaffee, "I'll hire you on spec. If you find the person who killed her, I'll give you a thousand bucks. If you don't find her, then you don't get a cent. Also, you don't tell anyone that I hired you unless you have to for some legal reason."

"I'll need a piece of paper."

"You'll get it."

"How come you changed your mind?"

Chaffee leaned against the door frame of the gazebo and folded his arms. "I got nothing to lose. I get you out of my hair and if by some slim chance you find the killer, then I get the credit, which would be worth far more than a thousand in advertising. Now beat it. I don't like Mazdas parked in front of my house."

Mrs. Chaffee interrupted her husband. "I need to talk to Mr. Bradshaw a little, Burke."

"Then you deal with him, but make sure he clears out afterward or he might swipe one of your precious Tiffany lamps."

Charlie and Mrs. Chaffee watched him walk back to the house. Charlie was tempted to make some rude remark, but instead he sat back down, folded his hands in his lap and tried to look full of love. Mrs. Chaffee glanced at him skeptically. Her little brown dog had gone back to sleep.

"I want to show you something," said Mrs. Chaffee. "Wait right here.'' She got up and walked toward the house, carrying the dog in her arms.

Charlie leaned back in his chair and tilted his head first one way, then the other, making the lawn with its hedges and pine trees and rows of ornamental purple cabbages move between a blur and clarity through the lenses of his glasses. It occurred to Charlie that in a few years he might have trifocals which would give him an even wider variety of confusion. And were there quadfocals? Then Charlie took hold of himself and wondered if Burke Chaffee was a serious suspect. And he wondered again where Chaffee had gotten the money to open the dealership and guessed he would have to look into it.

Joan Chaffee returned in a few minutes carrying a book in one hand and the dog in the other. Sitting down opposite Charlie, she put the book on a white wicker table and began patting the dog's head.

''You know, Mr. Bradshaw, when that note came supposedly from my aunt some months after her disappearance, I didn't believe it. I couldn't imagine her in another country and the words didn't sound like hers. Then, several years later, I happened to open one of my aunt's books. I had taken all of her books because we were both great readers. In any case, a letter fell out, a love letter which was written to my aunt. You'll see it in a moment, but after I read it, I thought that I had been wrong and that my aunt was happy someplace after all. That's what made the discovery of her body so horrifying, that and the realization that the letter had been written by her killer.''

Mrs. Chaffee picked up the book, which was Michener's *Iberia,* and removed a folded sheet of typing paper. She handed it to Charlie. There was no date and no signature.

''My dear Grace [the letter began]: It's been three days since I have seen you and your absence is like an ache in my heart. I've tried slipping out at night but my wife has become suspicious. You know how she watches me. I miss holding you in my arms so much. I think of you every minute and wonder what you are doing. Your dear face is always before my eyes. I wish I had the nerve to carry your photograph. All this pretending makes me very unhappy. But soon we will be free. If you only knew how I look forward to lying together with you without nervousness or fear. I'm extremely glad that you received your papers without trouble. Soon we will be in Vera Cruz. After that, who knows? Think how our whole lives lie before us. I'll try to see you Wednesday night or at least call.''

Charlie reread the note. He was struck that it said nothing that could connect the writer to any person or place, but at least it indicated that Grace's murderer had been a man, if indeed the note had been sent by the murderer. Charlie looked up at Mrs. Chaffee. Even though her face seemed as unperturbed as ever, she had begun to pat her little dog quite roughly, as if this were the single place where her emotions could be charted.

''Why didn't you take this to the police?'' asked Charlie.

''When I first found it, I believed what it said and believed that my aunt had run away with someone. I didn't take it to the police because I wanted her left alone. I imagined she was happy and I can't tell you how glad that made me feel. Anyway, I put the letter back in the book and more or less forgot about it. As for why I didn't give it to Sergeant Novack, I'm not sure. Partly I hardly remembered the letter, partly his attitude irritated me, as if the discovery of my aunt's skeleton was a nuisance for him. If you feel he should see it, then I'll take it to him.''

''I can do it,'' said Charlie. ''Did Novack show you the earrings that were found with the body?''

''Yes, I didn't recognize them. Actually, my aunt very rarely wore jewelry and the few things she had were quite simple. Certainly nothing like those turquoise-and-silver earrings. Do you think they can be traced?''

''After eighteen years? I doubt it. Are you going to have a funeral service?''

''Tomorrow afternoon from St. Peter's. That's the church she attended. It will be very private.''

''And tell me,'' said Charlie, looking around at the large lawn and handsome house, ''how'd your husband get the money to start his dealership?''

Mrs. Chaffee was silent for a moment. Then the growling of her little dog seemed to force her into speech. ''Burke had a grandmother in Saratoga who passed away in 1973. I expect her will is on file somewhere and you can look for it.''

''I shall,'' said Charlie.

9

"The trouble with crossword puzzles," said Victor Plotz, giving his section of the Albany *Union Leader* a shake, "is they ask you stuff that no person in his right mind could possibly want to know."

It was Friday morning and Victor and Charlie were in Charlie's office on Phila Street. The unseasonably warm weather had continued and the window was open, propped up with the telephone book to keep it from falling. The breeze riffled the papers on the desk and sent an envelope zigzagging to the floor. Charlie was reading his mail, mostly bills.

"For instance," continued Victor, "what's this supposed to mean: 'Famous Deadwood victim'? Six letters."

"Hickok," said Charlie without looking up from his mail, "Wild Bill Hickok. He was shot in the back of the head by Jack McCall while playing poker at Carl Mann's Number Ten Saloon on August 2, 1876, shortly after four o'clock in the afternoon. The bullet exited from his right cheekbone and struck Captain Massey, a Missouri River pilot, seated opposite Hickok, breaking his arm. McCall was later hung."

"Jesus, Charlie, what's the point of knowing that stuff?" Victor raised his eyebrows as if Charlie had committed some impropriety. "What kind of hand was he holding?"

"Ace of Diamonds, Ace of Clubs, Eight of Spades, Eight of Hearts and the Queen of Hearts: Dead Man's Hand."

"Charlie, did it ever occur to you that you got a lotta junk in your head?" Victor carefully penciled Hickok into the appropriate squares of his crossword.

"Some people know stocks and bonds. I know Western trivia." Then Charlie sat up straight as he read a sheet of paper which he had just removed from an envelope. "For Pete's sake," he said, rereading the letter.

Victor stared at him. Charlie appeared to be suffering from severe stomach pain. "Hey, Charlie, you look as serious as a dog in a boat."

Charlie handed him the letter across the desk. Victor groaned at the interruption of his puzzle, unnecessarily smoothed the page out on his knee, then began to read.

"To Charles Bradshaw: Don't think I've forgotten. I'm coming up to Saratoga to keep my promise. Make sure your prayers are said. Virgil."

"What's all this about?" asked Victor mildly.

Charlie retrieved the envelope from his desk. The letter had been mailed from New York City on Wednesday. "It's Virgil Darcy, the guy that was let out of prison the other day."

"The one you arrested?"

"That's right, the one who used to say he wanted to kill me. He'd been the driver on a bank robbery in Albany. Remember?"

Victor tossed the letter back on the desk and scratched his head. "I hope you got your insurance paid up. Am I still your beneficiary?"

Charlie was annoyed by his friend's lack of concern. "This could be serious. I mean, if he's been thinking about this for twenty years." And to himself Charlie asked: Is it really serious? Am I exaggerating?

"Maybe he's just pulling your leg," said Victor, grinning. "He'll probably come up here, hide behind a tree, jump out at you and shout: Boo-colic!"

Charlie didn't feel like joking. He realized he felt guilty about Virgil just as he felt guilty about Grace Mulholland. Even though Charlie had acted according to the book, Virgil was one of his mistakes as a policeman. Recently it seemed that mistakes were all he could remember, but surely there hadn't been many. Nor was it accurate to call them mistakes, Charlie thought, since each course of action had seemed correct at the time.

But this sort of wisdom made him feel no better. Even if they hadn't been mistakes that he had made as a policeman, they were mistakes he had made as a human being. It had been wrong to arrest someone with whom he had been friends and had spent years trying to help. Because of his guilt, Charlie took the threat seriously. Virgil knew that Charlie deserved to be punished and so Virgil had taken it upon himself to do the job, as if he were the punishment for Charlie's mistake about Grace Mulholland as well. Then Charlie told himself to stop thinking so negatively. He considered giving the letter to Peterson, but that would only get Virgil Darcy in further trouble. At best Charlie could stay more alert and he asked himself whether he should start carrying his revolver. And perhaps he should try to talk to Virgil's parole officer to see what Virgil was doing.

"I wonder if he's going to try to shoot you or knife you or drown you or poison you?" asked Victor pleasantly.

"How come you think this is so funny?" asked Charlie, wondering where he had put his revolver. Usually he kept it in the safe in his office, but maybe he had taken it home.

"I'm just pleased to see you looking so alert. A murder threat for you is like shooting you full of vitamins. It makes you full of vigor. This is the brightest I've seen you all week. Better than caffeine, better than cocaine. Maybe you should get yourself a bodyguard. Hire Eddie Gillespie. Since he's been on TV for discovering Grace Mulholland's head and had his picture in four newspapers, he feels he has finally broken out of the young-married-man-with-baby racket. His wife is furious."

"I don't need a bodyguard," said Charlie disagreeably.

If Virgil had been released from a Federal Correctional Facility, then most likely he would be supervised by a Probation/Parole Officer in Albany. Charlie imagined the danger of someone sneaking up on him, and again he told himself that he was worrying only because of his guilt about Grace Mulholland. It was another example of subjective vision. Yet, when events were occurring around him, how could he tell if his vision was subjective or objective? Immediate experience tended to be confusing. It was only after a certain amount of time had passed that he could be objective, or sort of objective because hadn't he been completely wrong about the person he had been eighteen years ago? And again Maximum Tubbs's description came to his mind: a miserable cuss.

Charlie had spent the previous evening with Janey Burris (he kept an extra toothbrush and a change of clothing at her house) but he hadn't been good company. He kept telling himself that he should feel optimistic after his interviews with Leroy Skinner and Joan Chaffee. The letter which Joan Chaffee had discovered in the book seemed to prove that Mulholland's murderer had been a man who had pretended to be in love with her. That was a definite step forward. Also, a private detective needs a client and now Charlie had a written contract. He even had the promise of future money, although he had little faith that any money would be forthcoming.

But Charlie had been unable to cheer himself. Basically he had felt distracted by what he saw as the ambiguity of immediate experience. He was following a course of action which he believed was correct, but perhaps he was wrong about that course of action just as he had been wrong about Grace Mulholland. Perhaps it was even wrong to be at Janey's when he should be doing all sorts of other things. Perhaps it was even wrong to continue a relationship with Janey if he was going to maintain a separate life out on the lake. Reading his old files had shaken his confidence. In the past he had had various theories about Grace Mulholland which had turned out to be mistaken. In the present he had believed he was just the same sort of person as he had been in the past and he was wrong about that as well. Now it seemed that all his ideas and opinions were in jeopardy and he could find no firm ground.

Added to these mental confusions had been the telephone calls from reporters which Janey's daughters had fielded. These reporters (some as far away as *The New York Times*) wanted clear statements about past events and Charlie had begun to think that the past was just as perplexing as the future.

"Charlie," Janey had said, "let's just get out of here." Charlie sat by the kitchen table and she stood before him with her hands on his shoulders. "I can take time off and leave the kids with someone. We'll go to Bermuda and make love on the beach. We could even go to Buffalo. Let's just go someplace and get undressed and to heck with the rest."

The idea was so tempting that it frightened him. To run off to Bermuda or Buffalo would be like getting drunk, like throwing aside his responsibilities just when a clear path was beginning to manifest itself. But was that path really the true path?

"I can't," Charlie had said, "I've got to straighten out this stuff about Grace Mulholland."

"You don't really care about her," said Janey. "You're just doing it because you don't want people to think badly about you. I don't think badly of you and none of the rest matter. Charlie, let's go to Bermuda."

"I do care about her," Charlie had said, "I really do. I mean, she's been lying under that damn pool hall . . ."

"Then at least stay at my house for a while. Don't just hide out at the lake."

"I'm fine," Charlie had said. "Chaffee hired me to get this business straightened out and I'm on the right track."

But Janey had looked at him skeptically and even Charlie knew that his words were not quite true.

Watching Victor mull over his crossword through the blurred bottom half of his bifocals, Charlie thought of Jack McCall and his reasons for shooting Wild Bill Hickok. McCall had given dozens of reasons: Hickok had threatened him (untrue), Hickok had killed his brother (McCall didn't have a brother), a man named John Varnes had paid him to kill Hickok (no John Varnes was ever found). And eventually it became clear that McCall had killed Hickok for the same reason that Bob Ford had shot Jesse James: the action changed an eminently forgettable human being into a famous person. "Take that!" McCall had shouted as he fired off his Colt at Hickok, then he ran out of the saloon yelling, "Come on, ye sons of bitches!" He leapt onto the nearest horse and immediately fell off because the owner had loosened the cinch and the saddle slipped over to one side, dumping McCall onto his head. He ran down the street and was later found hiding in the back of a butcher shop among slabs of beef. And in McCall's case there had been no friendly governor to pardon him. Although Hickok claimed to have shot thirty-six men, most of those killings had been as a peace officer.

Jack McCall wanted to be famous; Bob Ford wanted to be famous. And what about Virgil Darcy? Would killing Charlie Bradshaw transform him into a respectable person in the social circles which he had been frequenting, meaning prison? This idea struck Charlie as thoroughly possible but that was all. He felt surrounded by possibilities and he couldn't push any of them forward to where it would become a Truth, or even a probability. He was, Charlie thought, like a boat without a rudder: drifting loose in troubled waters. And once more he glanced at his picture of Jesse James—stern and hawk-eyed, a man for whom these uncertainties had never existed.

When he had originally picked up Virgil Darcy for stealing candy from the Grand Union, Charlie had given him the job of washing his car for a dollar a shot and Virgil had washed his car five or six times a month for over a year, creating a small expense that Charlie's wife had complained about. But the car washing at least gave Virgil money to buy candy for himself and his younger brothers and sisters. He had quit shoplifting, had stopped skipping school, and Charlie had even found Virgil some other small jobs: raking leaves, mowing lawns, which had finally led to his getting a job with a marina out at the lake. And now, Charlie thought, this same kid is a middle-aged man who wants to kill me.

At this moment there was a knock at Charlie's office door, immediately followed by the door being pushed open. It was Arnett Stroud, a reporter for the *Saratogian.* Charlie had known Stroud for some years and didn't like him, thinking of him as a parasite who depended on other people's bad luck. As that occurred to Charlie, he remembered that "parasite" had been Burke Chaffee's description of private detectives. The memory made Charlie's jaw tighten. Seeing Charlie at his desk, Stroud smiled a slow smile as if he had caught Charlie doing something that he shouldn't. He was a pudgy man in a brown suit who kept his belt cinched tight above his belly, which put his monogrammed silver belt buckle an inch or two beneath his heart.

"You been hard to locate, Charlie," said Stroud, taking a small tape recorder from his pocket as he crossed the office. "You mind if I ask you a few questions?"

Victor looked up from his crossword. "A newshound," he said happily. "Hey, Stroud, what's a 'Friend of Horace,' six letters?"

Stroud glanced at Victor as if he weren't entirely in the room, as if his presence were spectral. "The crossword," he said, "is not my section of the paper." He drew another chair up to the desk, then carefully set his tape recorder on the blotter. "Tell me, Charlie, why do you think you did such a bad job investigating the Mulholland disappearance eighteen years ago?"

"What are you talking about?" asked Charlie testily, then he stopped himself. He knew that Stroud had talked to Peterson and that Peterson had put Charlie in as poor a light as possible.

"You tried to convince everyone that she had run away to South America," said Stroud, checking his little tape recorder to see if it was working properly.

"All the evidence pointed in that direction," said Charlie, answering more calmly. "It was the probable conclusion." He went on to discuss the travel books, the brochure on obtaining false papers, the letter from Mexico. As he spoke, he asked himself, Why am I being so polite and reasonable? Why don't I just kick him out? In the meantime, Victor's cellular phone had rung (it made a mechanical buzz) and, rather loudly, Victor was discussing the merits of the Janus Fund as opposed to something called MFS Worldwide Governments Trust. Most likely he was talking to Eddie Gillespie and was attempting to impress the reporter from the *Saratogian* who seemed in his nature unimpressible. Victor leaned back with his shiny black shoes stuck out in front of him. Stroud leaned forward with his knees drawn up under his belly.

"So you thought she'd run off with somebody else?" asked Stroud, moving his tape recorder away from Victor.

"There was no evidence of another person," said Charlie. "If she had disappeared with someone, then presumably that person would have been reported missing as well. Look, Stroud, I know at this point it seems impossible that Mulholland would have fled the country, but at the time the weight of evidence pointed in that direction."

"Leroy Skinner didn't think so," said Stroud, with the air of a man laying down big cards.

"Not entirely, but his insurance company accepted my report over his."

"A wrong report," added Stroud. "And the FBI and Mexican police turned up nothing?"

"Nothing at all."

"Haven't you felt guilty about this over the years?"

"Oppenheimer Global looks good," said Victor. "I say we pop for fifty big ones."

"Until the skeleton was found, there was nothing to think about. Additionally, a policeman's job consists of collecting evidence and then drawing conclusions from that evidence. Your conclusions are only as strong as your evidence and obviously mistakes can be made."

"So you rule out the possibility of personal error?"

Charlie tried to look relaxed and felt he was failing. "You want a news story, the more dramatic the better. If I hammer my chest and say I'm guilty or if I throw you out of my office or if I confess to killing Mulholland myself. All that is more important to you than the truth.''

Stroud smiled at Charlie in such a way as to indicate that he forgave him for his ignorance about the workings of the news media. ''And are you going to investigate Mulholland's murder?''

''I have a client,'' said Charlie.

''Can you tell me who it is?''

''I'm not at liberty to say.''

''But you're hoping to be given a second chance?''

And Charlie thought to himself: Why do I hate this person? He's only doing his job. It's his duty to provoke me into saying something that I shouldn't. ''It's not a matter of a second chance. It's a matter of a murder having been committed and the murderer still being at large.''

''Any ideas about who the murderer might be?''

''Not yet. In fact, he or she might not even be still alive.''

''So you haven't settled on a sex for the murderer?''

''All we know for certain is that Grace Mulholland couldn't have buried herself.''

Stroud stayed for five more minutes but Charlie remained stubborn and unrevealing, speaking in a sort of official dialect that was so false that it burned his lips as the words left his mouth. At last Stroud gave Charlie a vindictive wink, shut off his tape recorder and left.

''Hey, Charlie,'' said Victor, ''the big story is about this Virgil Darcy guy making his way to Saratoga to scrag you. Just like that movie. I can still hear Hoot Gibson singing the theme song: DUM, da, da, DUM, da, da, DUM, DUM, da DUM!''

''*High Noon,*'' said Charlie unhappily.

10

Frank Augustine no longer worked for the Grand View Insurance Agency, which in any case had gone out of business. Instead he was president of his own agency that had offices on Church Street around the corner from the Adirondack Trust. He talked to Charlie in a paneled office. On the walls were the usual plaques and tokens of civic responsibility as well as color photographs of his wife and three children. Augustine didn't particularly strike Charlie as effeminate and he couldn't imagine why he had once suspected that Augustine might be gay. He was gray-haired and several years younger than Charlie. On a bookcase stood several racquetball trophies which explained how Augustine managed to keep so fit. Augustine was a cheerful man, perfectly at ease within the world he had created and he treated Charlie's visit with nothing more than mild curiosity.

"When Schwartz and DiAngelo died within a year of each other," Augustine was explaining, "I decided to strike out on my own. I've done pretty well for myself, I must say."

And almost automatically Charlie wondered if Augustine had been helped along by the money that Grace Mulholland had acquired through submitting false claims.

"You've struck out on your own as well, I gather," said Augustine. "I hope it's been profitable for you." Augustine sat at his desk. He was in shirt-sleeves and leaned back in his swivel chair with his hands linked behind his head.

"More peaceful than profitable," said Charlie smiling.

"Being a private eye would seem to be a strange place to find peace. You should have been a monk. Do they still use that term *private eye* or *shamus*?"

"Only in books. I'm a private investigator, or at least that's what my license says." He wondered a moment about being a monk—no sex life, that was the trouble with being a monk. "I guess the peace comes from being my own boss."

"So now you're investigating Grace Mulholland again."

"That's right." Charlie sat in a green leather wing chair. It was early Friday afternoon and Charlie's hair was still damp from swimming. "Did you ever see her outside of the office?"

"I remember you asking me that before. It wouldn't have occurred to me. She was a good office manager but the moment anything became personal it seemed to frighten her. She'd blush and stammer. The Christmas party, which was very low-key, was a torture for her. I guess like many men I always wonder what a woman, any woman, would be like sexually. It's a thought that just drifts through the mind. But what I found most striking about Grace was that I never had any sexual thoughts about her at all. When Schwartz and DiAngelo would kiss her on the cheek at Christmas, I thought she'd scream."

"And yet she seems to have been killed by a man who was her lover," said Charlie.

"That's hard to believe, although I'm sure you're right. For a while I thought she might be lesbian but even that seemed unlikely. She appeared frightened of her body and the whole sexual world. When it seemed that she'd run away to Mexico with that money, I felt like cheering, in secret of course. It showed she had spirit, that she had a life after all. In the past few days I can't tell you how many times I've thought of her under Jacko's Pool Hall. It struck me as so sad. And then when you think of the guy who killed her.

He must have really worked to gain her trust. I mean, she was like a frightened rabbit. He coaxed her along and coaxed her along, then he bashed her head."

"Who were her friends?" asked Charlie.

"As far as I know there was absolutely nobody except her niece. Mind you, it's been a long time. Occasionally, I'd tease her a little, ask her about her weekend, but she blushed and seemed so uncomfortable that I stopped. She read a lot but I don't even think she went to movies."

"Would it have been difficult for her to submit those false claims?"

"Not if she kept her head. It would have been easier for her than anybody. All the paperwork went through her. She dealt with the mail and saw that all the forms were copied properly. Certainly it was a risk to insure a whole house and then burn it, but if she had just done little stuff, she could have gone on for years. It required coolness and efficiency, that's all."

Charlie looked into Augustine's open face and wondered what could disturb it. He was impressed by the man's self-confidence. "Weren't you surprised that she had betrayed the agency's trust?"

"Not really. In my experience shy people sometimes have a lot of anger. They're repressing feelings that frighten them. The rest of us in the office were all perfectly conventional and led conventional lives. Grace Mulholland was a kind of cripple and, even though it didn't show, I sometimes thought she could have had the envy that cripples sometimes have. She knew she ran that office and she knew she was better than any of the agents, even me. She could have easily felt a kind of superiority."

"You've thought about this a lot."

"It's not as if it just happened. I've been mulling it over for nearly twenty years. I mean, this was an important event. The insurance company was furious. Schwartz, DiAngelo and I had to go to Albany and be dressed down by executives who knew nothing about it. Schwartz ended up retiring. We fired one of the secretaries. It was a lot of trouble for us, that's why I saw the whole thing as also an expression of Grace's anger. She really stuck a knife in us."

"You think she did it to hurt you?"

"She did it for the money, but she didn't mind its hurting us." Augustine smiled ruefully.

"What happened to the other women in the office, the secretaries?" asked Charlie.

It turned out that only one of the four was still alive or living in the area: Aurora Bailey, who Charlie had long ago considered reporting because she hoped that Grace Mulholland was happy wherever she was. In fact, Bailey worked for Augustine who hired her when he formed his own agency. Augustine took Charlie in to talk to her which was just as well because otherwise he wouldn't have recognized her, not because she was ugly or fat or had dyed her hair. Simply she was middle-aged where once she had been young. Again Charlie asked if she knew anything about Grace Mulholland's friends, but Aurora Bailey knew nothing.

"Sometimes she'd mention a book club or some kind of travel club," said Bailey, "but mostly she never spoke about anything outside of the office."

She, too, had been distressed to learn of Grace's murder and long burial beneath the pool hall.

"All those years I thought she was happy," she said.

At three o'clock Charlie walked over to police headquarters, less than a block away. Leaving the insurance agency, he felt invigorated by the warm weather—already people were speculating about a mild winter and an early spring—but then Charlie remembered Virgil Darcy and his threat. It occurred to him that by being out in the open he might be exposing himself to danger. Instead of swimming at noon, he should have driven home to look for his revolver or tried to track down Darcy's P.O. in Albany. And as these thoughts occurred to him, Charlie moved over toward the wall of the Adirondack Trust and into shadow. Minutes later, when he entered police headquarters, he gave a little sigh of relief. Then he thought: How foolish I am.

Charlie's old papers were still piled on the table in the empty office, apparently untouched by anyone else. There was only one window high up on the wall and covered with wire mesh, which made Charlie feel that being in this little room was like being in jail. He divided the files into the people who had known Grace through her book club, people in the Travel Bugs, people she had known through church, neighbors and acquaintances of her brother's, old school acquaintances and miscellaneous. Charlie began with the book club, which had had twenty members of whom thirteen were women. Of the seven men, four were over fifty in 1974. Charlie wrote down the names of the three remaining men on a sheet of paper and took it upstairs where he found an elderly detective with his feet up on his desk reading a comic book.

"Could you get me the addresses of these guys?" asked Charlie.

"I'm pretty busy right now," said the detective, whose name was Hale Tharpe, an oversized sprawl of a man who dreamt about retirement so much that he was half retired already.

"Just do it," said Charlie, dropping the list on Tharpe's large lap. He wondered if he was being unfair but realized Tharpe was getting paid to read that comic book, plus getting health and retirement benefits. Going back downstairs to his little room, Charlie knew he could be making one of three possible errors: the man who killed Grace Mulholland might have been over fifty, meaning he would now be over sixty-eight. Two, Grace might have been killed by someone other than her lover. Three, the murderer might be a woman who wrote the love letter to divert suspicion. But these ideas existed at the far edge of possibility and he wouldn't pursue them until he had learned more about the younger men. As he thought this, Charlie wondered, "Am I deceiving myself in some way?" but no possible self-deception came to mind (which, he thought, means nothing).

Still dissatisfied with himself, he turned to another stack of files to look through the members of the Travel Bugs. In 1974 the club had had thirty members. By removing the women and older men, Charlie was left with a list of five men. Charlie used a similar procedure on the people who had known Grace at St. Peter's church, her neighbors and all the rest, which gave him a list of twenty-five more names: thirty altogether, plus the three from the book club. At quarter to five he took the list up to Hale Tharpe.

"I was just going home, Charlie," said Tharpe, giving him the addresses of the three men from the book club. Tharpe had taken one of his thick legs off the desk as if in preparation for departure.

"This is more important."

"I have no authorization." Tharpe dragged his other leg off his desk and began struggling with his jacket. He was a swollen red-faced man whose body appeared packed with cholesterol. His comic book lay closed in the very center of an otherwise empty desk. It was a Classic Comic and its cover showed Greek soldiers battling with round shields and short swords.

Charlie picked up the phone and dialed Peterson's extension, then gave the phone to Tharpe. "Peterson will give you authorization."

Tharpe unhappily spoke with Peterson for several minutes, then gave the phone back to Charlie. "He wants to talk to you. Jesus, Charlie, my granddaughter's got her trombone recital tonight."

Charlie took the phone. "What is it?"

"Don't make this expensive for us, Charlie," said Peterson.

"I need some addresses. You could have done this two days ago." He felt impatient with Peterson and uninterested in his problems.

"We're understaffed."

"Yeah, and Tharpe needs time to read his comic book." Charlie hung up.

Hale Tharpe looked aggrieved. "You didn't have to tell him that, Charlie."

"It's okay. He's probably got one of his own. Look, just find some of these addresses." Charlie circled the five male members of the Travel Bugs. "The rest you can do tomorrow."

"Tomorrow's Saturday."

Charlie gave Tharpe a dissatisfied look. Tharpe had been a patrolman when Charlie had left the department. His nickname had been Otherway Tharpe, because when anything happened, Tharpe always seemed to be looking in the other direction. "You heard what Peterson said. Either you can find all thirty today or you can put off twenty-five until tomorrow."

Charlie went back to the little office to read the files of the three men whose addresses Tharpe had given him. Next to one of the names Tharpe had written the word *Deceased* and Charlie felt a surge of relief immediately followed by a pang of guilt. And he imagined the dead man's loved ones and how badly they must have felt. In any case, he would still have to read the man's file. On the off chance that the death was suspicious, Charlie checked back with Hale Tharpe and learned that the man had died of liver cancer.

Charlie read for an hour and again he was struck by the tone of his notes, as if his old self had found something silly about a book club, as if its members were too feeble to do anything but read dull books about which they would have dull conversations. Since moving out to the lake Charlie had begun to read more than in the past—history for the most part, but also novels and biographies. But even as a policeman he had read a little—history again but mostly Western history. Charlie found it hard to concentrate on the notes, hard to confront evidence about the person he had been, and without intending to, he kept putting down the files and letting his mind wander to pleasanter subjects: visiting Janey Burris or the geese he had seen on Saratoga Lake.

"William Slade [Charlie had written about the man who had died of cancer] teaches eighth grade, is married with two children. He claims never to have spoken to Grace Mulholland. He says he has no interest in sports or television and rarely goes out. His main interest, he says, is the contemporary novel, especially the novels of Samuel Beckett (look him up), and is working on a novel himself." There was more but in the margin, as a note to himself, Charlie had written, "What kind of teacher could such a guy make?" In those years Charlie had been deeply involved in Little League baseball and would have seen somebody's indifference to sports as a serious perversion.

"Ralph McMann [began another several pages of notes] works

at the library and is one of the officers of Readers Anonymous (the name of the book club). He is twenty-five and unmarried. When I asked about his relationship with Grace Mulholland, he grew defensive and said she never liked him and that they had disagreements. These turned out to concern a book on Kennedy's assassination. McMann favored the conspiracy theory; Mulholland didn't. 'It wasn't that she really disagreed,' McMann told me, 'but she looked at me crossly.' " As a note to himself Charlie had written: "Don't these people have anything serious to do?"

The third member of the book club was a forty-year-old pharmacist, Wallace Eliot, who two or three times had given Grace a ride home from the library. "If she hadn't known me for fifteen years, I'm sure she wouldn't have accepted. And after all, I'm a married man and we both go to St. Peter's." Even so, Eliot said, he rarely spoke to Grace. He had a large family and Charlie's note indicated that he had found something funny about Wallace Eliot spending time with a book club rather than with his kids. During those years Charlie had wanted children almost more than anything, but Marge hadn't gotten pregnant. It was one of the reasons they had begun turning away from each other.

Charlie pushed himself away from the desk. He would have to visit Eliot and McMann to see if anything about them was different (had they become mysteriously rich?) or if they could give him further information. Then he wondered if he had really been such a jerk eighteen years before, or just very different. But neither answer was satisfactory considering that he felt the same, that he was aware of no change. And if eighteen more years passed by, what would his seventy-two-year-old self think looking back at who he was now? More disappointment, most likely. Reaching for the phone, Charlie called up to Hale Tharpe to get the addresses of the five Travel Bugs. One of them had died as well—this time Charlie tried not to feel relieved—and another had moved to Missouri. Charlie thanked Tharpe, then gathered the five files and left the office. He could read them at Janey's that evening.

Before driving to her house, Charlie walked over to the Bentley to see if any more windows had blown open. Although it was only six-thirty, it was pitch dark. The warm wind was hurrying dried leaves and scraps of paper along Broadway. In the car headlights the dust had a yellowish tint. It was supposed to rain that evening and the air carried the flavor of faraway water. Charlie could hear distant thunder and just the rumbling pleasantly excited him. He unlocked the front door of the Bentley, then retrieved his flashlight from the reception desk. Again there were banging noises and various creakings. He left his old briefcase containing the files on the desk and headed upstairs.

As he walked through the dark halls, Charlie kept thinking of Virgil Darcy. Would it be possible that Virgil still hated him so much that he would try to kill him? Charlie remembered that he had bought Virgil his first baseball glove even though Virgil had been twelve years old. Pretty late for your first glove, he had thought. They played catch in Congress Park and Charlie had taught Virgil how to throw a curve. To Charlie's mind Virgil was the perfect name for a big league pitcher. As he made his way through the hotel Charlie gritted his teeth with embarrassment over his old self. Then he thought again about his revolver. Shouldn't he have gone home to get it? And for the first time the windy noises of the old hotel made him nervous and he considered getting somebody to take care of it for him. Again he gritted his teeth, muttering to himself that there was nobody here except the cat and his own guilty conscience.

That evening Charlie told Janey Burris about Virgil Darcy and getting the threatening letter as the two of them sat at her kitchen table drinking Jim Beam green. It was raining hard and the sound on the metal roof of the kitchen porch made Charlie think of dozens of midget snare drummers. Janey's daughters were watching television in the living room. It was nine o'clock and they had just finished a big spaghetti dinner.

"Did you tell Peterson about the letter?" asked Janey, growing serious.

"He'd call Virgil's P.O., who'd probably have him picked up. They could easily send him back to prison. I don't want to get the kid in any more trouble."

"He's not a kid." Janey sat with her elbows on the table and looked at Charlie with a mixture of exasperation and affection. "So are you just going to let him shoot you?"

"I'll look into it. I don't think he was really serious."

"Why not?"

"Well, why tell me about it? If he wants to kill me, then the best way to do it would be not to warn me first."

"Do you have any real reason for thinking that? Or do you think it just because you hope it's true?"

Charlie sipped some whiskey. "It's logical," he said.

Janey lit a cigarette, then blew the smoke away from Charlie. She was trying to smoke without inhaling and it made her smoke twice as much as usual. "Don't you know it's dangerous to try to do everything yourself? Are you going out to the lake tonight?"

"I was planning on it."

"Stay here. I'd feel better. I don't see enough of you as it is." She reached across the table to touch his hand.

"My revolver's out at the lake." He paused and glanced at Janey, who was giving him a worried look. She wore black running shorts and a black T-shirt. She kept jiggling her glass and the ice made a tinkling noise. Charlie gave her hand a squeeze. "If you see too much of me, you'll get tired of me. I wouldn't want that to happen."

"It's not seeing you that makes me tired of you," said Janey drawing her hand away, "it's not seeing you. Why do you have to spend so much time out at the lake?"

Charlie looked at her with surprise. He liked his own company, no matter how much he liked being with Janey as well. Or maybe it was his own solitude that he liked. He wasn't sure how to tell her this. "It's nice out at the lake," he said lamely. "And there are geese now. I can hear them honking all night long."

11

It sometimes occurred to Victor Plotz that in another life, if he were invited back to earth again in human form, he would like to be a writer. Not a poet or playwright, nothing serious. He would like to be a writer of Hollywood romances in which the young starlet half zonked on liquor and cocaine fell in love with the honest stuntman and, after three hundred pages of will-she-won't-she-will-she-won't-she, they get married and tumble energetically into the sack. And what was literature after all, Victor sometimes wondered, since most books spent most of their pages trying to get their heroes and heroines laid, which made the books not literature, but foreplay. Dickens, for example, wasn't copulation his secret destination? Even *Moby-Dick*—you knew perfectly well what Ishmael meant to do once he got off that boat. The purpose of his long stint on the *Pequod* was to give him a powerful sexual hunger. Oh, Victor had it figured out and if he got reincarnated as a writer of Hollywood thrillers he was going to pack each paragraph with squeezes.

It was this fantasy of being a writer which Victor later blamed for leading him into temptation, for having done something he shouldn't, for letting the burning authorial juices overrun his better judgment in the same manner that Mount Vesuvius once overran Pompeii. Let it be said right away that the letter from Virgil Darcy to Charlie Bradshaw was Victor's own creation. It seemed to Victor that Charlie was being too smug in the face of a possible death threat and so he decided to give his pal's adrenaline a couple of cranks toward the ceiling. As he often said later, he meant no harm in the least. He telephoned a friend in New York City, dictated the few simple phrases to stick in the mail and that was that.

Then, Friday evening, as Charlie had wandered through the dark of the Bentley, worrying about the possible intentions of Virgil Darcy, Victor was regaling his cronies at The Parting Glass, an Irish bar on Lake Avenue, on the cleverness of his practical joke. It should be said that Victor's cronies were like grains of sand upon a beach or like stars cast across the sky. Basically they included anyone within the range of his voice and Victor had a loud voice. Some were lawyers and some were bums; some were wealthy and some cadged drinks; some were flatterers and some were forthright. And perhaps Victor can be forgiven for exaggerating. It was the effect he wanted, not accuracy. If the truth were religiously adhered to, few jokes would elicit more than a wispy smile.

"And I said, 'Charlie, you look as serious as a dog in a boat.' But to tell the truth his hands were shaking. This is a man who I've seen relaxed under gunfire, who's faced odds of twenty to one. His hands were shaking and the paper was rattling and even the chair he was sitting in was banging against the desk so all the pencils rolled off onto the floor; and I said, 'Charlie, do you need a glass of water?' And he said, 'I could do with a shot of whiskey.' And he showed me the letter and said, 'This is the most dangerous man I've ever sent to prison and now he's coming to get me. It's just like the movie, *High Noon.*' And I said, 'DUM, da, da, DUM, da, da, DUM, DUM, da DUM!' 'No joking,' said Charlie, 'this could be the end of me!' "

There was more. Cronies contributed their own scenarios. At least a dozen people speculated on the degree of Charlie's fear. Could his gray hair turn white overnight? Would his hands continue to shake? Three or four times during the proceedings, Victor's cellular phone made its insistent buzzing, giving him a chance to shout out,

Buy low! or Sell high! before a crowd of witnesses. Several people remembered the bank holdup of twenty years before and several even claimed to remember Virgil Darcy. "Whitey," people had called him, although they hadn't. But others remembered Joey Damasco and Frank Bonita and how the $200,000 taken from the Marine Midland had never been recovered. There was speculation about where they were now and how pissed Virgil Darcy must be. They imagined Charlie sneaking around full of anxiety and this amused them because although they liked Charlie, he had been too successful and too independent and now he had been made to feel fear. He was just like they were, after all. Victor saw these peripheral subjects and he didn't quite like them. So he tried to draw the conversation back to his own cleverness and speculation about what Charlie might do next. "I wouldn't walk up on him from behind," Victor said. "He's too uptight. A nervous man is a dangerous man."

But all and all it had been very pleasant and Victor saw no reason why it couldn't be repeated. It was now Saturday morning and Victor was in his top-floor apartment in the Algonquin on Broadway seated at a table surrounded by crumpled-up sheets of paper. With mussed hair and wrinkled brow, he was in the throes of artistic creation. If truth be known, Victor was not entirely satisfied with his first letter ("To Charles Bradshaw: Don't think I've forgotten. I'm coming up to Saratoga to keep my promise. Make sure your prayers are said. Virgil"). It lacked those elements of the flamboyant and ornate to which Victor found himself naturally drawn. By being subtle it fell into the trap of being dull. Its very credibility rendered it lackluster. And although Charlie had been clearly startled, his socks were not knocked literally off. Like any writer, Victor wanted his reader to look up with dazed eyes and say, "My life has been changed."

So now Victor was sitting with a stack of paper, a dictionary and a Thesaurus and he was striving for the perfect articulation of menace. "Dear Bradshaw: I am drawing closer with an ax with which to chip away your kneecaps. . . ." "Dear Bradshaw: I'm going to boil your eyeballs to make soup for my dog. . . ." "Dear Bradshaw:

I'm going to use your ribs as a fork and spoon with which to eat the meatloaf I plan to make out of your brain. . . ." Victor had many variations on this theme of violence and cannibalism, and the writing of them kept him happily occupied throughout the morning. And when Eddie Gillespie called on the cellular phone—just because Victor had asked him to call regularly—Victor said, "Don't bother me. I'm making great art."

The only sour note in all this happy creation had come from Victor's girlfriend, Rosemary Larkin. She had called his joke "mean" and Victor had been shocked. "Me mean? Captain Kangaroo is an ax-murderer compared to me." In the past such criticism would have led Victor to seek out greener female pastures, his motto being: "Girls will come and go—they're just like streetcars." But Victor liked Rosemary more than most, perhaps because she also entrusted him with her investments. She was a pink-faced fifty-year-old woman who ran a lunch counter on Route 29 just west of Saratoga. "The queen of softness," Victor called her.

"I thought he was your best friend," she had said.

"Sure he's my best friend and we'll have a big laugh about this later. It'll take his mind off his troubles."

"I still think it's mean."

"A joke without teeth ain't funny," said Victor.

And because of Rosemary Larkin's criticism, Victor wanted his next letter to be an absolute riot and so he toiled and wadded up sheets of paper and threw them around the room. But beyond Victor's worries about his budding literary career, he was aware of Charlie's preoccupation with Grace Mulholland and the mistake he had made eighteen years earlier. The Saturday *Saratogian* had had Charlie on the front page in a venomous article by Arnett Stroud in which Charlie was quoted as saying that he never felt guilty for past blunders and anybody could make a mistake, but that now he had a serious client and he hoped to be given a second chance to find the murderer, who he expected to arrest in no time. The article concluded with Charlie's remark: "All we know for certain is that Grace Mulholland couldn't have buried herself," which Stroud had been able to frame in a context that made it seem cynically humorous.

Victor firmly believed that his practical joke would distract Charlie from his other troubles and give him a kind of breather. Hey, he was actually doing the guy a favor. Anyway, Charlie was taking this Mulholland business too seriously and there probably wasn't even any money in it. Certainly no big bucks. So what if Charlie had made a mistake? People made mistakes all the time. Even I make mistakes, thought Victor. If the first threatening letter from Virgil Darcy had been a simple joke, then the second one would be an even bigger joke. Even if it turned out to be a mistake to have written them, no harm had been meant, none in the least. And this was what Victor kept arguing for months afterward when everything had turned out to be troublesome and misunderstood.

12

Friday evening when Charlie had been making his way through the darkness of the Bentley, he had had every intention of spending the night with Janey Burris. But then, leaving the hotel, he thought again about the reports he had written eighteen years before and changed his mind. He wanted to read them in private. He didn't want Janey to know about them. So he decided to visit her just for an hour or so and then go home. Charlie felt embarrassed by his younger self and wanted to keep him a secret, at least from Janey. But was this all true? This was a question that Charlie had been asking himself a lot lately: Is it possible that I am lying to myself? And he had to tell himself that he thought it was true, but he wasn't certain. On the other hand, he was afraid that Janey would read the reports and say, "Oh, Charlie, what a jerk you used to be!" because that might lead her to change her mind about who he was right now in the present. Then her feelings about him might change entirely and it would be a real mess. Charlie had broken up with women before but he didn't see how he could break up with Janey Burris without being seriously damaged. It wasn't simply that he loved her, she had gotten under his skin in some way he couldn't explain.

It rained all night and the sound on the roof soothed Charlie's dreams, as if the orderly drumming lent structure to his sleep. He had found his revolver in a kitchen drawer and, after cleaning and loading it, he put it on his night table next to his bed: far enough away to reach in an emergency but not near enough so that he might knock it off in the night.

The next morning he was up at seven. The rain had stopped and there was a thick fog over the lake. Hung with wet, the leafless birches and maples looked like mourners at a funeral. Charlie stood at the end of his dock and listened for geese but the only sound was the lap of water against the pilings and from somewhere a barking dog. After making himself some hot oat bran for his cholesterol, he lit a fire in the stone fireplace and sat down in his easy chair to read the files of the five men who had been members of the Travel Bugs, between thirty and thirty-five pages. Within minutes he was gritting his teeth and squinting his eyes as if to put more distance between who he was now and who he had been in 1974.

It was clear that his younger self had found the Travel Bugs a bunch of foolishness: full-grown men and women spending fortunes on Airstream trailers so they could take bad snapshots of petrified wood. Considering how much he had disliked his own life at the time, Charlie thought his younger self should have had more patience with a group of harmless people engaged in a mild form of escapism. But this was not the case. ''Herman Evans's hardware store is on the verge of bankruptcy,'' Charlie had written of a man who had since died of leukemia, ''and yet he spends several hours a week with the Travel Bugs. He is treasurer, collects the dues and buys refreshments. He claims that he hardly knew Grace Mulholland, although once he got her to bake some chocolate chip cookies for a meeting. He says that she always paid her dues on time and never needed to be reminded. He called her a good citizen. I asked him what he meant by that and he said, 'Why, a member in good standing.' My cousin Jack [who also owned a hardware store in Saratoga] says it's only a matter of time before Evans's store is auctioned off to pay his debts.''

''Robert Hendricks,'' Charlie had written of the man who had moved to Missouri, "objected to my questions and said he planned to consult his lawyer. He is a travel agent in his mid-thirties. He said he had never exchanged a single word with Mulholland, and when I doubted that, he grew angry. He is married with five children but that doesn't mean anything. I asked him if he knew where Mulholland lived and that was when he said he'd have to consult his lawyer. I'll keep the pressure on him."

Hendricks and his family had moved to Columbia, Missouri, in 1980. Charlie guessed that he would at least have to ask Peterson to send a query to the Columbia police to see if any money had come into Hendricks's life.

The remaining three men still lived in Saratoga. Charlie wondered if the travel club was still in existence and if these men were still members. "Leon Futzel wears a cheaply made brown wig which must have cost about ten dollars. He is produce manager at the Grand Union and you'd think he could afford a better wig. He said that Mulholland used to shop at the Grand Union but after he spoke to her, she stopped coming. Futzel said that Mulholland had never given a presentation at the Travel Bugs and always sits in back. I asked what he had said to her that made her stop going to the Grand Union and he claims that he can't remember. Futzel is thirty-eight and divorced. His ex-wife lives in Albany with his daughter. I asked him about the reason for the divorce and he said 'incompatible differences.' I bet he plays around, or tries to."

"Vince Reardon is twenty-seven and a waiter at the Firehouse Restaurant on Broadway. He moved to Saratoga in the fall and hopes to work at the track this summer. He is married and his wife works as a waitress somewhere. No kids. He says he joined the Travel Bugs around Christmas because he was bored. He has spent a lot of time in the Southwest and did a slide presentation about Santa Fe. He says that Grace Mulholland asked him for a copy of one of his slides showing a Mexican church. He asked her if she was going to give a presentation and if she had visited any interesting places. She said that she hadn't been anywhere yet but that she knew some Spanish. He said in the time he had been there, she had never missed a meeting. All of the members of the club are older than Reardon and I can't see what he's doing there. Maybe he's bored, as he says. Maybe he's lonely."

"Frankie Manelli is a big fat Italian with a black mustache and thick black hair. He was a year ahead of me in high school and I remember he once got in trouble for sneaking into the girls' locker room and stealing Jean Potter's white sneakers. He acted as if I were an old friend but he knows I've never liked him. Three years ago he was arrested for drunk driving and he joined the Travel Bugs shortly afterward, probably to make himself look good if he got arrested again. He claims that he never spoke to Grace Mulholland and that she was scared of him. I asked what he had done to scare her and he claimed not to know. She was probably scared he would accidentally sit on her."

On each of these five men Charlie had written between six and eight pages of notes which included bits of interviews, musings and detailed information. From each he had later typed up a condensed report. The three men still in Saratoga he would have to visit. Manelli was a plumbing contractor who had several white Ford vans with his named printed in big black letters across the side. Charlie saw them all the time. Vince Reardon owned an upscale bar and restaurant on Caroline Street called Mother McDougle's. Leon Futzel worked at the Shop and Save, where he was manager or assistant manager. Charlie had seen him there as recently as a month ago.

But to Charlie the most mysterious character in this whole business was himself, or rather who he had been in 1974. He disliked the person who had written these notes but perhaps he was being unfair. His younger self was clearly unhappy and maybe this alone explained the difference. He hadn't necessarily been wrong or foolish or bad. Just cheerless. But it also unnerved Charlie that he didn't recognize this younger self who seemed so eager to find fault; and Charlie imagined his younger self as a person who loved to seek out the foibles of his fellow creatures. But was that really true? He was a cop and people didn't come across his line of vision unless their foibles had blossomed into serious problems. Hadn't it been his job to find foibles?

Still, there was something smarmy about this younger self, something a little superior. He seemed both intellectually fastidious and barren: one of those people who keep their buttons always buttoned and their arms always crossed. But then Charlie thought it was perhaps unfair to blame this younger self for the quality of these notes. He was no writer and the notes were no more than jottings. Certainly they hadn't been intended for the critical attention he was now giving them. In the written reports, he hadn't mentioned how Frank Manelli had once sneaked into the girls' locker room or that Leon Futzel wore a cheap wig. Perhaps it was only his younger self's lack of literary ability that he disliked and perhaps any notes he wrote now would look equally unattractive. Perhaps it wasn't his former personality that Charlie objected to but the abbreviation, the subjective shorthand he had used to sketch the psychological dimensions of each of his possible suspects. Then he again recalled Maximum Tubbs's description of him: a miserable cuss. But as a gambler Tubbs was on the other side of the law. Perhaps he would have been equally critical of all policemen.

Somewhat bravely Charlie decided to visit his ex-wife. He had hardly exchanged a word with her in sixteen years and if he sometimes caught sight of Marge downtown, it was only by accident. In fact, he had gone out of his way to avoid her and for years had bypassed Broadway so as not to cross her path. Long after their divorce Marge had continued to criticize him to practically everyone, describing what she called Charlie's laziness and childishness, but now she seemed to have quieted down. Charlie still felt reluctant to see her. And what was he afraid of? Stern stares and critical looks.

Occasionally he heard about Marge from his cousins. Lucy, her partner in the boutique, was the wife of his cousin Robert. But Charlie knew little about Marge. Did she have a boyfriend or belong to a bridge club or bet the horses or have a dog? He realized with surprise that they had been divorced far longer than they had been married. Originally she must have had something that appealed to him. She was a strong-minded woman who never lacked an opinion and she had been physically attractive in a military sort of way. In any case she had been the wife of the man—this younger self—who had written these reports. It was only after Charlie had decided to change his life that they had gotten divorced.

But now it seemed to Charlie that if his inability to discover what had happened to Grace Mulholland in 1974 was due to something in his psychology—perhaps a flaw, perhaps a virtue (no, not a virtue, he thought)—then perhaps Marge could give him some clues. For not only was he trying to track down the person who had killed Grace Mulholland, he was also trying to discover the character of the overcritical policeman who had originally handled the investigation: that is, himself.

At precisely nine-thirty, Charlie hesitantly opened the front door of his ex-wife's boutique on Broadway with the sense—certainly irrational—that a truckload of bricks was about to fall on his head. But the taboo of not seeing her had grown so great that to break it made Charlie feel endangered. It was a large store with a maze of clothing racks and white wicker furniture. On the walls were movie posters and Indian wall hangings. At first Charlie thought the store was empty. Then he noticed a middle-aged woman in back sorting through a stack of Indian blouses. Then he realized that the middle-aged woman was his ex-wife.

At fifty, Marge had become as solid as a punching bag. Although she wasn't fat, she had no waist and seemed the same width from her shoulders to her thighs. Marge had dark brown hair of a color not originally her own which was curled and swooped up on one side in a way to remind Charlie of birds in flight. She wore a brown skirt and matching jacket with a colorful red silk scarf at the collar of her white blouse. Marge's ambition had always been to be a high-minded, no-nonsense woman whom people took seriously and in this she had succeeded. As he approached her across the store, Charlie tried to remember having had sex with her, of having lain naked with her side by side. The memory felt more like a fantasy, yet surely it had happened and surely he had loved her. As an event, however, it was like an object on Mars: very far away and invisible without the best scientific equipment. Charlie found nothing unattractive about his ex-wife. After all, being fifty was nobody's fault and to look like a Marine sergeant in drag had perhaps been a secret desire. It was just that she looked so foreign to what he had known and so distant from the years they had shared together.

As Charlie approached her between the racks of colorful skirts and blouses, he saw Marge's dark brown eyes widen slightly and he knew this would be the only evidence of her astonishment. Indeed, her features were already relaxing themselves into an expression which suggested that she had been expecting this visit for a long time. Marge closed her lips more firmly and waited for him to speak.

"You're looking well, Marge," said Charlie, trying to keep his voice relaxed.

She didn't answer right away and her silence seemed to ask if he had made this first visit in sixteen years just to comment on her appearance. "You look well yourself," she said at last. Her voice had grown huskier and wrinkles appeared around her lips when she spoke.

"I'm working on a case that I was first involved with as a policeman. Maybe you heard something about it: Grace Mulholland? She'd disappeared back in 1974."

Marge nodded toward the cash register and Charlie noticed a newspaper on the counter. "There was an article this morning in the *Saratogian.* They seemed pretty hard on you."

"They see it as my big mistake, my goof-up. It's just a way of selling papers."

Marge didn't respond to this but continued to look at Charlie expectantly. He noticed the crow's-feet around her eyes, the slanting furrows running from her nose to the sides of her mouth. She wore a lot of makeup and her rosy expression seemed almost unhealthy.

"My mistake was in thinking she'd left the country and was living happily ever after," said Charlie. "Now I want to find out who killed her."

"I have only the vaguest memory of the case," said Marge. She folded her arms, then unfolded them and held her hands at her sides as if they made her uncomfortable.

"I thought perhaps I could get a better idea about the nature of my mistake if I had a better idea about who I was back then. And I thought you could help me. Of course I know you have a lot of anger . . ."

"You seemed very unhappy," said Marge, quickly brushing aside his attempt to describe her feelings. "I know I didn't deal with it very well. I saw your unhappiness as criticism and it made me angry with you. I tried to make a perfect house and a perfect place for us within the community and you seemed to want no part of that. It took me a long time to realize that I made mistakes as well. I wanted you to be a certain way and if you refused to be that way, then I saw it as your fault."

Charlie was so touched that he wanted to reach out and take her hand, to apologize for thinking badly of her. Instead, he rubbed his brow and looked away. "Well, I couldn't have been very easy," he said. He realized that she was making a sort of explanation, even an apology, and he felt guilty for having misjudged her.

"You wanted another kind of life. You were right to ask for a divorce. I wasn't ready to change and I refused to see anything was wrong. In many ways, we were just incompatible but I wish we'd been more patient with each other."

"I tried to be patient."

"When you grew unhappy, you'd pull away," said Marge more sharply. "You wouldn't talk. You'd just mope around the house. It was like living with a stranger. You tried not to react to anything and I did things to make you react. Once you didn't speak to me for two weeks."

"I'm sorry."

"None of it matters now." Marge turned away. The store was

still empty. Muted Muzak based on rock and roll themes drifted down from speakers in the ceiling.

"I remember being unhappy," said Charlie, "but I'm sorry I was so unfeeling about your own unhappiness." Now Charlie had become uncomfortable with his hands and he shoved them in his pockets. Even though he was glad for this conversation, it would have been easier if she had been simply mad at him.

"You disliked almost everything you did and felt bitter about the people around you. All you liked was coaching Little League, and I criticized that just to get even with you. It's no fun living with an ill-tempered ghost. Your cousins helped me a lot during that time, but you seemed to despise them."

"I did," said Charlie. "They were always critical."

"Everyone has a different idea about what someone needs, and if the person is someone you care about, then it's even harder. Do you remember how you went to movies all the time? You'd go by yourself, your cousins thought that was crazy."

"I'd forgotten," said Charlie. He'd always liked movies but he could remember nothing that struck him as obsessive. "My cousins are sometimes too businesslike. I guess they saw going to movies as a waste of time."

Marge laughed abruptly. "James used to call you a dreamer. He made it sound like a perversion."

"I think it took me a long time to get through adolescence," said Charlie, trying to smile but not feeling like it.

"And I couldn't get through it fast enough," said Marge.

"I'm sorry it's taken so long to get around to talking to you," said Charlie.

"No, I hated you and thought I was right to hate you. Now I don't care. I don't particularly like you but I wish you well. I'm only sorry I didn't have more sense at the beginning. I used to think I could do things and feel things and change things just by willing them, by wanting them hard enough. That was a mistake but none of it seems to matter now."

Charlie felt some apprehension at the seriousness of their talk and wished he could make a joke in order to change the tone. That was something that Victor could do: radically change the tone of a conversation without causing serious offense. Then Charlie thought that Marge had probably wanted to say these things for a long time. Perhaps they even needed to be said. As for who they were and who they had become, each was still an unfinished story for the other and their talk that morning was a kind of conclusion. Again, Charlie was struck that for years he had been frightened of seeing her.

"It seems to me," said Charlie, "that I was certain Grace Mulholland had run away to start a new life because that's what I wanted to do myself."

"Possibly," said Marge, "but it seems an easy explanation. You must have had some evidence."

It occurred to Charlie that Marge was the sort of person who would always disagree, no matter what was said. Even if you said something that she passionately believed, she would rephrase to make it more exactly her own. But is that really true? Charlie asked himself: isn't that just my old defensiveness again?

"Whoever killed her," said Charlie, "tried to make it seem that she had run away to Central America or somewhere. He offered the bait and I took it."

"But since you know that, won't you find him more easily? Whatever your faults, Charlie, you're certainly the most stubborn person I've ever known." Marge smiled slightly and Charlie realized that she was trying to make a joke.

He tried to think of some neutral thing to say. Glancing around, he noticed the cutouts of pumpkins and turkeys in the window. "How's your store been?"

"We're depending a lot on the week after Thanksgiving. Indian blouses aren't as popular as they were." She paused. Two young women entered the store and a little bell tinkled in back. "So do you have what you wanted?" Her tone had changed, becoming a little harder, as if she wanted him to go.

"A friend of mine described me back then as 'a miserable cuss' and I was hoping that wasn't really true.'' Again Charlie tried an uncomfortable smile.

''I'd say no to the 'cuss' part,'' said Marge. The two young women were standing by the cash register. ''I've got customers.''

Charlie took a step toward the door. ''Thanks for the help. Maybe I'll stop by again for a talk.'' Looking at her, Charlie realized that she didn't believe him. Then he realized that he didn't believe it himself.

13

Leon Futzel still wore a wig but it seemed expensive and had a gray color that was almost natural. Dressed in white with a white apron, he stood back by the meat counter of the Shop and Save explaining to a young male clerk how to make a pyramid out of packages of hamburger. The clerk was listening as attentively as if Futzel were telling how to build the Eiffel Tower. Charlie stood nearby, waiting for the opportune moment to interrupt. He had first driven by Futzel's house and had been told by a middle-aged woman (presumably Futzel's second wife) that Leon "had gone to the mines today," meaning he was at the supermarket.

"Your husband ever gamble?" Charlie had asked.

"Only when he married me," the sprightly wife replied.

Futzel had laid out a row of hamburger packages. He was a vigorous-looking man in his late fifties. "The trick is to stagger them," he was saying, "with about an inch between, and you start out with a platform of twenty-four—six wide and four deep—then you work your way up. But don't use bloody packages. A good customer hates blood. . . ." There was more. Charlie wondered what his own life would have been had he worked in a supermarket. Maybe he too would be jolly and wear a wig. How could he have thought that this man might have killed Grace Mulholland? He was tempted to sneak away, but decided he still had a few questions. Weren't there always questions? Also, he had felt stunned by his conversation with Marge, what it said about her, what it said about himself.

When Futzel was finished with the clerk and turned toward the mysterious back rooms of the supermarket, Charlie stepped forward to introduce himself.

"I read about you in the paper," said Futzel cheerfully, "and how you'd been wrong about that poor dead woman. And of course I remember you from years ago. You're older."

"That's right," said Charlie, wondering what the man had expected after eighteen years. "I've aged."

"Tell you the truth, I'd thought the woman had run away as well. I mean, don't we always hope that people's lives get better? Sometimes when it's been snowing hard and the wind's blowing I'd think of Grace down in some sunny country, smelling the jasmine and honeysuckle. What a shame."

"Why'd you think she'd run away?"

Futzel seemed surprised. "It's what everyone seemed to think. And maybe you said she did."

"Do you still go to the Travel Bugs?" Charlie followed Futzel into the back, where brown cardboard boxes were stacked to the ceiling. A yellow forklift glided toward a semi-trailer parked at a loading dock.

"No, they petered out eight years ago. Tell you the truth, I think we got killed by the video stores. People started renting movies. In fifty years, I bet no one'll ever leave their houses. And they'll look just like slugs, big fat white slugs. Bet you're glad you won't be around. I know I am."

"I was wondering if you'd ever talked to Grace Mulholland," asked Charlie.

"Not really. I addressed some remarks in her direction but she never responded. Of course it's been a while but that's how I remember it. I'm a man who likes his joke and Miss Mulholland was of a serious demeanor. So I would say something witty about the weather or about something funny in the newspaper and she'd pretend she hadn't heard. Maybe sometimes she'd blush. Once I offered to show her my wig and she became upset. After that I decided to let sleeping dogs lie. Am I a suspect?'' Leon Futzel seemed happy with the thought.

''More a vague possibility than a suspect.''

''I've always liked crime,'' said Futzel cheerily. ''I mean I like reading about it. Take Agatha Christie, for example, I bet she'd have made a wonderful ax-murderer. We're lucky she wasn't born seven feet tall with a mean disposition, right? Well, maybe in another life.'' He drew a pack of Luckies from his shirt pocket and offered one to Charlie, who declined. Then he lit one himself with a shiny silver Zippo and blew the smoke out of the corner of his mouth. The Zippo clicked shut.

''Do you remember Grace Mulholland talking to anybody?'' It seemed to Charlie that Futzel was an entirely different person than he had been eighteen years earlier. Had he always been so aggressively humorous?

''Sometimes she talked to the women, but not much. She liked the slides and seeing faraway places. And I think she liked being near people, having them nearby without having to talk to them. Sometimes I thought she was dying to talk but just didn't know how.''

''What makes you think that?''

''Well, she'd stand at the edge of conversations and listen, and sometimes she'd nod her head or shake it a little. She wouldn't look at the person who was talking but she'd have her ear cocked.''

''And she went often?''

''Never missed a meeting as far as I could tell.''

''Did she ever talk to any of the men?''

''I suppose she must have but I don't remember seeing it. Maybe some of the women could tell you better.''

Charlie had been afraid of that. It had been wrong to think he could restrict his investigation to just men who had been under fifty at the time.

After leaving Leon Futzel, Charlie drove over to the police station and spent an hour making a list of the women members of the Travel Bugs and the book club and checking their addresses. Then he called Eddie Gillespie and said he needed his services as an assistant private detective.

"Do I get to carry a gun, Charlie?"

"I want you to talk to a number of older women. Do you have a suit? Wear it and wear a nice tie as well, nothing flashy." Charlie could hear a baby crying in the background and the sound of a TV turned up too loud.

"This doesn't sound like fun, Charlie."

"These are all women who knew Grace Mulholland. I want you to ask them who she talked to, but especially if she talked to any men. This is very subtle work, Eddie, I'm trusting you."

"And you don't think I'll need a gun?"

Charlie sighed. Hiring Eddie was like employing a baseball bat to do the work of a dental pick.

"You've got to be very quiet on this one, Eddie. You like police work. With something like this, you'll have your foot in the door. It's a big opportunity."

"And will I get paid this time, Charlie?"

"Only if you don't frighten anybody."

"Where're the laughs, Charlie?"

"They come after you get paid. Come on, Eddie, I need your help. After all, you're the one who found the skull."

Mother McDougle's on Caroline Street was located about two blocks east of Broadway in a two-story brick house which gave the restaurant an intimate quality. Downstairs was the bar, upstairs were about six rooms where food was served. Like all Saratoga restaurants it made most of its money during the summer, but unlike some it remained open the entire year. Charlie had never eaten at Mother McDougle's but he had had drinks in the bar, which prided itself on a wide variety of expensive wines. Charlie hadn't tried the wine. Maybe he'd had a Budweiser or a Jim Beam Manhattan. Whatever it was, he felt the drinks were overpriced and he hadn't gone back.

Or maybe he hadn't gone back because the patrons tended to be lawyers and business types with high-priced neckties. Around noon Charlie found Vince Reardon in the bar going over the specials being offered that Saturday evening.

"I thought I might see you," said Reardon, reaching out to shake Charlie's hand. He was a handsome blond man in his mid-forties who Charlie had sometimes seen playing basketball at the Y. "The paper said you were investigating the Mulholland case."

"Well, it was my case when I was a cop."

"Amazing to think of her under Jacko's all those years." The pool hall had stood a block and a half from the restaurant.

"Do you remember what the two of you used to talk about when you belonged to that travel club?" Charlie asked. He had sat down on a stool. Reardon stood behind the bar. At several small tables some people were having lunch. Everyone was dressed very nicely. Charlie wondered whether it should bother him that he bought most of his clothes from JC Penney's.

"I'm not sure I ever talked to her at all," said Reardon. "It's been a long time."

"You told me before that she had asked you for a copy of a slide, some Mexican church."

"Then I must have, but I don't remember it. I mean, I remember that she seemed to be particularly interested in Spanish and South American stuff." Reardon shrugged pleasantly. He had an easy smile and the sort of friendly face that seemed to shine. He wore a white shirt with a blue polka-dot bowtie. On the wall by the mirror hung some kind of baseball trophy. Charlie tried to read what it said but was too far away. The trophy showed golden crossed bats over a pitcher's glove.

"Do you remember if Grace Mulholland had any friends in the group or if there was anyone she talked to?"

"Not really. Possibly she talked to the women."

"Do you know if she ever missed any meetings?"

"Again, I don't know. I mean I remember her as shy and rather plain. I hardly thought about her at all before she disappeared. Then when she apparently took off with that insurance money I couldn't imagine it. Who would have thought she'd been a crook? Wasn't the FBI looking for her?"

"They didn't find anything. No one figured she was dead."

"Can I give you anything?" asked Reardon. "I've got a nice Australian chardonnay."

"A Budweiser's fine, unless you have Rolling Rock."

Reardon drew a green bottle of Rolling Rock from the cooler, opened it and began to pour it into a glass.

"I can pour it," said Charlie. Noticing Reardon's surprised look, he added, "I guess I like to pour it myself. Less foam."

Reardon pushed the glass and bottle toward Charlie. "I'm probably the same way," he said grinning.

"What's that baseball trophy on the wall?"

"My team won their division championship two years ago. It was a big deal."

"Your team?"

"The restaurant sponsors a kids' team. We buy uniforms, equipment, then volunteer as coaches. My headwaiter's a great pitching coach. The chef coaches first base."

"That seems like a nice thing to do," said Charlie somewhat enviously. "How long have you had this place?"

"My wife and I opened it in '82 so it's been about ten years. We split up a few years ago and I was able to buy her out."

"Kids?"

"Nope."

"Did she stay around here?"

"She went back to Santa Fe. We were from there originally, then we went back in the late seventies for about five years. She hated the winters up here."

"Her name was Irma, right?"

"No, Mary Rose."

"Is Santa Fe where you got the money for this place?"

"I'd always wanted a restaurant. I saved a lot working as a waiter, both here and in the Southwest. You can make a bundle at the right places. I bought this place at the right time when interest rates were down. After that, prices really started to explode.''

''You have any ideas who might have killed Grace?''

''The whole thing astonishes me. Maybe someone she worked with, maybe a relative. I've got no ideas. I mean she seemed so mild, almost as if she wasn't there at all.''

''D'you think she had a lover?''

Reardon looked astonished. ''I can't imagine it. You mean a man? She seemed too frightened, but who knows? That part of a person's life has always been a mystery to me.''

''Me too,'' said Charlie.

Frankie Manelli still had a thick mustache but it had gone gray and he was now almost bald. He was still fat, however, and just as loud as ever. He and Charlie were in Manelli's basement rec room where Manelli had been watching the Michigan–Notre Dame game on a big Sony. It was now halftime and the sound was off. On the screen miniature Michigan band members were duplicating the shape of an angry wolverine with precision marching.

''Sure,'' Manelli was saying, ''we were in shop class together. Mr. Perkins. You were making a coffin for your dog.''

''I never made a coffin for a dog,'' said Charlie indignantly. He was drinking a Beck's dark and his mouth was half full of potato chips.

''Sure you were. You had this old dog that you said was dying and so you were making a coffin. I remember you saying that you just hoped the dog lived long enough for you to finish the coffin. The teacher thought you were nuts.''

''I never made a coffin for a dog,'' repeated Charlie. Had he? Had he really made a coffin for a dog? He couldn't remember. In fact, he could hardly remember shop class.

''It even had little silver handles, although maybe they were chrome. You put on a couple of coats of poly so it really shown. And a red interior. Pillowy, if you know what I mean. I thought it was too nice for a dog, even a good dog.''

"I never . . ." Charlie began to say and then he gave it up. He'd had a little dog named Mike which had died when Charlie was in his late teens. Could he have made a coffin for it? Surely if he had done it in shop class, he was only showing off. He thought of all the people who had crossed his path over the years and how they all carried a small piece of his history which he himself might have forgotten. He imagined gathering all these people together in order to reconstruct himself.

"Grace Mulholland," said Charlie, "what do you remember about her?"

"Not a thing," said Manelli, eyeing the Michigan cheerleaders, who were kicking up their long legs. "She seemed like a mouse and I bet she even squeaked."

"You told me before that you had frightened her. Do you remember why?"

"Jeez, Charlie, I hardly remember talking to you. And I sure can't remember frightening her. She was a nervous little thing who always sat in the back of the room. Maybe I sneezed at her or something." Manelli kept watching the cheerleaders. He wore a blue RPI sweatshirt and drank his Beck's from the bottle.

"Do you remember anyone talking to her?"

"Tell you the truth, I haven't thought of her for eighteen years. When I read about her skeleton being dug up, I at first didn't even know who it was. I mean, the name drew a complete blank. You think I got her to embezzle all that money and then scragged her? I sure the shit wouldn't be hanging around here if I had. I'd have gone to Trinidad or someplace like that."

"I'm just trying to get some kind of lead," said Charlie, trying to keep the complaint out of his voice.

"So you think she was killed by one of the Travel Bugs?"

"Not necessarily but it was certainly someone who knew her and it was most likely a man."

"Well, I quit that group, oh, way back in the seventies. Just too boring. I figured I'd rather go to the track instead of travel. I don't even know if it's still going on."

"It's not. Did you have any friends in the group."

"Nah, I mean there're people I still run into. Maggie Henry, the librarian, a couple of others. Vince Reardon, who's got the restaurant, Ruth Robinson down at the Chamber of Commerce. I got my hands full being a plumbing contractor. How come you're still fussing with this if you're not a cop?"

"Unfinished business, I guess."

"I remember in school you were a stubborn sort of guy. What was that fellow, Jerry something, who told you to wash his car or he'd punch you out. Every day you told him no and every day he'd bash you one. Remember that? Finally he just got depressed and gave up. You had a bunch of Band-Aids on your face. What was that, tenth grade? I could never figure if the Band-Aids covered real bruises or if you just put them on to make him feel bad."

"I wanted to make him feel bad," said Charlie, who remembered nothing about the incident. All the fights he had in school had blended into an unpleasant blur. If he had won any, then perhaps he would remember them more clearly. And hadn't it been nearly forty years ago?

The game was starting. Manelli pressed the mute button and turned his attention to the screen. Michigan was kicking off. The announcer was talking excitedly and tiny cheering swelled in the background. "Hey, hey! Ten bucks that Notre Dame clobbers them!" said Manelli, finishing his Beck's.

"I remember you snuck into the girls' locker room and swiped Jean Potter's white sneakers," said Charlie, just to show that he remembered something.

"Yeah," said Manelli, as he watched a Notre Dame receiver make it to the twenty-five. "I had the hots for her. I was a real cutup, always having fun. These days it's all trouble and backaches. Who would've thought it could happen?"

14

There came a point in most cases which Charlie thought of as the pick-and-shovel part of the case. It was simple slogging, sometimes days of talking to one person after another as he tried to get a handle on what the case was all about. He compared it to swimming: when you jump in deep water and for a moment don't know if you are upside down or right side up, a period of darkness and confusion. But in investigations it came in the middle, an analytical floundering which would be worse if Charlie hadn't learned to be patient and follow his leads and wait for that mental prickling that told him that somehow the case was declaring itself even if he wasn't yet conscious of it. Suddenly one day there would come an alertness and Charlie would cheer up because he knew that from now on it was all downhill.

But this case was more troublesome because of Charlie's doubts about what he had done eighteen years earlier and what he was doing now, doubts that kept him from seeing clearly, which made him think that seeing clearly wasn't possible. And always, like an alarm clock jangling in the background, was Charlie's awareness of Virgil Darcy and his possible grim plans.

For the remainder of Saturday and most of Sunday Charlie talked to men and women (but mostly men) he had interviewed eighteen years before: neighbors, members of Grace Mulholland's church, people she knew in school, her family and friends of her family. He even drove out to Great Sacandaga Lake to see her older brother, Fred Mulholland, the retired electrician. Halfway to the lake was a smaller lake by the name of Lake Desolation, while on the opposite side of Saratoga was a small lake called Lake Lonely. And sometimes when Charlie was feeling blue, he liked to think of Saratoga as the town situated between Lake Lonely and Lake Desolation. He slowed as he passed the lake. No one was in sight, not even any bass fishermen. "Desolate," he said to himself, then pressed down firmly on the accelerator.

Years ago in his old notes Charlie had described Fred Mulholland as a potential gambler and his wife, Gladys, as a potential drinker. Visiting their small house on Great Sacandaga Lake, Charlie looked for signs of gambling and drinking, but there were none. The house was tidy and its occupants seemed sane and conventional.

"My sister was not a sociable woman, Mr. Bradshaw," Fred Mulholland told him as they sat on the front porch. "Even as a child she had few friends. Grace had a pretty tough shell and people had a hard time getting through it. It took years for her to accept my wife, Gladys, who's the kindest soul in the world. Actually I wasn't surprised to learn she was dead, even though it was terrible news. I couldn't imagine Grace going off on her own. What was she going to do in Costa Rica once she got there?"

"So you've had no new ideas?" Charlie asked. It was Sunday afternoon and Mulholland had given Charlie a bottle of Miller's and took one for himself. He was a thin, angular man with a shock of white hair and he wore a blue work shirt with the name "Fred" stenciled on the pocket. His wife, Gladys, hovered nearby, nodding whenever her husband spoke. A pro-football game was on the TV.

"New ideas? I don't know. We buried what was left of Grace on Friday and I've been thinking a lot about her, certainly more than in the past eighteen years. Somebody obviously robbed her, killed her and stuck her under the pool hall. There's no way to deny that even if I want to. But I've been thinking about the people she knew or might have known and there's just one fellow who comes to mind, a young man who used to mow her lawn. When she disappeared, of course, I didn't even think twice about him."

"Who was it?" Charlie asked.

"Ward something, but I don't know if that was his first or last name. He lived over on York Street. He went to jail in the late seventies for a couple of robberies down in Albany. He cut my sister's lawn for years when he was a teenager."

"You have any reason to suspect him?"

"Only those robberies. I never met the fellow myself."

When he got back to Saratoga, Charlie stopped by police headquarters. The desk sergeant knew nothing about anyone by the name of Ward. He was a red-faced, pear-shaped man known as Doofus O'Dwire. He had seen the recent articles describing Charlie's mistake of eighteen years earlier and felt it was a shame that Charlie should be mixed up with police business.

"The records section is closed, Mr. Bradshaw. You'll have to talk to Chief Peterson Monday morning."

"Thanks," said Charlie, half relieved to be done with the business for the day.

Early Sunday evening Charlie visited Maximum Tubbs, whom he hadn't seen for several days. He felt guilty about this and he hoped it wasn't because Tubbs had called his younger self "a miserable cuss."

"You went and visited your ex-wife, Charlie?" Tubbs said in a wheezy whisper. "That's probably the bravest thing you've ever done. She throw anything at you?"

"Actually, I felt sorry for her. I mean, it was fine but she seemed brittle and of course she's older and I don't think her store's doing well. It's too bad I didn't see her years ago, just to lay the whole thing to rest."

"Like you're laying me to rest?"

"I'm here because you're my friend."

"I appreciate that. Just don't forget my wake, that's all that counts. We'll have a great time." Tubbs was propped up on pillows with his thin hands resting on the counterpane. He spoke without looking at Charlie, who sat on a chair by his side. "Victor was here earlier, laughing about something. He wouldn't say what. What a happy barrel of pork that guy is."

"He'll end up as mayor of Saratoga."

"He said you were upset about Virgil Darcy, is that true?"

Maximum Tubbs's temples were peculiarly prominent and shiny and Charlie kept staring at them. The hair on his head was no more than fuzz. "Well, I probably haven't thought about it as much as I should. I received a threatening note from him. But I just can't believe he'd try to kill me."

"I remember him as a nice kid," said Tubbs.

"Prison will change a person. I found my revolver, oiled it and loaded it, then I forgot it and left it out at the lake. This business with Grace Mulholland takes all my attention. One woman told me that Grace used to read romantic novels and a man told me she always kept her shades drawn and a fellow who fixed her car said she'd write him letters saying what she wanted done but she'd never talk to him in person. I don't know why I felt she'd left the country. It would have been impossible for her."

"How'd she run that insurance office?"

It occurred to Charlie that Tubbs wasn't asking out of interest but because he was trying to keep one foot in the world, trying to keep the world alive to him. He mulled that over for a moment before answering. "I think basically she was a little bossy—one of those people who pride themselves on knowing what's best. But she wasn't friends with anyone in her office. Maybe she was cordial, but she'd never chat and shoot the breeze. She was efficient and they trusted her and then she went and embezzled $233,000."

"I wonder if she played cards," said Tubbs. "I like a girl with a stake of over two hundred grand."

"Maybe solitaire," said Charlie. "You have any games here?" He could never bring himself to pronounce the word "hospice."

"You kidding? With this morphine I couldn't even play gin rummy. Maybe I could manage a game of old maid. I'm not here to gamble, I'm here to die." Tubbs turned his head slightly and fixed his pale eyes on Charlie, then he tried to smile.

"I keep hoping you'll get better."

"And I keep hoping my shit will turn to hundred-dollar bills. Nobody gets better in this place, Charlie. With the morphine I keep drifting along, sort of dreaming while being awake. Sometimes people who've been dead for years, come and visit and it takes a while to realize it's just a dream. I can't decide if I like it or don't like it."

"You ever see my father?" Charlie asked.

"Not yet, but I'll keep my eye out."

"If you see him, give him my best."

Sunday evening Charlie went over to Janey's, promising himself he would be on his best behavior. But his visit with Maximum Tubbs and his interviews with the people who had known Grace Mulholland had left him melancholy and, he felt, somewhat illogical. For instance he found himself thinking that it was unfair that people had to die. He didn't mind about his own death so much—perhaps because he imagined it far in the future—but he didn't like Tubbs dying and he didn't see why it had to happen. "Unjust" was the word he used to himself. Then he laughed at his foolishness even while being at the edge of tears.

"We've got to make plans about Thanksgiving," Charlie told Janey. "You want it out at the lake?"

"Your stove can't cook a turkey," Janey said suspiciously. She hadn't trusted his good mood and she told him later that his eyes had looked sad.

"Then we'll do it here. Can I bring anything? Yams, I like yams. Or cranberry sauce. I'll do anything to make you happy."

"Charlie, why are you acting so cheerful, when you don't feel like it?" They sat at the kitchen table. Janey leaned toward him to see him better. A bottle of Jim Beam green and a bowl of dry roasted peanuts stood between them. All the things that are bad for me, Charlie thought.

"I've decided to be more upbeat."

"You just leave Maximum Tubbs?"

"That's right."

"Poor Charlie."

"That's what people keep saying about Grace Mulholland. 'Poor Grace.' I'm not that bad." He ate some peanuts. He sometimes thought he could eat buckets of dry roasted peanuts without stopping.

"Is that what you've been doing all day, learning about Grace Mulholland?"

Charlie nodded as he chewed the peanuts.

"Make anyone mad?"

"Only Burke Chaffee—you know, he married Mulholland's niece. I went over to his house to needle him, ask him again where he got the money to open his Toyota dealership."

"Do you really suspect him?"

"It's a long shot. Apparently he inherited the money. I was just trying to stir him up to see if he'd let something slip, also so he can be indignant about it around town. Make complaints about me."

"Why do you want that?" Janey had her elbows on the table and stared at Charlie. She wore a red V-neck cotton sweater and Charlie could see that she wasn't wearing a bra.

"If the murderer's still in the vicinity, I'd like to make him nervous. Maybe he'll do something to reveal himself."

"Like shoot you?"

"Nothing so radical, I hope."

"Have you heard anything more about that Virgil person?"

"No. I'm sure that was just a one-time threat. Actually, I heard about another ex-con today." He told Janey about the man named Ward who used to cut Grace Mulholland's lawn.

"And you think he might have killed Grace Mulholland?"

"I don't think anything, I just want to learn more about him. Grace hardly talked to any men but she talked to this guy. I mean, everyone else I've talked to says how nice Grace was and how shy and how she liked books and loved to fantasize about taking trips to South America and this Ward guy is the only person I've turned up who seems to have a dark side."

Janey sipped her whiskey and looked at Charlie over the edge of her glass. "Can you see people's dark sides?"

"Sometimes."

"Can you see mine?"

"I'd rather not comment." Charlie laughed and looked away.

"Charlie, let's go upstairs and go to bed. We've been forgetting each other too much recently. I'll show you my dark side and you can show me yours."

For a moment Charlie hesitated. He was still full of Grace Mulholland and wanted to think about it some more. Then he glanced again at Janey's red sweater. Finishing his drink, he stood up abruptly. The kitchen chair fell over behind him with a crash. "Let's go," he said.

"Attaboy, Charlie." Janey's chair tumbled over as well.

By late Sunday three elderly women had called the police department to complain about Eddie Gillespie and the first thing Monday morning Chief Peterson telephoned Charlie at his office.

"It was his tie, Charlie. Seen from one direction it shows a cutie in a bathing suit, seen from another direction she's nude. So it's always, you know, on and off, on and off. This is a guy you're employing? Come on, Charlie, be professional."

"I'll talk to him about it."

"And his manner, Charlie, tell him not to be so threatening. Why act like a tough guy? These are old women."

"Eddie tends to get enthusiastic."

"I'd hate to have to pick him up."

"I'll call him," said Charlie. "By the way, I have to come by in a while about this Mulholland business."

"I'll be here all day."

Hanging up, Charlie looked pensively at the poster of Jesse James. After Bob Ford and his brother had received the ten-thousand-dollar reward for killing Jesse, they made a tour of variety halls back east where Bob Ford told large audiences how he'd shot the famous outlaw. Sometimes the event would be acted out with Jesse reaching for his gun and Bob Ford being faster on the draw. It was all hokum. In two years they squandered their money and Charlie Ford committed suicide, apparently over guilt about Jesse. Bob Ford moved to Colorado, settling eventually in Creede, where he opened a saloon and whorehouse called the Creede Exchange. By that time he had picked up a common-law wife by the name of Dottie, who was in charge of the whores. Ford wore the widest-brimmed hat anyone had ever seen and he carried a brace of Colt .45's, the biggest and most expensive available. He talked a lot about killing Jesse and it was in Creede that he began to say, "I know what I done and what's going to come of it."

Charlie picked up the phone and dialed Eddie Gillespie's number. After half a dozen rings Eddie's wife, Irene, answered. In the background a baby was trying to imitate a police siren. "Charlie Bradshaw," said Irene crossly, "all you do is get Eddie in trouble."

"Just let me speak with him," said Charlie soothingly.

Eddie had just woken up. "I talked to fifteen women, Charlie, and I bet they were lying. Like they acted nervous."

"Did they remember Mulholland talking to any men?"

"They said she didn't talk to much of anyone. One woman, the librarian, Maggie Henry, said she'd invited Mulholland over to dinner once but she didn't know anything about any men. You want me to tackle them again?"

"No, that's okay. Look, Eddie, I want you to find the address and phone number of Vince Reardon's ex-wife in Santa Fe. Her name is Mary Rose and maybe she kept the name of Reardon. Don't let Vince Reardon know that you're interested."

"You don't want me to call her?"

"Just get me her phone number and address."

"Doesn't sound like fun, Charlie."

"Some things aren't fun, Eddie, but this will have to do for now."

Putting down the phone, Charlie thought of Eddie badgering the fifteen elderly women and how each had probably described the visit to a dozen other people. Surely if Grace Mulholland's murderer was in Saratoga he must feel increasingly anxious.

Five minutes later Charlie left his office for police headquarters. The weather had turned cool and the sky was gray. There was a sense of snow not far off. When he passed Marge's store, he looked in the window but didn't see her. He felt good about looking in the window. Even if the discomfort wasn't gone at least an easier sort of discomfort had taken its place.

Peterson was at his desk reading when Charlie looked around the corner of his door, almost hoping that he wasn't there. Charlie rapped on the frame and Peterson glanced up from his papers. His face was expressionless, maybe it grew just a little more tired. There was nothing welcoming about it.

"The name Ward ring any bells with you?" asked Charlie, entering the office. He told Peterson about the young man who used to mow Grace Mulholland's lawn and who had lived on York Street. "I heard he had committed some robberies in Albany in the late seventies and was sent to prison. I don't even know if Ward is a first or last name."

Peterson picked up the phone and called down to records, then passed on the information that Charlie had given him. When he hung up, he said, "Now I got some information for you. D'you remember the people who owned the pool hall back in the seventies?"

"I've no idea." Charlie remembered that the old guy in charge had had a big beer belly and favored black T-shirts.

"Louie and Bill Schaaf." Peterson said this as if naming a brother team as famous as Jack and Bobby Kennedy.

No lights flashed on in Charlie's brain. "Aha," he said. "Crooks?"

"Car thieves. Don't you remember about seven years ago they got sent to Auburn? They'd swipe some Skiddie's Jag and drive it to Florida for shipment to Venezuela or someplace like that. And back in the seventies they ran a sort of chop shop, dealt in stolen auto parts."

"Didn't they steal your wife's car?" asked Charlie, remembering a little.

"Damn right they did. That was their Waterloo."

"And they owned Jacko's?"

"It was their dad's place but they worked there. The father's dead now."

"What connection was there between them and Grace Mulholland?" Charlie was impressed by the gleam in Peterson's baggy eyes.

"Other than proximity, I don't know. Mulholland lived half a block away and was buried in their basement. I mean nobody had a better opportunity than Louie and Bill Schaaf."

"What's the motive?"

"Let's say she knew something about these stolen auto parts. Maybe we're making a mistake by assuming that she was killed by this guy she was involved with. She could have been connected to the Schaafs in all sort of ways. They could have got her false papers or helped her with some of the false claims she submitted. Car fires were their specialty. Then when she got the money, they killed her and dumped the body in the basement and covered up the spot with a pool table. What's her boyfriend going to do? Or maybe he thought she'd left the country without her." Peterson leaned back in his chair and seemed to puff up a little.

"Do you have one piece of hard evidence?" asked Charlie. It occurred to him that Peterson was still angry with the Schaafs for stealing his wife's car.

"Charlie, it's a connection. Are you suggesting it's not worth investigating?"

"Of course not. Where are these guys now?"

"That's what I'm in the process of finding out."

The door opened and a plainclothesman entered carrying a folder. "Here's that file you wanted. Paul Ward."

Peterson put on his reading glasses. "Paul Ward, born July 8, 1956, Saratoga High School, no graduation, Army, bad discharge. Robbed three convenience stores in Albany during the summer of '79. Got shot in the leg, sent to Auburn, paroled in '88. No present address listed. Mother, Kathleen Ward, lives on York Street. And this guy used to mow Mulholland's lawn?"

"That's right."

"Looks like we both got ourselves some ex-cons, right, Charlie?" Peterson gave Charlie one of his cheerless smiles.

Charlie took the file and jotted down Ward's mother's address and the name and phone number of Ward's Parole Officer in Albany. "By the way," asked Charlie, "you heard anything about Virgil Darcy since he got out of jail last week?"

"No, I was notified that he'd been released but I haven't heard anything else. He was pretty mad at you, wasn't he?"

Charlie winced. "I should have stayed out of it."

"You were a cop then."

"And nothing's ever turned up about Joey Damasco or Frank Bonita, the guys who got the money?"

"Nothing." Peterson laughed abruptly. "Maybe they're under Jacko's Pool Hall as well."

Charlie seemed to take the remark seriously. "That's an idea. By the way, do you have those earrings that were found by the skeleton? I'd like to see them."

"The state police lab still has them. Turquoise and silver. Big dangling things."

Kathleen Ward's house on York Street was a narrow wood frame house squeezed in between two bigger brick houses. Its light-blue paint was faded and the front porch sagged. Charlie climbed out of his Mazda and approached the house looking at the windows, which were covered with drawn shades. As he climbed the front steps, a dog began barking inside, a big dog. An old-fashioned bell was set into the front door. Charlie gave it a twist and the jangling brought the dog to the verge of canine apoplexy. On the top half of the door was a pane of glass covered with a white curtain and suddenly it began jerking and being pushed aside by big black paws. The dog's nose left a curved smear across the glass as it leapt up to get a better look at Charlie, who stood waiting patiently, trying to appear friendly and calm.

The door opened four inches, then was stopped by a chain. A black muzzle shoved itself out at the level of Charlie's knees and snarled.

"What is it?" came a voice.

An elderly woman stared at Charlie through the crack. She was short, about five feet tall, and beneath her the dog also stared up at Charlie, who found the woman's expression and the dog's expression not dissimilar: suspicious and angry.

"Hi," said Charlie, smiling broadly. "My name's Charles Bradshaw and I'm looking for Paul Ward. He's your son, I think?" Charlie poked one of his cards toward the woman and the dog furiously chewed the air near Charlie's knees.

After the dog had quieted a little, the woman said, "You're the detective." There was nothing nice about how she pronounced the word. She could have been saying, "You're the pervert" or "You're the mass-murderer."

Charlie kept his smile, which made his cheeks ache. "That's right. Is your son around?"

"Why don't you leave him alone?" said the woman.

"I just want a few words."

"He's not here." The women pushed the door shut.

Well, thought Charlie, I didn't particularly want to go inside that house anyway. The dog's muffled barking continued on the other side of the door.

Charlie drove back to his office so he could call Ward's Parole Officer in Albany. On Charlie's answering machine were several calls from reporters, a message from Janey Burris saying that she liked him, and a message from Eddie Gillespie. Charlie dialed Eddie's number and his wife, Irene, answered.

"He's at work, Charlie. Normal people work during the day," said Irene. "If it weren't for you, Charlie, Eddie would be a wonderful husband. You just rile him up."

Charlie began to say something soothing but Irene slammed down the phone. He thought of the large blue lamp he had given Eddie and Irene as a wedding gift. It had been made by a local potter. The shade was a kind of parchment with pressed violets and cornflowers. It had been expensive but Charlie wanted Eddie and Irene to have something nice. Charlie scratched his head and looked thoughtfully at his picture of Jesse James. Then he called Paul Ward's Parole Officer, whose name was Nick Belotti. A secretary told him that Belotti was out of the office and wouldn't be back until after lunch. Charlie checked the Saratoga phone book to see if there was a listing for Paul Ward. There wasn't. There wasn't even a P. Ward. It was eleven forty-five. Charlie decided to walk over to the YMCA and swim some laps.

Thirty minutes later Charlie was pulling his body back and forth the medium-speed lane at the Saratoga Y, passing the oldsters, getting passed by the youngsters. He thought of the dog that had wanted to bite him and the old woman who had hoped he would fall off her porch and break his ankle. He thought of Chief Peterson's cold expression and Irene Gillespie's claim that he was leading her innocent husband down the path of wickedness. And as he swam all this unpleasantness seemed to slide from him. No wonder they call it the crawl, he thought: humility's what it's all about. Then he wondered again about Joey Damasco, Frank Bonita and about the ten thousand dollars being offered by Marine Midland for the return of the money. Later, in the locker room, three acquaintances asked him about Grace Mulholland and his goof-up nearly twenty years ago.

Charlie stood before his locker in his JC Penney's underwear. "I made a mistake," he said. "It happens."

Nick Belotti had a friendly booming voice that forced Charlie to hold the phone away from his ear. It was three o'clock and the Parole Officer had just returned from lunch.

"Paul's not in trouble, is he? I'm sure he's been keeping his nose clean."

"This concerns something that happened eighteen years ago," said Charlie. He tilted back his chair and looked out the window. "I want to ask him some questions." Above the red-brick building across the street, the gray sky was getting grayer.

"That's what they all say," said Belotti with a laugh. "You a cop?"

"Private. Tell me why he got sent up in the seventies."

"Paul had a drug problem," said Belotti. "He's clean now, as far as I know. He's a good guy, a little temperamental but a good guy. He had a hard time at Auburn. I can't believe he'd do anything to get himself sent back."

"Where can I find him?"

"He works out at the flat track on the grounds crew and he's got a room in town." Belotti gave him the address of a rooming house on Oak Street on the west side of Saratoga. "Hey, Bradshaw, you a big guy?"

Charlie was surprised by the question. "Not particularly."

"Paul Ward has trouble with big guys. Go easy with him, will you? He's sensitive."

Hanging up the phone Charlie thought, I'm sensitive myself, my feelings get hurt, I get sad easily and I'd rather be at the beach. He decided that was another thing he liked about Jesse James: if he was sensitive, he kept it under his hat. If Jesse was sad, it never showed. Charlie decided to take a ride over to the track and see Paul Ward. Just as he reached the door, the phone rang and he ignored it.

The gates were open at the racetrack but no one was around. Charlie drove in and parked by the ticket booths. Then he made his way to the main office. The tall pines were blowing back and forth and dried leaves skittered across the ground. Some workmen were putting a coat of white paint on the clubhouse. The jockeys' scales had been wrapped in plastic.

In the office, a fat man was seated with his feet on a desk reading a copy of *Racing Form.* His hair was brushed straight back, like Charlie's used to be when he had more hair. As the man glanced up inquiringly, he licked his hand and wiped his palm across a recalcitrant brown frond, effectively sticking his hair in place with a drop of saliva and a remnant of lunch.

"I'm looking for Paul Ward," said Charlie.

"We don't like personal business being conducted during business hours," said the man. His voice was disinterested and he waited to get back to his paper.

Charlie thought for a moment. "This isn't personal."

The man opened his mouth, then closed it.

"On the other hand," said Charlie, "we hate to cause our clients undue embarrassment by publicizing their misfortunes." It was a meaningless sentence that was sometimes effective.

"He's supposed to be with a painting crew over in the grandstand," said the man, somewhat sheepishly.

Charlie strolled over to the grandstand. The previous July and August he had been to the track about six times, following the fortunes of a horse called Charlie's Revenge which Victor swore had to be a winner and which went absolutely nowhere. No win, no place, no show and Charlie had been out twelve bucks. Next season he promised himself he would only bet a combination of top jockey and top trainer and post position. To heck with the horse. No more broken hearts for him. At least Charlie made sure he never came to the track with more than twenty dollars and he always saved enough for a beer, a hot dog and sometimes a big pretzel. His ex-wife, Marge, consistently did well at the track. It had always been a sore point between them.

The foreman of the painting crew said that Paul Ward had gotten a telephone call shortly before lunch and had left for the rest of the day.

"Some kind of trouble at home?" Charlie asked innocently.

The foreman had a splotch of white paint on his pink chin. "He didn't confide in me," he said.

Around nine-thirty Charlie was wandering down the third-floor corridor of the Bentley. The gray cat accompanied him, yowling every so often. Charlie kept telling the cat that he would feed it when they were done.

Before coming to the hotel, Charlie had spent two hours with Maximum Tubbs, who had seemed worse: half conscious and drifting in and out of morphine dreams. At one point he called out, "Hey, Henry, don't play that card!" Charlie had felt he was doing no particular good sitting with Tubbs, but he kept staring at him, trying to fix his face in his memory so he could always keep it with him, even though Charlie knew that faces and memories didn't work like that. Tubbs's breathing had been extremely shallow; at times it didn't seem his chest was moving at all. Charlie would see no movement and hold his own breath until it felt his lungs would burst. Then Tubbs would breathe and Charlie would breathe as well. At nine he had left to drive over to the Bentley. He had been angry and drove too fast and squealed his tires around the corners.

Despite a slight nervousness, Charlie found something soothing about walking through the darkness with only his thoughts and the gray cat. He kept wondering about Joey Damasco and Frank Bonita and how strange it was that they had managed to hide themselves for over twenty years. Could they have made the two hundred thousand last for that long? He decided if he ever saw Virgil Darcy, he would ask about them. And as he remembered Virgil, Charlie thought again about his gun, which he had left out at his house at the lake. And he also thought about the other ex-con, Paul Ward, whom he had spent much of the afternoon trying to find, visiting his rooming house on Oak Street, revisiting his mother's place on

York and drawing a blank at both places. Charlie was certain that Ward's mother had warned her son that Charlie was looking for him, but why should Ward hide if he was innocent? Charlie hated to bring in Peterson, but if he couldn't find Ward tomorrow, then he would go to the police.

Charlie made his way down to the kitchen with the cat mewing behind him. The beam of the flashlight swung across the stairs, then across the dark furniture of the lobby. Charlie wondered what it meant to be afraid of the dark and if the fear was a response to some other guilty feeling: something done badly or not done at all. And he imagined Grace Mulholland's spirit drifting slowly after him until the hair rose on the back of Charlie's neck. He had all the files in the trunk of his Mazda and shortly he would drive over to Janey's and read them once again.

15

The next morning when Charlie left Janey's something frightening occurred. Later he realized he could have easily been killed. Charlie was in a rush because he was supposed to meet Victor at his office at nine o'clock and it was five of. He imagined Victor's complaints, the long-suffering sighs, the irritated rustlings and shakes of his crossword. Charlie hurried to his red Mazda, jumped in and turned the key. The Mazda had a design improvement which had always irritated him, meaning that he had to put in the clutch before the ignition would engage. Charlie popped the clutch and spewed gravel as he shot away from the curb. At the end of the block was a stop sign where a blue Ford pickup was waiting for traffic to clear.

The Mazda accelerated quickly, swerving slightly as Charlie tried to steer with his knees and buckle on his seat belt. Then, approaching the corner, Charlie touched the brake. Nothing happened. Harder, he put his foot down again, pumping several times. Still nothing. The pickup was twenty feet ahead and Charlie was doing about thirty-five. Abruptly, he shifted to first, dragged up on the emergency brake and yanked the wheel to the left. The Mazda gave out a pained scream, swerved across the road and up over the curb into a yard where a thin gray-haired man was raking leaves. Seeing the red Mazda skid across his grass, the man dropped the rake. The car slid across the lawn toward a small white house and at last stopped by a row of holly bushes. Charlie let out a breath. The world seemed suddenly silent. Half a dozen people stared open-mouthed, frozen as motionless as if they were playing statue.

Charlie climbed out of the car. His knees felt rubbery and he put a hand on the roof. "My brakes failed," he told the man who had dropped the rake.

"You should get them inspected," said the man.

"I just did," said Charlie, "or at least pretty recently." There was an unsightly gouge across the man's front lawn. For the next few minutes Charlie was busy giving the man his driver's license, insurance card and the name of his insurance agent.

"I'm sorry about this," said Charlie.

"Hey," said the man, "let the insurance bozos rake my lawn. It means I can watch 'Ozzie and Harriet' on the cable. Care to join me?"

"I got to get to work," said Charlie.

"Retirement's where it's at," said the man.

Charlie drove the rest of the way downtown at five miles an hour, keeping one hand on the emergency brake. Occasionally, he pumped the brakes but nothing happened. Charlie left the Mazda at a garage on Putnam. "My brakes failed," he said.

"Shoddy foreign goods," said the mechanic.

By the time Charlie reached his office it was past nine-thirty. Victor was sitting on the hall floor working on his crossword and eating poppy-seed bagels with cream cheese from Bruegger's Bagel Bakery on Broadway.

"I could've had a heart attack here," said Victor, "and there would've been no one to help."

"My brakes failed," said Charlie, scooping up his mail and unlocking the door.

"You're just trying to compete," said Victor, entering the office.

Charlie felt out of breath, although not from the stairs or his hurried walk from the garage. He kept remembering the blue tailgate of the Ford pickup getting closer and closer. He sat down and began sorting through his mail. He breathed deeply, trying to relax.

"You're making quite a bit of noise, Charlie," said Victor. "Puff-puff-puff, you should get a stress test."

Charlie began to say that he'd just had a stress test when a plain white envelope without a return address caught his eye. The postmark indicated that it had been mailed from Albany on Monday. Even before opening the envelope, it occurred to Charlie that this was going to be a difficult day. Across from him Victor had gone back to his crossword puzzle and his poppy-seed bagels with cream cheese. For some weeks Charlie had asked Victor not to buy poppy-seed bagels because the seeds got all over his desk and created what Charlie thought of as the wrong ambiance for prospective customers. After all, this was a private detective's office. But there really weren't enough customers to worry about and so Charlie had stopped saying anything, leaving Victor and his poppy-seed bagels undisturbed.

"For crying out loud," said Charlie. He had opened the envelope, withdrawn a single sheet of paper and cast his eyes over its contents.

"Bill collectors?" asked Victor without glancing up from his bagel.

"Listen to this," said Charlie. " 'To Charlie Bradshaw: I'm going to cut out your eyes for scrambled eggs and eyes. I'm going to cut out your liver for liver pancakes. I'm going to cut out your heart to eat all by itself. I'm coming to get you and I'm getting closer. Virgil.' "

"I like the food motif," said Victor.

"Don't you ever take anything seriously?" asked Charlie angrily. He recalled lying in bed with Janey that morning and he wondered what foolishness had led him to get up.

"Only fast women and big cars," said Victor, "and sometimes big women and fast cars. When this Virgil guy breaks in here with his machete, you're going to have to throw sandwiches at him: Big Macs and Kentucky Fried Chicken."

Charlie ignored his friend and reread the letter. Could it be serious? Was Virgil threatening to eat him? If the letter was serious, then it was also insane. But maybe it was a joke, maybe someone was trying to stick a pin in him. Whatever the case, Charlie blamed himself for not tracking down Virgil's P.O. in Albany. At least the man could say whether Virgil was crazy.

"Cannibalism is increasingly popular these days," said Victor. "Films, books, real life. I once had a girlfriend who was into biting but we split up before she drew blood. 'Long pig' was what the sailors used to call the edible midshipman. Maybe that's how Virgil thinks of you: Long Pig Bradshaw. You be careful wandering through that empty hotel, Charlie. If he catches you there, he can fry you up right in the kitchen."

"I thought you were going to help me with the hotel," said Charlie, deciding the letter was a joke after all.

"The stock market's too jumpy, Charlie, and I gotta look out for my rental property. And I got my clients."

"You mean your girlfriends?"

"Whoever they are, I gotta hold a lot of hands. What about Eddie?"

"Eddie's afraid of the dark."

After Victor left, Charlie swept the poppy seeds off the surface of his desk, then he began making some calls to Albany to see if he could track down Virgil Darcy's Probation/Parole Officer. After twenty minutes of being put on hold, then having his call transferred, then being cut off, then redialing, he reached a nasal-sounding man by the name of Leo Angier, who identified himself as Darcy's P.O.

"He took a job up with GE in Fort Edward, but I don't think he likes it much. He'd like to relocate to Saratoga. And who are you?"

"I was the arresting officer twenty years ago," said Charlie. No point in mentioning that he was no longer a cop. "How does he seem to you?"

"Confused, scared, but otherwise okay. You're name's Bradshaw, right?"

"That's me. Has he said anything about me?"

"Not a word, but I'd leave him alone if I were you. He's still got a lot of bitterness."

"At me?"

"At everything."

"Does he seem crazy?"

"Just pissed off. Why do you ask?"

"Just wondering."

Charlie hung up and leaned back in his chair. The call had reassured him but not completely. It was understandable that Virgil felt bitter, but it seemed a long way between bitterness and deciding to eat Charlie's eyeballs with scrambled eggs.

Until eleven Charlie reread his files, digging into the notes he had made about people he had interviewed eighteen years earlier and whom he had seen again in the past few days.

Of Grace Mulholland's next-door neighbor, Bennett Blakeslee, Charlie had written: "Blakeslee is assistant manager of the Adirondack Trust out on Route 29 and extremely boring. For him to open his mouth and say three words seems almost beyond his ability. His wife left him four years ago and I'm surprised she lasted so long. She probably has permanent yawn scars. Blakeslee claims that he never even glanced at Mulholland's house and her shades were always drawn. There might be a contradiction there and perhaps she kept her shades down because she spotted him watching her house. Blakeslee can't see why Mulholland would have gone to South America. In fact, he can't imagine why anyone would want to leave Saratoga."

Sunday afternoon Charlie had visited Blakeslee again. Blakeslee had retired from Adirondack Trust a few years before but he still lived on Henry Street. "I was horrified to think of her under that pool hall," he told Charlie. "I'd quite gotten used to the idea of her being off in another country." Blakeslee was a tall baldheaded man who had given Charlie a cup of coffee. This time he hadn't seemed so boring. "Grace and I sometimes would leave our houses for work at the same time in the morning but if she caught sight of me, she'd always duck back inside. And if I caught sight of her I'd hurry away quickly so as not to make her uncomfortable.''

About Ralph McMann, one of the officers in Readers Anonymous, Charlie had written, ''McMann suggests that Mulholland wasn't smart enough to falsify those claims. He suggests she was working with somebody else. He says the only time they ever talked was about books on Kennedy's assassination. He says Grace didn't believe any of the conspiracy theories. He told me that there's a good chance that Oswald was a CIA agent. It was probably thinking about Kennedy conspiracy theories that led him to think about Mulholland conspiracy theories. One of his smart ideas (ha, ha) was that Grace would have gone to Europe instead of South America.''

Years before McMann had worked at the library. Now he worked for a public television station in Albany but still lived in Saratoga. ''I didn't mean she wasn't smart,'' he had told Charlie on Sunday. He was a bearded heavyset man in his late forties whose small living room was full of canaries. ''I just didn't see her as having enough energy or gumption or courage to steal the money on her own. And the reason I thought she might have gone to England was that it seemed easier to imagine her living in England than living, say, in Ecuador.''

About another member of Readers Anonymous, Wallace Eliot, Charlie had written: ''Eliot says that he and Mulholland hardly talked during the three or four times he had given her a ride home. I asked if they hadn't talked about the books they were discussing in the book club and he said that whenever he tried to have a conversation, she would answer with only a yes or no. I asked why she had stopping accepting rides from him and if he had done anything to upset her. He got angry and said he always treated her as a lady. He said he found it more likely that she'd turn up in California instead of South America. I asked if she had ever mentioned California and he said No.''

On Sunday Eliot had explained, ''It just seemed too hard to go to South America. I mean the language and the different society. I couldn't see Grace doing it. California seemed a lot easier.

Even Canada, for Pete's sake.'' Eliot was a pharmacist at a drugstore on Broadway. Charlie had seen him off and on for years and the two would usually exchange comments on the weather when they met.

"When she disappeared, what did you think happened to her?''

"I had no idea, but after a while a lot of people talked about her going to either Mexico or South America and I figured they had more information about it than I did.''

"Who talked about it?''

"Well, you did for one. I don't know who else did, but soon all the members of the book club were talking about it. I mean, I think we were all glad that Grace had gone off to start a new life. We wanted her to be happy, and the embezzling or fraud or whatever it was, who did it harm?''

Sitting at his desk Tuesday morning, Charlie wondered who had come up with the idea that Grace had gone to Mexico or South America. Had he been the one to suggest it? But surely there had been those books on South America in her living room, even though the general opinion had been that no one could imagine Grace going anyplace. When it appeared that she had actually left the country, then people were glad for her and approved of her adventurous spirit at the expense of the insurance company.

Charlie also continued to be bothered by the tone of his notes: critical, snide and somewhat superior. The notes offended him and he read them with the very edge of his bifocals, switching to blur when he found something he didn't like. It was as if they burned his eyes. He wanted to take his younger self by the lapels and say, Now listen here!

The previous night he had been reading the files in Janey's kitchen and she had leafed through several. At first Charlie hadn't wanted her to, but then he thought it would be good for her to understand what he was upset about.

She had read for about ten minutes, then said, "Charlie, I don't think I would have liked you back then.''

"That's all right,'' said Charlie, "neither did I.''

"I'm glad you stopped being a cop."

"It was more than being a cop," Charlie had said. "I just didn't like the life I was leading."

"A cop life," Janey had said.

Charlie left his office around eleven to pick up his car from the garage and to look for Paul Ward. Briefly, he considered driving out to the lake and getting his revolver but he had now pretty much convinced himself that the letter from Virgil Darcy was a prank. Besides, he didn't have time to go out to the lake. There were still a number of people connected to Grace Mulholland whom he hoped to see.

When Charlie reached the garage, he found two mechanics arguing in the office. They were young men in blue coveralls with grease smudges on their faces. Seeing Charlie, they looked embarrassed and the younger (the name stitched on his pocket was Marcello) nudged the older one (the name on his pocket was Frankie) and said, "You better tell him."

Frankie looked down at his feet, then out the window, then said, "You have any enemies, Mr. Bradshaw?"

The phrase that leapt into Charlie's mind was "Is the Pope Catholic?" Instead he asked as calmly as possible, "Why do you wish to know?"

"The push rod in the master cylinder was snapped," said Frankie excitedly. "I don't know how it happened, I wasn't there."

Even as Charlie was articulating Virgil Darcy's name to himself, he asked, "Could it have been an accident?"

"Fat chance," said Marcello.

"Possibly," said Frankie.

And the two men resumed the argument that Charlie had interrupted minutes before: was it possible that the push rod had broken accidentally. The eventual ruling was that Marcello said, "One chance outta one million." And Frankie said, "One chance outta one hundred thousand."

Charlie considered the difficulties of someone tampering with his car left overnight on a side street. "How long would it take to break it?"

"If you know what you're looking for," said Marcello, "five minutes. You'd need a chisel and a hammer. It's tricky."

Leaving the garage, Charlie drove back to Janey's to look at the spot where he had parked the previous night. Janey was at work, which was just as well because Charlie wasn't sure that he wanted to talk to her. The street was tree-lined and the houses had big lawns. Charlie got out and paced back and forth on the pavement. There were no footsteps or telltale clues, no accidentally dropped business cards with Virgil Darcy's name. Even so, someone could have easily tampered with the Mazda without being seen.

Still, thought Charlie, it might have been an accident.

Somewhat gloomily he drove over to the track to look for Paul Ward. It upset Charlie to think that someone might want to hurt him. Would I have been hurt? he asked himself. And once again he saw himself rushing toward the back of the blue Ford pickup as he uselessly pumped the brakes.

Charlie parked near the ticket booths, then walked between the pines to where a paint crew was giving the Club House a coat of fresh paint.

"Ward didn't show up today," the foreman told him. "He called in sick. And this is a busy time, too."

Charlie drove over to Ward's rooming house on Oak Street. Occasionally he pumped his brakes and each time he was thrown forward against the seat belt. He tried to imagine a structural flaw that would cause the push rod to snap. But wasn't that too much of a coincidence? Paul Ward wasn't at the rooming house and the landlady was certain he hadn't slept there the previous night. His mail hadn't been picked up and no one had seen him.

Maybe Ward screwed up my brakes, thought Charlie. Maybe it wasn't Virgil.

As Charlie drove over to Ward's mother's house on York Street, he found himself becoming increasingly angry. He stomped up the front steps and gave the bell a twist. Again the large black dog enacted a version of canine hysteria. Charlie wondered if he should have gone home for his revolver just for the dog. At last the door opened three inches stopped by its chain.

"I want to talk to Paul Ward," said Charlie.

Ward's mother glared at him. "He's not here." She slammed the door.

Charlie rang the bell again. He kept ringing it for five minutes until the door opened again. The dog's hysteria expressed the conviction that never in its canine life had it encountered such human effrontery.

Charlie didn't give the woman a chance to speak. "I want to talk to your son and I want to talk to him fast. Either I can find him or the police can find him. It's his choice. Tell him to make it quick." Charlie turned and walked back to his car. He wondered what his life would have been like if he had taught third grade or if he had somehow gotten involved in baseball as a coach, maybe a minor league third-base coach. Perhaps he could have helped put the Syracuse Chiefs on the map.

Charlie drove over to police headquarters. He still felt cross, as if his skin were too tight or if he had sand under it. He found Peterson dusting the trophies of his prize Irish setters. Fleetingly, Peterson looked embarrassed, then he stuck out his jaw. "Don't you ever knock?"

"If you knock," said Charlie, "it only makes you responsible for what you find. If you just push your way in, it's okay."

"I never like you when you're in a bad mood, Charlie. I never know what you're going to do."

Charlie had no wish to tell Peterson about the snapped push rod. He saw it as his business rather than police business. Anyway, like Victor, Peterson would only make wisecracks.

"Where'd we get the idea that Grace Mulholland had gone to Mexico or South America?"

"That was your idea, Charlie." Peterson sat down at his desk, then leaned back in his chair and linked his hands across the front of his blue vest.

"But those books and then that letter . . ."

"She had books about Hawaii as well. And Spain, Greece, New Zealand. Whoever killed her had that letter sent from Mexico. Have you found Paul Ward? He sure didn't send any letter."

"He's been avoiding me. He could have sent it, anybody could have."

"You want me to grab him?"

"I told his mother he had one more day." Charlie sat down as well.

"I tracked down Louie and Bill Schaaf. They're over in Herkimer running a bar. I can't decide whether to go over and see them and just haul them in."

"You have any evidence they did anything or are you just hoping to beat me to the punch?"

Peterson leaned forward in his chair. He tried to look imposing but he only looked uncertain. "I'm Commissioner of Public Safety, Charlie. I have a civic responsibility."

"Has your guy Novack found anything? Anyone with money? Any secret gamblers? Anyone living a soft life in California?"

"Nothing." Peterson kept his jaw shoved forward. Charlie thought it made him look like he needed a tetanus shot.

Heading for the door, Charlie said, "Tell me if these Schaaf brothers amount to anything. If you're right and I'm wrong, then I'm going to fly down to Key West for the winter and you can stay up here in the snow."

Charlie drove back to his office to pick up his bathing suit and towel so he could make the noon swim at the Y. He needed time to think about what had happened to the Mazda and if Paul Ward might have been responsible. Sometimes it seemed that he did his best thinking underwater: relaxed and purposeful and burning calories all at once. Charlie's phone was ringing but he ignored it. Just as he was opening his door to leave, he bumped smack into Eddie Gillespie, who was reaching for the doorknob. Eddie was dressed in brown coveralls and carried a yellow hardhat in his left hand.

"Hey, hey, hey," said Eddie. "Here's the guy who never picks up his telephone."

Charlie began to say something rude, then stopped himself. He wondered if he had been acting badly because of his brakes or badly because he felt badly about himself. And he wondered if he felt badly about himself because of how he appeared in his old Grace Mulholland notes.

"Come on in, Eddie, let's have a chat," said Charlie in his friendliest manner.

Eddie hunched down a little. "Once burned, forever watchful" was his motto. "That's what you say when you've got something unpleasant for me to do."

"Not unpleasant, Eddie, something exciting, something to keep the adrenaline flowing."

Eddie remained in the doorway. "I told you, Charlie, I'm not going to wander through that old hotel in the dark. I don't like the dark and I don't like ghosts. Being terrified is not the same as being excited. It's nastier."

Charlie deflated a little. "You've been talking to Victor."

"Sure. I mean, he pays me to call him every hour."

"It'd be a big help to me."

"No can do, Charlie. I'll face fifty guys with guns but I can't walk through that empty hotel at night. I'd wet myself."

"I don't mean to force you. Maybe I'll have something else for you to do later. What were you trying to call me about?"

"I got the phone number and address of Reardon's ex-wife in Santa Fe. She calls herself Mary Rose Reynolds now." He handed Charlie a piece of paper.

"It almost slipped my mind. By the way, do you know a Saratoga guy by the name of Paul Ward? He was sent up for some holdups in Albany in the late seventies and got out a few years ago."

"A short guy?"

"That's what I'm told. He works on the grounds crew out at the track."

"I seen him around. As far as I know he's gone straight."

"I want to talk to him but he's avoiding me. Can you put the word out that I have to speak to him? I don't like to ask the cops to bring him in."

"You want me to haul him in for you?"

"I'd rather he showed up of his own free will."

After Eddie left, Charlie telephoned Mary Rose Reynolds in Santa Fe. The phone rang and rang. There was no answer. He wondered why it was in books that when people made phone calls, they always got through. No telephones ringing in empty rooms, no busy signals, no answering machines.

That evening Charlie had dinner at Janey's house, sharing a sort of stew with Janey and her three daughters. "I call it Strange Stew," said Janey, "because I put in everything strange I find left over in the ice box." The oldest daughter liked the pineapples, the youngest liked the mushrooms and the middle daughter thought the pickles added a nice touch.

"You put in the cat food, ma?"

"No, no cat food."

Charlie had locked his car in Janey's garage and was uncertain whether he should mention his failed brakes. Mostly he was quiet. He had spent the afternoon looking for Paul Ward without success as well as talking to men and women he had visited years before in connection with Grace Mulholland. Apart from small details that he learned about the dead woman—a fondness for yellow flowers, blue sweaters and lavender-scented notepaper—he heard nothing to help with her disappearance. None had guessed what had happened to her, all were surprised yet pleased with the possibility that she might have gone to Mexico or South America, all were horrified by the news of her death.

Grace Mulholland had never drawn much attention to herself and people had no strong feelings about her. What people liked best was that she embezzled the money and apparently ran away to start a new life. With each person he talked to, Charlie was confronted with his opinions of 1974 and how they conflicted with what he thought now. And repeatedly he was disheartened by the contrast. "Susan Hanney still lives with her mother," Charlie had written about a thirty-year-old librarian. "I wonder what she's afraid of." "Ron Wallerby has terrible acne," Charlie had written of a young man who had gone to Mulholland's church. "No wonder women don't like him, but maybe Grace did if she couldn't get anyone else." These notes also made Charlie worry about the subjective elements that existed in any reasoning process: elements that were invisible at the time but which became obvious later. For instance, what mistakes was he making now?

After dinner, while Janey's daughters were washing the dishes, Charlie showed Janey the second letter that had come from Virgil Darcy. "I'm sure it's a hoax. That stuff about cutting out my liver for liver pancakes is silly."

Janey looked at him seriously. They were sitting in the living room, which was furnished with stuff that Janey had bought cheaply from a motel that was going out of business: mustard yellow, broken down and none of it comfortable. "But what if it's not a hoax, Charlie?"

"But I'm sure it is."

"How do you know?"

"I feel it, that's all. Somebody's pulling my leg."

"Somebody wants to eat your leg."

"Come on, Janey, it's a joke." They were sitting side by side on the couch. Whatever temptation he had had to tell her about the failed brakes of his Mazda slipped away. Ward must have done it, or maybe Virgil, or maybe it was an accident after all.

"Take the letter to Peterson."

"It would only get Virgil in trouble."

They argued about this some more. Charlie was sure it was a joke, but he couldn't help remembering all those things he had been positive about eighteen years ago and which had turned out to be wrong.

Afterward they talked about Thanksgiving. "Don't you really

want to come out to the lake? I'll even buy a new stove. It's pretty. Woods, water, countryside, it's more like Thanksgiving."

"Your TV's broken, Charlie. It's been broken for two years. If it was just us, it would be fine, but the kids are bored stiff if they can't swim. And your place is small. You don't even have any games. No TV, no swimming, no sex—all you can do is read, think and look at the water."

"That's what I like," said Charlie.

Janey stroked his cheek. "Any self-respecting twelve-year-old would think you were outta your gourd."

16

The outline of Maximum Tubbs's sleeping body beneath the thin blue blanket reminded Charlie not so much of a mountain range as a low ridge between two valleys. Soon even that ridge would be gone. Then the bed would be stripped, the room would be made ready for someone else and Tubbs would be no more than a spirit hovering in the autumn air. If that, thought Charlie, and he considered how his own life would then become even more solitary.

It was Wednesday morning, still before nine o'clock, and Charlie had come to the hospice straight from Janey's "on a business matter," as he told himself.

Tubbs's head and shoulders were propped up on pillows. His eyes had become increasingly sunken and the skin on the forehead and temples was paper thin, as if the skull were asserting itself and taking possession of the whole. Only the tubes inserted in his nose seemed to link him to the world. The rise and fall of his chest was slower than ever. And just when Charlie thought that it had stopped for good, Maximum Tubbs opened his eyes.

"Crazy dreams, Charlie." His voice was a whisper and Charlie had to lean forward to make out the words.

"See anyone I know?"

"Worrety Greenfield had himself a horse that was no more than four feet tall which he claimed was a Derby contender. We all laughed. Then the damn thing won: a mere midget." Then Tubbs laughed: a sound like a cat clearing its throat. "You cleared up that woman's death yet?"

"I'm still talking to people."

"It's been months, hasn't it?" Tubbs's eyes looked uncertain.

"Eddie dug up her skull just a week ago yesterday."

"Time gets funny in here. It must be the drugs. Learn anything new?"

"I don't have a handle on it yet. Each person I see makes me think of who I was back then and I don't like what I find. I have my notes on these different people and all my ideas, yet when I talk to someone now I see how mistaken I was. Sometimes not mistaken, just different. So instead of learning who might have killed Grace Mulholland, I have to face who I used to be: a person I dislike and disapprove of. It makes it hard to know what's there. In fact, I start doubting it's possible to know what's there, like the world's always a mirror for what we're feeling and thinking, and so what we always see is ourselves."

"You got yourself all worked up, don't you, Charlie."

"It's like there's always a loud noise in my ears."

"You know, I think of you as a young guy, although you're not. You're over fifty but I got thirty-three years on you and it makes you seem like a kid." Tubbs spoke staring up at the ceiling. Now and then he slowly lifted a hand to adjust one of the oxygen tubes entering his nose. "You look at a person's life: some people change, some never change. I always followed the game and it made me who I was: everything was odds and percentages and making the important decision. I never had a regular life, never wanted it. In a way, I was never in the world. I was in the game and so I never had to change. I just adapted myself to different games, different rules. Your father followed the game but he also had a wife and kid. And when he got stuck to the bookies, he couldn't change himself. He got stuck to the bookies and stuck in himself as well." Tubbs paused and cleared his throat, a dry raspy noise. "I've never said this to you, Charlie, but to my mind your old man was gutless. People hammering on the bathroom door and he puts a bullet in his head. If you don't like life, that's one thing, but to put a slug in your head because you're scared, well, that's another. He needed to do something but he couldn't do it, so he ran away. You're not like that. Eighteen years ago you were like your old man locked up in the bathroom with angry people hammering on the door. And what'd you do? You quit your job, divorced Marge and started another life. It doesn't so much matter what you were back then. I mean, to me you were an asshole, but basically you were just different: neither worse nor better, but you couldn't live with it. So what are you griping about now? You're upset because you used to be an asshole? You're afraid you might secretly be an asshole now and don't know it?''

''I don't think I'm an asshole. I'm just bothered by the foreignness. I don't recognize myself back then.''

''So what? Give me some of that water, will you?''

Charlie lifted Tubbs so he could drink from the glass. He could feel Tubbs's knobby bones through his gray silk pajamas and he was surprised by how light he was.

''Think of your life like a curve,'' Tubbs continued, ''like a half circle: the view from each part is different. You start reading these old notes and suddenly you got the view you had in those days. You don't like it? Forget it. Sure you had a problem with your life back then, but you solved it and if you didn't completely solve it, at least you moved around it. As for that stuff about seeing yourself reflected in the world around you, maybe that's always true. When I bet the horses and find I want a horse to win, then I don't bet. I don't trust the desire part. It fucks up the reasoning part. Same way with cards. If I find myself wanting something, I never raise. I never bet. The mirror's always there, Charlie, but you don't have to stare into it. You can turn away a little.''

''So what should I do?'' Charlie began to feel sorry at having further tired the old man.

''You gotta relax with it. It's the game, Charlie, you gotta stay limber. You gotta be ready to move. You gotta feel like a winner. You take your cards and play them, that's all. And if you get beat? Well, fuck it. The rest doesn't matter. Your old man went down because he started chewing at himself. The drinking didn't help. When he put that bullet in his head, he was wound as tight as a spring. You gotta stay agile. You gotta be ready to jump in any direction."

"Thanks for the advice," said Charlie.

"I can't play cards when I'm all pumped up with morphine, Charlie, I can't do anything but chew the fat. It makes me tired, that's all. That's the trouble with taking such good care of myself for so many years, it makes it hard to die. I tell the body to let go, but it keeps hanging on. I always hoped I'd drop dead at the card table holding a good hand, just let my head fall down to the green felt."

Charlie waited a moment, then he said, "There's something else you can help me with concerning this Mulholland woman."

"Make it short, Charlie, I need my beauty sleep."

"I've got a list of about sixty people who knew Mulholland. I need to know if any were gamblers. Tell me some people I can show the list to."

"Willie Hartwick, Solly Hurlwitz, Hugo Schwartz, Rodger the Beagle and Pete Mendecino."

"Where can I find them?"

"You know that list of names I gave you? People I want to come to my wake? They're on that. Names and addresses, everything you need to know. You think that woman was killed by a gambler?"

"Possibly. If one of the names on the list turns out to be a gambler, it'll give me some new ideas." Charlie considered telling Tubbs about the second threatening letter from Virgil, his search for Paul Ward and the fact that someone had disabled his brake cylinder. Then there were his problems with Janey Burris: the lake versus the town. Why couldn't he be the person Janey wanted him to be? Tubbs had helped Charlie with one problem, maybe he could help him with all his problems. But Tubbs's eyelids were drooping and he seemed to have forgotten that Charlie was in the room. And then, once more as a shock, Charlie realized that soon Tubbs wouldn't be there at all. He'd only have the memory of his voice: a voice getting farther away.

When Charlie got to his office at nine o'clock that morning, he found a rather short red-haired man with an angry expression waiting on the stairs. He appeared to be in his mid-thirties. Charlie guessed it was Paul Ward before the man opened his mouth.

"Why the hell can't you leave me alone?" said the man. "Why've you been bothering my mother?" Ward wore a green work shirt and work pants spotted with white paint.

"Let's go into my office," said Charlie. "D'you want a cup of coffee?"

"I don't want anything," said Ward as Charlie let him into his waiting room. Ward's body seemed stiff and he moved jerkily as if his anger were like sharp strips of metal inside of him.

Charlie walked to his desk, turning his back on the other man. Sitting down, Charlie motioned to the visitor's chair but Ward preferred to stand. Side by side, Charlie was several inches taller; sitting down put Ward several inches above him.

"You used to cut Grace Mulholland's grass," said Charlie, "I'd like to ask you a couple of questions about her."

"You mean you want to know if I killed her?" Ward leaned over Charlie's desk with his hands gripping the edge. He had a hard red face spotted with freckles: the sort of face that never relaxes, a face like chipped pieces of stone.

"Well, sure, if you killed her, I'd like to know that, but let's start with something easier. Did she ever talk to you?"

"Sure she talked to me. I mean, she was a nice lady."

"What'd she talk to you about?"

"I don't know. Sometimes the weather. What she needed me to do. That I'd done a good job on her lawn and when she wanted me to come back." As he spoke, Ward's anger seemed to decrease.

"She ever talk to you about anything else?"

"Like what?"

"Like what she was interested in. Books or traveling or movies or other people."

Ward thought a moment. "No."

"She ever talk about going anyplace."

"Not that I remember."

"What'd you think when she disappeared?"

"I was surprised." Ward stepped back from the desk and crossed his arms. He had large brown eyes and small even teeth. His face didn't relax but it grew less wary.

"You have any ideas as to what happened to her?"

"No. People said that money had been embezzled and that she'd taken off. After a while people said she'd gone down to South America."

"Did you have any thoughts about that?"

"Like I said, I was surprised. I mean, I mowed her lawn a few days before she disappeared. It was April. Mostly I raked up old leaves and cleaned out the flowerbeds. It was warm for that time of year. She gave me some lemonade and asked me about baseball because she knew I was a baseball fan. The season had just begun."

"Anything else strike you?"

"Yeah, she seemed happy. Really cheerful. I don't mean that she ever seemed depressed but she was never cheerful, just polite and sort of friendly. That day she seemed on top of the world. She asked what I was going to do when I graduated from high school and if I had a girl. She even blushed when she said that. And her hair was pretty and she was wearing earrings."

"D'you remember the earrings?"

"Just that they were noticeable and dangling and had color to them. Mostly she just wore little pearl earrings. Then a couple of days later I heard she was gone."

"Anything else?"

Ward turned away, thinking. "Nothing I remember. Just that she was happy."

"When did you get involved with drugs?"

Ward started to get angry again and Charlie interrupted him. "I need to know."

Ward stared at Charlie as if he hoped to hurt him with his eyes. " 'Seventy-seven a little bit. 'Seventy-eight, worse. 'Seventy-nine, real bad. You talking to me because I'm an ex-con?"

"I'm talking to you because you're one of the few people that Grace Mulholland talked to. Were you running away from me because you're an ex-con?"

"I could bust you one." Ward again leaned over the desk.

"You could try," said Charlie, not moving from his seat.

"Every time there's a stickup or some drug stuff, the cops come to me to talk about it and they always want to know where I've been."

"That's not going to change. Because you once broke the law, you'll always be suspect. There's nothing fair about that, but that's the way it is. You're on a computer and whenever there's a certain type of crime, your name'll pop up. That'll continue until you're in a wheelchair someplace. The cops may even know you had nothing to do with what they're investigating. But if they don't solve a case right away, then they'll come knocking on your door, just because they've got to cover all the angles. You can either accept it or chew yourself to pieces. Cops don't care. You're just part of their working time."

"So I should sit back and take it?"

Charlie shrugged. "Like I say, there's nothing fair about it. It's just the way things are."

Ward stepped back a little. He seemed about to sit down, then changed his mind. "So you don't think I killed her?"

"If it'd been five years later and you'd been heavy into drugs, then I might spend more time with you. But what were you, seventeen or eighteen? I figure you're safe. By the way, did Grace ever mention anything to you about South America or studying Spanish or how she'd like to go to Mexico?"

"No, nothing like that, ever."

"You ever see her with anyone else?"

"Not really."

"What d'you mean?"

"Well, I never saw her with anyone but one Saturday when it had snowed I came by to see if she wanted her walk shoveled and she was real nervous. She hardly opened the door more'n a crack. I had the sense there was someone inside her house that she didn't want me to know about. And there were no prints in the snow. If someone was really in her house, then that person had been there all night."

"You think it was a man or woman?"

Ward seemed surprised. "I guessed it was a man but maybe I had no reason for thinking that."

"Anything else?"

Ward shook his head and Charlie stood up. "I appreciate your coming over here," said Charlie. "I'm sorry I got you all upset by looking for you."

Ward tried to smile but he wasn't a man to whom smiles came easily. Instead he twitched his jaw. "I liked Miss Mulholland. It made me sick to think of her under that pool hall."

"Did you shoot pool there?"

"Sure, everyone shot pool at Jacko's."

"By the way, you know anything about foreign cars? I'm having trouble with the brakes on my Mazda."

Ward twitched his jaw again. This time it was more of a smile. "Never learned that stuff. Gardening, yes. Painting and maybe Sheetrocking, yes. But cars are a mystery. I don't even have one. I gotta two-fifty Honda."

After Paul Ward had left, Charlie again telephoned Vince Reardon's ex-wife in Santa Fe. Once again he waited patiently as the phone rang a dozen times. He had also called her four times the previous day without success. After a minute, he picked up the phone again to call Eddie Gillespie.

Irene answered. "He's not here, Charlie. He's at work. Some people have to earn an honest wage."

"Just ask him to call me, will you, Irene?"

Charlie hung up again, then leaned back in his chair and looked over at Jesse James.

Bob Ford's big trouble had been his need to call attention to himself. If he could have been satisfied with killing Jesse and keeping quiet about it, then he might have lived a long life. But he had to buy the biggest hat and biggest guns anyone had seen and he had to brag about all the big things he had done. Worse, he was a bad drunk and liked to shoot out the streetlights when he got loaded. One night he forced everyone off the main street of Creede by nine o'clock, shooting his guns and roaring back and forth. Soon other businessmen had had enough and Ford was told if he didn't leave town, he was a dead man. Ford fled to Pueblo and immediately began writing letters back to Creede begging to return. He promised to become a leading citizen and sent a public apology to the newspaper. After a few more weeks he returned quietly, having been told that nothing would happen. But although he stopped shooting up the town, he couldn't keep his mouth shut, couldn't stop talking about what he had done to Jesse James. "I know what I done and what's going to come of it."

It was shortly past 10:00 a.m. Trying to steel himself against what he would find, Charlie dug into his briefcase for another handful of notes.

"Maggie Henry invited Mulholland over for dinner in January," Charlie had written about the librarian. "She claims that they didn't discuss traveling even though both belong to the Travel Bugs. Maggie Henry gave a talk about the coast of Maine the previous fall. Henry is a big mannish woman of the sort that always become librarians. She's single. She said that she and Mulholland discussed ways they could raise money to buy a movie projector for the club. They decided to arrange a bake sale. No traveling was discussed, no books were discussed, no men were discussed. It must have been lots of fun."

Charlie ran his tongue across the roof of his mouth. The process of reading made his mouth so dry that it felt like eating sawdust. He had seen Maggie Henry the other day. She had retired from the library and was preparing to travel down to Key Largo, where she now spent her winters. "When Grace disappeared, I was really too astonished to think much of anything," she had told Charlie. "It was so unlike her. Certainly it was wrong to take that money, but it also seemed very brave. Much braver than I would have ever thought her." She hadn't struck Charlie as particularly mannish: just big.

Charlie glanced through the files of the people Grace Mulholland had worked with, then began rereading the files on the members of the Travel Bugs. When he came to Vince Reardon's file, he was stopped by the following sentences: "He says that Grace Mulholland asked him for a copy of one of his slides showing a Mexican church. He asked her if she was going to give a presentation and if she had visited any interesting places. She said that she hadn't been anywhere yet but that she knew some Spanish." Later in the file, Charlie read: "I like Reardon. He seems affable and willing to help. Maybe he belongs to the Travel Bugs because these people and their passions for other places strike him as funny."

Charlie reached for the phone and dialed Joan Chaffee's number. She answered right away and told him she was in the midst of making lunch for her husband and some of the salesmen at the Toyota dealership. Charlie could hear a machine whirring in the background. He wondered if she held her little dog while she cooked. "Did your aunt ever study Spanish?" asked Charlie.

"I don't believe so," said Chaffee, surprised. "I mean, I don't think I ever knew about it."

"Maybe in high school?"

"I think she told me she took French."

"Did she go to college?"

"She spent a year at Union but was so homesick that she didn't go back."

"Were there any Spanish books or dictionaries or grammar books in her bookcase?"

"I don't remember anything. In fact, I'm sure there weren't."

Shortly after twelve o'clock, Charlie walked over to Vince Reardon's restaurant on Caroline Street. The air was cold and windy, even though the sky was blue. The only time that Charlie could swim during the day was between twelve and one. He had already missed swimming once this week and he hated missing it twice. It made him feel slow and porky. It made him feel that he shouldn't eat ever again. And just that thought alone made him hungry.

Mother McDougle's was full of wonderful smells and Charlie could feel his stomach knotting up. He clenched his jaw and swore he wouldn't eat anything. But as he sat in the bar, waiting for Reardon, he found himself automatically reaching for the little goldfish crackers.

"Just a Vichy," he told the waiter.

After a few minutes Reardon ducked behind the bar, then took up a position in front of Charlie. He was smiling but seemed hurried. "You caught me at a busy time." Once again he was wearing a white shirt and blue polka-dot bowtie. Charlie guessed it was a kind of owner's uniform.

"I won't take long. When I talked to you years ago, you told me that Grace had said that she knew some Spanish. Do you remember anything else about that?"

"Jeez, Charlie, I don't remember any of it. Spanish?"

"That what my old notes say."

"Then I must have. It's gone completely out of my mind. You said the other day that she'd asked me for some picture of a Mexican church. Maybe it was connected with that." Reardon pushed a hand through his blond hair. Someone called hello to him and he smiled and nodded.

"Did she give you the impression that she wanted to travel?"

"I guess so. Eighteen years, she's just a vague picture for me. Since the other day I've been trying to remember more. I can sort of remember where she sat at the back of the room. And I remember that she tended to wear dark colors, dresses and suits, mostly. I don't remember if she ever said anything."

"You told me on Saturday that she seemed particularly interested in Spanish and South American stuff. How'd this interest show itself?" Charlie polished his glasses on a napkin to distract himself from the goldfish crackers.

"Well, she seemed to like this presentation I gave on New Mexico. And I remember someone else gave a talk about Machu Picchu. And there was also a talk about Seville." Reardon smiled again like a kid in school who liked to get the answers right.

"But what did she do that made her seem particularly interested in these subjects?"

"I don't remember. I suppose when everyone decided she'd gone off to Mexico, then I remembered she'd asked for that picture of a Mexican church, and maybe I remembered her at those talks on Peru and Spain. Maybe that's all the interest I ever saw. I just don't remember."

Charlie wondered what he remembered from that time. But didn't he already have sufficient evidence that his own memories were false? It seemed that either a person had forgotten what had happened or he remembered something that hadn't existed in the first place.

"You said you left Saratoga in the seventies, when was that?"

" 'Seventy-six. We went back to Santa Fe."

"And you worked there?"

"Not at first. Then I worked as a waiter, then I managed a restaurant."

"What sort of places?"

"Pretty fancy. Nouvelle cuisine. We catered to a lot of business types, lawyers, even the art crowd, and we had a good chef."

"And you saved a lot?"

"Both me and my wife, yes."

"So how long did you do that?" The bar was getting full and Reardon kept nodding to people. Charlie was impressed by how friendly he looked.

"Till about 1981, then we came back here."

"And when did your wife go back to Santa Fe?"

"Four or five years ago. She was born in the Southwest." Reardon laughed. "She told me once that she couldn't get used to so many trees."

"What's she doing now?"

"I have no idea. She got some money when we split up but I don't know what she did with it."

"Did she remarry?"

"I just don't know."

"Did you quarrel?"

"Not really, but we'd certainly had enough of each other. And when you're splitting up property, there're bound to be disagreements."

"You think she thinks badly of you?"

"I don't know. We were together about fifteen years, then split up. After so much time, it's hard to split up gracefully."

"Had either of you been involved with other people?"

"It was nothing like that. She just wanted to go back to the Southwest. And maybe we were tired of each other as well, didn't find each other exciting anymore."

Charlie started to reach for the goldfish crackers, then stopped himself. "You ever shoot pool at Jacko's?"

"Sure, I'd go over there now and then. Didn't you?"

"I guess everyone did," said Charlie. "By the way, what happens to your kids' baseball team during the winter."

"We play some basketball. At the end of the season they have an evening at the restaurant, about fifteen kids and their families. This year we also sponsored a team trip to Washington, D.C., over the Columbus Day weekend."

"It must set you back some," said Charlie.

Reardon smiled. Even his teeth seemed friendly. "I write it off as advertising."

That night around ten Charlie was sitting on the stairs at the third-floor landing of the Bentley thoughtfully scratching the jawbone of the gray cat, which, in the near dark, appeared as a darker smudge. During the day Charlie had tried five times to telephone Vince Reardon's ex-wife in Santa Fe. The phone had rung and rung. Now Charlie was considering calling a Santa Fe private detective to track her down, but he hated the expense since he only wanted to talk to her for about five minutes. However, perhaps it couldn't be helped.

The wind was making the old building rattle. Charlie thought about each noise and how it had a specific cause: loose window frame, a broken latch, the pressure of the wind against old wood. But without much effort he could imagine the ghosts that terrified Eddie Gillespie and he could imagine that these creaks and bangings were caused by malignant spirits. Along with these explanations lay Charlie's discomfort about Virgil Darcy and again, with little effort, he could attribute the noises to Virgil's presence in the hotel: a presence that was searching for Charlie with the most dire of intentions. The cat made a fretful squeak and Charlie realized that his grip had tightened.

"Sorry, cat," he said, getting to his feet. They descended the stairs.

During the afternoon Charlie had given Eddie Gillespie the list of sixty people who had had some contact with Grace Mulholland and the names and addresses of the five gamblers that he had gotten from Maximum Tubbs.

"I gotta do all this, Charlie?" Eddie had asked. He had been leaning against his backhoe surveying with some pride a ditch he had just dug.

"You have to find each of these five guys and see if they recognize any of the names on the list. I'll give you a hand later if I have time."

"Jesus, Charlie, when does the fun start?"

"Detective work isn't all fun, Eddie."

"It is on TV."

"They only show the high points."

"I guess that's what I want too: just the high points."

"Don't we all," Charlie had said, "don't we all."

For much of the afternoon, Charlie searched through old wills at the courthouse to see if Burke Chaffee had really inherited the money to start his Toyota dealership from his grandmother. He didn't particularly doubt Chaffee, but he wanted to make sure, and when he at last found the document and saw that Chaffee had indeed received a large sum of money, Charlie felt pleased. It meant that one potential theory as to what had happened to Grace Mulholland had been shut down, a door had been closed. And if none of Tubbs's five gamblers recognized any of the sixty names, then another door would be closed as well.

But could he really eliminate Chaffee? Chaffee knew about cars, which might mean that he also knew about brakes. Even though he had inherited his grandmother's money, he might have needed, or wanted, even more. Chaffee hadn't been disqualified, he had only been downgraded a notch or two and perhaps even that was a mistake. For Pete's sake, thought Charlie, why don't I trust any of my thinking? But he knew the reason for that, or thought he did. No firm ground anymore, nothing certain, just lots of maybes and maybe nots.

Reaching the dark kitchen of the hotel, Charlie sought out the box of cat food. That day at lunch time, Reardon had been busy, yet he had answered Charlie's questions without protest. He had also answered questions about his private life which were clearly none of Charlie's business, again without protest. Charlie liked Reardon. He was agreeable and bright-looking. But Charlie wondered what he himself might have done if someone had asked him similar questions about his divorce from Marge. He doubted that he'd have been so patient. Then Charlie wondered if any of this meant anything.

17

Thursday morning the weather had again turned warm and there was the sense that something was broken in the sky. Charlie had spent the night at Janey's and when he got up about four-thirty to go to the bathroom, he could feel that the wind had shifted back around to the south.

"Wasn't there some year back in the 1880s when there wasn't any winter?" asked Victor. "Old guys used to talk about it." They were sitting in Charlie's office, where Victor was working on his crossword and eating poppy-seed bagels. A light rain was misting the window looking out on Phila Street.

"I don't remember," said Charlie. Out of his mail he had selected a plain envelope with no return address which had been mailed from Glens Falls the previous day. He looked at it, half knowing what it would contain. He wondered what would happen if he didn't open it, if he would be able to proceed through his day with the knowledge of the letter lying unread on his desk.

"I don't mean that you in particular were around at that time, Charlie. Don't be foolish." Victor's gray hair quivered indignantly. "Maybe Maximum Tubbs has some idea. I'll ask him later. You know, I saw him last night. He didn't look good."

Charlie glanced up. "I saw him in the morning and he seemed okay. We talked a lot."

"The nurse said he'd had a bad turn. They're always so vague about everything. When I die I want to know exactly what's happening. I bet ninety percent of the people die thinking, How peculiar. They probably think it's something they ate."

As Victor talked, Charlie continued to look at the plain white envelope on his desk. He decided he couldn't leave it unopened. Reaching for it, he ripped open the flap and withdrew a single sheet of paper.

"To Charlie Bradshaw: I'm getting closer. You're almost a dead man. Virgil."

"For Pete's sake," said Charlie, "I'm getting sick of this!"

Victor looked up bemusedly from his crossword. "Irate widows?"

"Another threatening letter from Virgil."

"What?" Victor was on his feet and reaching for the letter so quickly that he knocked over the chair. He read it standing up. "This could be serious!"

Now it was Charlie's turn to feel bemused. "You weren't bothered by the first two letters. In fact, you made fun of me for worrying about them. Like it was a joke."

Victor opened his mouth and briefly it remained half ajar as if ready to receive a hard-boiled egg. Then it snapped shut with a little click, and Victor glanced away and looked embarrassed. Charlie was impressed by this because Victor almost never looked embarrassed. In the world of upset and perturbation he tended to be the perpetrator rather than the victim of embarrassment.

"It's just that this letter doesn't make any jokes."

Charlie took the letter and compared it to the other two, which he had been keeping in the belly drawer of his desk. All three had been badly typed on different typewriters, using different paper. All three were mailed from different places.

"You should take it to Peterson," said Victor after a moment. He was still standing and seemed indecisive.

" 'It?' " said Charlie. "Don't you mean all three?"

"It's the last one that seems the most dangerous."

"You're not making much sense today. All three threaten to kill me and the second one threatens in the most violent terms. Cut out my eyes for scrambled eggs? Good grief."

"Then take them all to Peterson."

"I'll wait to see what happens."

Victor scratched his chin and looked around the room. "You got your revolver?"

"It's still out at the lake."

"Want me to drive out and get it for you?"

"Jesus, Victor, what's gotten into you?"

Again there was that openmouthed expression and again Victor's mouth closed abruptly with a little click. Then he asked, "Where you goin to be today?"

"I'll probably have to help Eddie check this list of names with some gamblers. And I want to talk to some members of the Travel Bugs again. First of all, I'll go see Maximum Tubbs."

"You going to do anything about Virgil Darcy?"

"Maybe I'll talk to his P.O. in Albany."

Victor sat down on a corner of the desk. He wore a gray suit with a crimson silk tie. "Want me to stay with you today, just in case there's any funny stuff?"

"How come you're so worried?" And Charlie found himself wondering if his own perception of his possible danger was false. But having decided that the first two letters were a hoax, he didn't set much store by the third letter. Still, Victor's concern made Charlie ask if he was making a mistake. And once again he saw the back of the blue pickup rushing toward him as he uselessly pumped his brakes. Had that been Virgil? Charlie couldn't make any sense of it.

"I just don't like the tone of that letter," said Victor. "If you got killed, I wouldn't have anyplace to do my crossword. You gotta think of me for a change. Don't go into that empty hotel, okay?"

"Victor, it's part of my job."

Charlie drove over to the hospice around ten. He kept his windows open and felt the warm breeze touch his face and riffle the remnants of his hair. As during the previous week, there were convertibles with their tops down and Skidmore students wearing shorts and T-shirts. Frisbees were being thrown, skateboards and roller blades zipped along the pavement. Gray squirrels chased each other through the leafless branches.

Before leaving his office Charlie had again telephoned Mary Rose Reynolds in Santa Fe without success. It had been eight o'clock in Santa Fe. Charlie had also called her from Janey's that morning at seven thirty, meaning five-thirty a.m. in Santa Fe. Wherever Mary Rose Reynolds was spending her time, she didn't seem to be sleeping at home. In his office Charlie had an old directory listing the names and addresses of private investigators around the country. He had found five in Santa Fe. Briefly he imagined going to the bank and taking out a loan so that he, a private detective, could hire a private detective at two hundred a day plus expenses.

Charlie parked his Mazda behind the hospice near the rear door. Almost without thinking, he was being more cautious. He had driven across town with one eye on his rearview mirror and had made several unnecessary turns. No one had been following him and he mocked himself for his nervousness.

Maximum Tubbs was asleep. Moving quietly, Charlie drew up a chair to the side of the bed and sat down. His friend's face seemed hardly alive, just a touch of color on each cheekbone. His mouth was half open but there was no sound. Charlie considered holding a pocket mirror above Tubbs's open mouth to see if it would mist over. From somewhere in the building he could hear a phone ringing and bottles clinking together on a cart being wheeled down the hall. Charlie leaned forward with his elbows on his knees and waited for Tubbs to breathe. Tubbs had been born around 1905 and Charlie thought about all the events that had passed before his eyes, all the changes. Soon the century would change again and it seemed to

Charlie that in a short time there would be no one alive who could remember the world before television and rock and roll.

Tubbs remembered the celebrations at the end of World War I. He remembered Prohibition and speakeasies and rum-running. He remembered Charlie's father. Charlie wanted to wake him and say, "Tell me about those things once again." Why was he bothering about Grace Mulholland and Virgil Darcy, when he should be trying to get Tubbs to help him understand the fabric of the world, the fabric of his own life? Charlie thought of his own tendency to slide into solitude, to spend his days out at the lake reading and looking out at the water instead of joining in the friendly chaos of Janey's house. Had his own father had any of that? And his mother living in the south of France, wasn't that also a chosen solitude after the rush and bustle of the summer months when the Bentley was packed from one week to the next? Charlie worried that with Tubbs gone, he would no longer be able to know himself, to learn about himself.

Maximum Tubbs turned his head slightly. His eyes were still shut. "The horses are slow getting into the gate," he said. The voice was a whisper, almost not speech at all.

"Pardon?" asked Charlie. Then he saw that Tubbs was asleep.

"They're all jammed up," said Tubbs more loudly. "There they go!"

Charlie sat back in his chair. Tubbs's thin hands were on the blanket. The fingers of his left hand moved slightly. "He's never going to break out of there!"

Charlie found himself listening for double meanings, as if the words spoken out of Tubbs's morphine dreams were actually communicating deep truths designed to help Charlie free himself from some existential predicament.

"If it's not one thing, it's another," said Tubbs. "He should be breezin."

Charlie sighed and got to his feet. Walking to the window, he stood with his hands linked behind his back. Whatever his difficulties, he would have to solve them himself. Out on the street, a young blond man in blue running shorts was racing a golden retriever to the end of the block. The dog trotted in affable circles around the man, seemingly touched by the man's desire to compete on a doggy level. Charlie turned and made his way to the pay phone at the end of the hall. He had to call Virgil Darcy's P.O. and there was no point putting it off.

This morning Charlie reached Leo Angier right away. "I need to know where I can find Virgil," said Charlie. "I may have to talk to him."

"You're no longer a police officer," said Angier suspiciously.

"That doesn't make any difference."

"I don't need to tell you anything," said Angier. "Virgil's having a hard time and I can't see that a visit from you would do anything but make it worse. He's got a lot of anger toward you."

"Has he mentioned me?" asked Charlie, surprised.

"There've been those articles about the woman whose skeleton was found under the pool hall. Virgil read them. He called it another Bradshaw fuck-up."

Charlie leaned his forehead against the cool metal of the telephone. "This is a complicated situation," said Charlie. "I need to know where I can find Virgil because I may have to talk to him concerning something you know nothing about. If you refuse to tell me where I can find him, then I'll have to ask Chief Peterson to bring him in."

There was silence on the other end of the line. Charlie could just barely hear the sound of the typewriter. "You're really a hardass," said Angier after a moment.

"Actually," said Charlie, "I'm doing him a favor."

"Virgil's got a room in Glens Falls." Angier gave him the address. "But he's looking for another job so I don't know if he's still up there or not."

"Why in particular is Virgil having a hard time?"

"Twenty years in the slammer. No friends, no money, bad job and he's trying to stay straight, and now the guy who sent him to jail wants a friendly chat with him—you figure it out, buster."

A few minutes later Charlie was back in Maximum Tubbs's room. Tubbs was still asleep. Charlie stood at the window and looked out at the weather. All the passing cars had their windows down and people looked happy.

"This jock was muscling the nag down the lane and it dropped dead," said Tubbs. "Sometimes, Bobby, you gotta ride chilly."

Tubbs's eyes were still shut. Charlie looked back out the window in time to see Victor's lime-green Mercedes 190 turning into the Forest Gardens parking lot.

"Watch out, Jacko," said Tubbs in a whisper, "he's got two queens showing."

Charlie walked to the door and after a minute he saw Victor hurrying toward him down the hall. "I was hoping I'd still find you here," said Victor. "How's Tubbs?"

"Talking in his sleep. What's up?"

Victor looked over his shoulder. They were alone in the hall. "I brought you this," he said. He drew Charlie's .38 out of the pocket of his gray suit coat.

"You went out to the lake?" asked Charlie, hardly believing it. He stuck the revolver in his belt. "You must have broken in."

"Nah, I've had a key for a long time."

"Why'd you do this?" asked Charlie. He was equally touched and astonished.

Victor walked over to Tubbs's bed and bent over to look at him. "I felt you should have it. I felt you're not watching out for yourself."

"You going to stay here for a while?" asked Charlie.

"Yeah, I like sitting with him. Makes me think I'm looking at my future. What about you?"

"I'm going to try and find Virgil Darcy." Charlie told Victor about talking to Darcy's P.O. "Virgil's supposed to be living in Glens Falls, a place on Maple Street."

"That's where that letter was mailed."

"That's right." Charlie walked to the door.

"Charlie . . ." said Victor.

Charlie turned. Victor's mouth was half open. "Ahh, it's not important," he said. "I'll talk to you later."

That evening Charlie was at Janey's. He was making a point of spending more time at her house but he worried that she would become sick of him if she saw him too often. After dinner Charlie sat at the kitchen table sipping whiskey as Janey finished the rest of the dishes. Sometimes Charlie cooked Chinese food for everyone, but Janey's daughters didn't like it. "It's the kind of food where someone could slip in a cockroach," the fourteen-year-old Emma had said, "and you'd never know." Macaroni and cheese was what Janey's daughters preferred: nothing surprising, nothing dangerous.

Charlie was describing how he had spent his day while trying to avoid getting any deeper into an argument they had been having.

"I went to his place up in Glens Falls, but he wasn't there. Then I went over to GE in Fort Edward but they said he hadn't come to work for a couple of days."

"Charlie, go to the police." Janey was wearing blue sweatpants and a blue sweatshirt and looked a little like a policeman herself.

"He hadn't been working at GE long enough for anyone to know him so there wasn't anyone to talk to. I went back to his room and spoke with his neighbors but they hadn't seen him since Sunday."

"Did you look in his room?"

"Too many people around. I couldn't just break in. The landlady stayed with me the whole time." The landlady had been a suspicious old woman who had reminded Charlie of dried fruit, maybe prunes or raisins. "Actually there was a guy there who Virgil apparently hung out with and who he'd known in prison, but he was at work and I didn't have a chance to find him what with Eddie letting me down."

"I don't blame Eddie's wife for being angry," said Janey as she dried her hands on a dish towel. "He's got a wife and baby. Those are big obligations and he doesn't take them seriously."

"She didn't have to attack him."

"I can't believe she really hurt him."

"He's in bed and he refuses to get out. His feelings are hurt."

Eddie had not had a chance to visit any of Maximum Tubbs's gambling friends. When he had told Irene that he wouldn't be driving the backhoe because Charlie had asked him to talk to some gamblers instead, Irene had kicked his leg. There was some disagreement as to how much damage this had caused. Eddie had shown Charlie the spot, swinging his leg out of the big double bed decorated with stickers of Bambi and Thumper. Eddie's legs were covered with thick black hair but at the place to which he had pointed, the skin had been slightly inflamed. "She kicked me, Charlie. She kicked me with a shoe!"

For twenty years Eddie had been breaking women's hearts. Puberty for him had been the beginning of a long and satisfying meal. He had jilted women. He had two-timed and lied and snuck around. He had let women buy him clothes and feed him. He even let them wash his car. And now his chosen woman, the one he had led down the aisle of the Pacified Jesus Methodist Church, had kicked him in the leg. "I'm a battered husband, Charlie. It's not that I can't walk, it's just that I don't feel like walking."

"You gotta get up sometime," Charlie had argued.

"Who says? I could stay here until Christmas. I got health insurance. This could be a home injury. Charlie, she kicked me with a *pointed* shoe."

And so Charlie had been forced to visit the gamblers himself, not that he had been able to locate all five. Solly Hurlwitz had been in the eighteenth hour of a twenty-four-hour card game in a room at the Holiday Inn. He gave Charlie five minutes as the other five cardplayers took a pee break. "So how is Maximum?" Hurlwitz had asked. "Still dying?" He was a big soft-looking man with parchment-colored skin and dyed black hair. Maybe he was about sixty.

"He seems worse."

"I'd visit him, but it'd fuck up my luck. I'll say goodbye at the wake. Am I supposed to recognize any of these names?"

"Not necessarily. But if any of them are gamblers, then I need to know."

Hurlwitz returned the list to Charlie. "They all look like virgins to me."

Around three-thirty Charlie had found Pete Mendecino organizing a football pool in the backroom of a bar in Ballston Spa. Mendecino had a big black beard, a big belly and a big booming voice. "So's Max keeping the Reaper at bay?"

"Temporarily."

"How's he taking it?"

"He's tired."

"You tell him I got a band lined up for his wake. Joey Lucetti will play horn."

"Do you recognize any of the names?"

"Nah, they mean nothing to me."

Rodger the Beagle owned a news shop in a shopping center in Clifton Park, less than ten miles from the Albany airport. He was a jowly man with soft-looking ears who must have been in his late sixties. Curled up on the counter beside him was an oversized brown cat with a mammoth head. The cat was so big that it looked like a dog wearing a cat costume. "This is Mrs. Beagle," Rodger the Beagle had said, introducing the cat.

"Maximum Tubbs thought you might be able to help me with this list of names," Charlie had said. "I need to know if any are gamblers." By then it was past six and Charlie had been driving around for most of the afternoon.

"Poor Tubbs, I saw him last week. No more card games for him. Once I saw him lose a hundred grand and never blink an eye. Mr. Unflappable, we used to call him. Who's going to handle the wake? It'll be a blast. Maybe I can get a roulette wheel."

"I guess I am," Charlie had said. "Pete Mendecino has lined up a band."

"Let me know when the time comes. There's a lotta people I need to call, a lotta people who'll want to show up." Rodger the

Beagle glanced over the list of names. "Nobody here rings any bells," he said.

Leaving Rodger the Beagle, Charlie drove back to Saratoga, reaching Janey's house around seven. Although he had spent most of the day doing work which he had hoped that Eddie Gillespie would do, he still felt satisfied. Another door was shut. It now seemed unlikely that Grace Mulholland had been killed by a compulsive gambler who had squandered the two hundred thousand dollars on a series of bad bets. And the search for the three gamblers had also taken Charlie's mind off Virgil and the threatening letters. By the time he got to Janey's the threats seemed inconsequential and he even felt embarrassed about the .38, which was still stuck in his waistband. But then he had told Janey about receiving the third letter and her exasperation made him feel like he might be making a mistake.

"Charlie, if you go and get yourself killed, I'll never forgive you!"

Charlie was struck that her words were similar to Victor's. "I'm sure it's a practical joke."

"Come on, Charlie, call Peterson."

"If I don't find Virgil tomorrow, then I'll call him."

"Tomorrow might be too late," Janey had said crossly.

When Janey finished the dishes, she poured herself some Jim Beam and sat down on the other side of the kitchen table. "So you've missed swimming three days in a row, Charlie. You must be ready to pull your hair."

"That's about right. Also, I've got to hire a private detective in Santa Fe and I may have to take out a loan to do it. Vince Reardon's ex-wife lives down there and she's not been answering her phone."

"Why do you want her?" Janey sipped her whiskey. A bowl of apples stood on the table. Charlie took one and began tossing it lightly in the air. In front of him, he could see his reflection in the darkened window: the shine of his glasses.

"Reardon says he earned the money for Mother McDougle's as a waiter in Santa Fe and I want to check it with her. I mean, it's probably true but I want to be sure. So I'll have to spend about a hundred bucks learning something which I think I know already. First I have to hire a private detective. Next, because of these letters, you're going to make me hire a bodyguard."

Janey stuck out her tongue: a friendly gesture. "Did you see Maximum Tubbs today?"

Charlie nodded. "These gamblers I saw today, they're already planning his wake. One guy's got a band lined up."

"I bet it's a Dixieland band. You want some ice?"

"That's okay. They talked about Maximum Tubbs as if he was already dead. I go in there and watch him. I tell myself that in one day or maybe two or three, he'll be gone, but I can hardly imagine it."

Janey stood by the refrigerator. "He's had a long life, Charlie."

"He'll still be gone. I'll want to ask him something and he won't be there."

Charlie was still tossing the apple. At that moment, it hit the edge of his palm and bounced away. Charlie bent down to retrieve it. Suddenly there was an explosion and the window burst apart, sending fragments of glass all over the kitchen. Charlie dove forward onto the floor. There was a second explosion and more breaking glass.

"Charlie!" Janey had ducked behind the refrigerator.

Charlie rolled over on his belly and tugged his .38 from his waistband. Hardly aiming, he pointed the gun toward the demolished window and fired twice. The noise seemed huge in the small kitchen. From another room he could hear one of Janey's daughters screaming. Charlie crawled across the bits of broken glass to the light switch and flicked out the light.

"Charlie, are you all right?" Janey sounded terrified.

"Stay where you are!" Making his way to the window, Charlie looked over the sill. There was no sound, no evidence of any person. The window looked out on the backyard by the garage. Charlie was angry at himself for shooting. He could have hit another house.

"Call the police," said Charlie, "but keep your head down."

"Charlie, what was it?"

"A shotgun."

While Janey telephoned, Charlie sat on the floor by the window. The whiskey had spilled and its smell mixed with the smell of cordite. Charlie listened to the sound of his beating heart. From the hall he could hear Janey talking on the phone and her daughters' frantic questions. Whoever had fired must be long gone by now. Not "whoever," thought Charlie: Virgil fired, just like he had wrecked the brakes on the Mazda. Virgil was trying to kill him.

When Janey came back in the kitchen, she was furious. "I told you to call Peterson, but no, you knew better! I hate this, Charlie. You got those letters and did nothing. You thought you had it all figured out. Well, Charlie Bradshaw, you almost got killed, that's how smart you are! And my kids could have been hurt too. I'm sick of you trying to be smart all by yourself. I want you to get out of here and not come back till this whole thing is over. And maybe not even then. I'm sick of worrying myself sick about you."

During this, Charlie had pulled the shade and drawn the curtains. Then he crossed the room and turned on the light. The shotgun blast had left a circular scar on the white wall, gouging great chunks out of the plaster. The second blast had smashed the cupboard over the sink, splintering the doors and breaking the window. The shots had passed right above Charlie, but the glass from the window had cut him and when he withdrew his hand from the back of his neck, it was red.

"Oh, Charlie," said Janey, "you're bleeding! Sometimes you irritate me so much I hardly know what to do with you."

18

Harvey L. Peterson, Commissioner of Public Safety, was a man who liked to be right, a man who saw the truth as his little companion. The discovery that Charlie had received three letters threatening his life and had the brakes disabled on his pokey little foreign car yet had done nothing about it but feel vaguely skeptical was shocking news. After all, the police department existed to safeguard the citizens of Saratoga.

But then had come a kind of retribution: someone had indeed tried to kill Charlie, and in Peterson's mind that attempt was caused by Charlie's very refusal to notify the police in the first place. "What goes up, must come down," said Peterson ponderously. And the people with whom he shared this sentiment nodded their heads while not being entirely clear about its meaning.

"Charlie, you mean that someone threatened to eat your eyeballs with scrambled eggs and you didn't come to us?" asked Peterson in a voice hushed with disbelief.

It was shortly after nine o'clock Friday morning and Charlie was sitting in Peterson's office. For an hour the previous night a doctor had picked bits of glass out of Charlie's scalp and the back of his neck. The back of his head had been partly shaved in a way that

Charlie disliked and now his neck was constrained by a bandage that felt like a tight turtleneck sweater. What Charlie disliked most about being shot at was the indignity of being patched up. At last he had been given a sedative and put in a room with a man who shouted out the names of trees ("Birch!" "Maple!") in his sleep. Charlie's last thoughts had dealt with the financial setback that the attempt on his life had inflicted.

"I thought the letter seemed like a joke," said Charlie.

"But don't you think that's something for the police to decide? Who but a crazy person would say such a thing? Liver pancakes, Charlie, that's not sane." Peterson seemed to balance on the very tip of his job description like a tightrope walker perched on a high wire.

"Did you turn up anything outside of Janey's?"

"A couple of shotgun casings, twelve-gauge. I had a squad car outside her house all night."

"I appreciate that."

"I didn't do that for you, Charlie. She's a citizen of Saratoga. This Virgil Darcy character must be nuts."

Charlie's bandage itched, and each time he touched his neck he felt a burning sensation. "Have you got a line on him yet?"

"He hasn't been to his place in Glens Falls in a couple of days and he hasn't showed up for work. I figure he's been hanging around Saratoga waiting to catch up with you."

"I haven't seen any trace of him."

"Have you been looking?"

Charlie considered how he had been checking his rearview mirror now and then. "Maybe not." What had he in fact done? He had found his revolver, cleaned it and loaded it, then left it out at the lake. Peterson was staring at Charlie like a high-school principal who has had about enough. Charlie decided to change the subject. "Have you learned any more about the Mulholland case? What about those ex–car thieves who used to run the pool hall: Louie and Bill Schaaf?"

Peterson leaned back in his chair. A little pain seemed to settle between his eyebrows. "Novack drove over and talked to them in Herkimer."

"And?"

"They laughed."

"What?"

"They thought it was the funniest thing in the world that a body had been found under the pool hall. They claimed they'd never heard of Grace Mulholland and said they knew nothing about those fake insurance claims and her disappearance. The cellar of the pool hall had been used for storage, junk mostly. It had a dirt floor and a door leading to the outside. Nobody was in the building after midnight and it would have been easy to break in."

"So you don't suspect them anymore?"

"Sure I suspect them, Charlie. I mean, they're crooks. It's in their blood. But it's going to be hard to prove. What about Paul Ward?"

"He might have seen Mulholland on the very day she was killed. He said she had seemed very happy. She'd also been wearing the earrings that were found with the skeleton."

"Should we bring him in and talk to him?"

"No, he didn't do it. Besides, he's touchy." Charlie described Ward's anger and dislike of the police.

"If he didn't want trouble, then he shouldn't have knocked over those convenience stores. What are you going to do now, Charlie? I don't want you just running around irresponsibly."

Charlie had a brief image of himself naked on a skateboard. "I'm going to see Frank Augustine again, he was the insurance guy who was about Mulholland's age. He's got his own agency now."

"You have any reason to suspect him?"

"I just want to go over some stuff." Charlie decided not to mention that he also had to hire a private detective in Santa Fe.

"Charlie, I want to keep a man with you, just to be on the safe side."

Charlie was impressed. He couldn't decide if Peterson's offer was intended to help him or make him miserable. He tried to imagine some sullen plainclothesman watching him swim laps. "I don't need anyone. Don't you have men looking for Darcy?"

"Every man on duty has seen his picture and we've alerted neighboring towns from Lake George to Albany."

"Let it go at that," said Charlie. "I don't want anyone tagging after me."

"I'd hate to see anything happen to you."

Charlie wondered if Peterson was sincere, then he thought that the question was irrelevant. After all, protecting Charlie was part of Peterson's job.

By eleven o'clock Charlie was seated at his desk. His .38 lay on the green blotter by the telephone next to a glass of water and a bottle of aspirin. The cuts on his neck hurt but he tried not to dwell on them. Instead, he was thinking about Frank Augustine, the insurance agent, whom he had visited that morning. Eighteen years ago Charlie had thought he was a jerk. Now he thought he was a nice guy. There seemed to be a lesson here but Charlie couldn't quite put his finger on which among many lessons it was. Charlie had wanted to ask him if Grace Mulholland had seemed particularly happy in the days before her disappearance.

"I don't know if she seemed happy," Augustine had said, "but she started wearing lipstick and that surprised me."

"Did she look pretty?"

"She didn't know how to put it on. Sometimes my six-year-old daughter puts on her mother's lipstick and gets it crooked. Grace's lipstick was a little like that. But certainly she was trying to look pretty."

Charlie tried to imagine Grace Mulholland preparing to run off with someone, ready to begin a new life as somebody's lover. The ex-librarian Maggie Henry had described her as brave. If not brave, she was certainly daring. She was in love and ready to run away. Then her lover crushed her skull.

Also that morning, Charlie had engaged Ben Howard, a private investigator in Santa Fe. "Her name's Mary Rose Reynolds," Charlie had said, "I got her address and phone number but nobody ever answers. For all I know she's on vacation."

Ben Howard said he'd look into it. "You got snow up there yet?" he asked. He had a cowboy drawl that Charlie envied.

"No, it's hot."

"It's raining here. I swear somebody's screwing up the atmosphere. It must be all those satellites. I'll try to get back to you this afternoon."

Before going to his office that morning, Charlie had briefly visited Maximum Tubbs, whom he had found awake but very weak.

"I'm still here, Charlie." His voice was like a sigh.

"I saw some friends of yours yesterday. They asked about you." He described his visits with the three gamblers.

"They planning my wake?"

"They mentioned it." The subject had embarrassed Charlie. How do you talk to a person about his own funeral?

"You know, Charlie, I been thinking I'm going to beat this but I don't think it anymore. Now I just want to call it quits. You still got the money I gave you?"

Charlie felt surprised, then embarrassed, as if he might have spent the fifteen thousand for the wake in looking for Grace Mulholland's murderer. "Sure. It's in my safe."

"You're in charge of the party," said Tubbs. "Make it big."

Charlie had thought of a number of dreary things to say—that he wouldn't feel like dancing and how much he would miss his friend—but he finally said nothing. He just nodded his head.

"Get some young girls," said Tubbs. "I've always liked parties with girls. And make sure everyone has plenty to drink."

"Rodger the Beagle said he'd try to get a roulette wheel."

"Damn," said Tubbs, "I'd like to be there."

Sitting at his desk, Charlie felt confused about the party and how he could carry it off if he was filled with grief. He wanted to call

Janey and consult with her, then he remembered that she didn't want to see him, didn't want to talk with him, didn't want him coming to her house.

"And no Thanksgiving either, Charlie," she had said. "I can just see someone shooting through the window when we're eating turkey. I don't need this excitement in my life and I don't need a man who thinks he can do everything by himself."

Charlie again found himself thinking about Bob Ford as if there were something there especially meaningful to Charlie's present dilemma. Some days before Ford's death, a fire in Creede had destroyed the downtown, taking Ford's Creede Exchange with it. Ford managed to save his whiskey and a grand piano. Two days later Ford set up a new bar in a large tent with wooden floors. The next day, June 8, 1892, a woman came to the bar asking for contributions to bury a dance-hall girl who had committed suicide the previous evening. Ford pledged ten dollars and next to his name he wrote, "Charity covereth a multitude of sins." It was just ten years after he had killed Jesse James. As Ford turned away, a cowboy named Ed O'Kelly entered the bar carrying a double-barreled shotgun. O'Kelly called, "Ho, Bob!" and when Bob Ford turned, O'Kelly emptied both barrels into him. O'Kelly then grabbed one of Ford's pistols and ran out to the street, where he was arrested minutes later. Ford was dead and Dottie knelt by his side. "A shotgun's a coward's gun," she said. "Bob wouldn't shoot a coyote with a shotgun. When he killed Jesse James, he did it with a forty-five."

Charlie had seen a photograph taken minutes after the shooting showing several hundred men posed before Bob Ford's tent saloon. All knew that Ford's death was an historic event and by having their picture taken they were seizing possession of their own particular snippet of posterity. Ford received a big public funeral. Then, several years later, Dottie returned to town and gave some dances to raise money to take Bob Ford's body back to Missouri. Charlie had been touched by that.

O'Kelly was sentenced to life imprisonment but was pardoned after serving two years. Sometime later he was shot to death by a police officer in Pueblo. There was no clear reason why he had killed Bob Ford. There was talk of quarrels and bad dealings between them, but the general feeling was that O'Kelly wanted the distinction of being the person who had killed the killer of Jesse James.

Charlie had always been impressed that Ford had been shot only minutes after pledging ten dollars to the dead dance-hall girl. Ten dollars was a lot in 1892. ''Charity covereth a multitude of sins'' —the phrase repeated itself in Charlie's mind in a way that seemed important but he couldn't grasp how.

There was a bumping at the outside door and Charlie grabbed for his .38. Someone tried the handle. It was locked. There was a knocking. ''Hey, Charlie,'' called Victor. ''You in there?''

Charlie slipped his revolver into his belt, then went to open the door.

''How come you lock yourself in here?'' asked Victor. ''You having trouble with wild women?'' Victor wore a gray silk suit and looked as distinguished as a banker. Only the sparkle in his eyes showed a certain shiftiness of soul.

''Virgil Darcy tried to kill me last night.''

''You're fucking kidding!'' Victor's face knotted up in alarm. ''Is that what happened to your neck?''

Charlie sat down again behind his desk. ''I got cut by glass from the kitchen window. I was at Janey's.'' Charlie described what had happened. Victor sat down in the other chair and his expressions ranged from guilt to astonishment. ''No,'' he kept saying, ''I can't believe it!''

Charlie was moved by Victor's response. He knew of course that Victor liked him, after all they were best friends, but never before had Victor shown this degree of concern.

''But the guy missed,'' said Charlie. ''I'm okay. Just some scratches.''

"Charlie," said Victor, looking down at his hands, "you're my buddy, right."

"Sure I'm your buddy."

"And you'd be my buddy no matter what happened, right?"

"Of course."

"And you'd be my buddy even if I did something I shouldn't, because you'd know I didn't mean it, that I really liked you, right?" Victor kept staring at his hands.

Charlie grew suspicious. "Tell me what you did, Victor."

"Charlie, I wrote those first two letters."

"You!"

"But I didn't write the third! Virgil must have written the third." Victor looked up and nodded so that his hair shook.

"You!"

"I should of told you yesterday but I couldn't bring myself to do it. If I'd told you yesterday, then you would have called Peterson and none of this would've happened. I feel terrible and you got an ugly-looking haircut too."

"But why'd you do it?" Charlie could hardly believe what he was hearing.

"It seemed like a funny idea at the time."

"Funny!"

"I admit it doesn't seem so funny now. I was talking to Eddie Gillespie. He said I should tell you. I don't want you to be mad at me, Charlie."

Charlie didn't say anything. He looked over at his poster of Jesse James. He was positive that people hadn't played these pranks on Jesse. "I thought Eddie was in bed," he said at last.

Victor held up his cellular phone. "He is, but he calls me now and then. He's still very depressed. I'm depressed too, Charlie, I did a bad thing."

"What if I went to bed?" said Charlie gloomily. "What if I got depressed?"

"You want me to do anything?"

"Yes, go up to Glens Falls and try to get a hold of that friend of Virgil's who lives in his building. His name's Montgomery. There's a chance that he can tell you where to find Virgil." Charlie gave him the address. "You do that and maybe I'll forgive you." Or maybe not, he thought.

That evening Charlie returned to his house on the lake, taking all his files with him. Then for four hours he read over his notes. Even though the weather was mild, he built a fire in the fireplace and he put on a tape of Benny Goodman quartets because the music made him feel good. After five minutes, he took the music off again. He wanted to be able to hear any strange noises, any cars pulling up along the side of the road, any footsteps. And when the fire died down, he didn't add any more wood.

By ten o'clock he decided there had never been any real evidence that Grace Mulholland had left the country. In fact, the only evidence was the letter from Mexico mailed three months after her disappearance: a letter which could have been written by anyone. There had also been the books on Mexico and South America, but as the old insurance investigator had said, the books made it seem too tidy, as if someone was trying to make it seem as if she had left the country.

What had happened was that Grace Mulholland had a lover who convinced her to submit the false claims and who promised to run away with her, a lover who made her happy and gave her flashy earrings. And Charlie almost knew who the lover was. It had something to do with Bob Ford and something to do with his conversation with the insurance agent Frank Augustine that very day. Usually Charlie was a little vain about his analytical abilities, but now whenever his mind relaxed he thought of Janey's anger or Maximum Tubbs's impending death or Victor's jokey betrayal or Virgil Darcy trying to kill him with a shotgun: "a coward's gun," Bob Ford's common-law wife had said. And what else was important about Bob Ford? "I know what I done and what's going to come of it.'' But it wasn't that statement nagging at Charlie's imagination, it was another.

Charlie stood up, went into the kitchen and poured himself a slug of Jim Beam. It was Janey's favorite whiskey and it made him feel close to her to drink it. He got two cubes of ice from the freezer and swished them around the glass with his finger.

Just before coming home that afternoon, Charlie had talked to Ben Howard, the Santa Fe detective. Howard told him that Mary Rose Reynolds worked for a restaurant-supply company and was occasionally out of town delivering glassware to distant bars and restaurants. He promised to discover her exact whereabouts the next day. ''Even though it's Saturday,'' he had said. And Charlie had wondered if Ben Howard charged overtime.

Returning to the living room, Charlie picked up the notes he had written about Vince Reardon. ''He says that Grace Mulholland asked him for a copy of one of his slides showing a Mexican church,'' Charlie read. ''He asked her if she was going to give a presentation and if she had visited any interesting places. She said that she hadn't been anywhere yet but that she knew some Spanish.''

Charlie went to the back door and looked out. The wind was blowing and he could see whitecaps near the shore. He opened the door and went outside, letting the screen bang behind him. He was half expecting a call from Victor but he had heard nothing. And he was also hoping that Janey would call, although he knew that she wouldn't. She was too stubborn to call.

Charlie walked out on the dock, which extended about a dozen feet into the lake. Several summers earlier he had bought an old aluminum rowboat but he had already taken it out of the water for the winter. He sat down on the end of the dock and set his whiskey beside him. His feet dangled above the water which swirled beneath him. The wind was making too much noise for him to hear anything, like geese for instance. By now the geese had presumably completed their journeys. He hoped it was nice wherever they went: warm weather and fat little fish.

Then Charlie turned abruptly, stretching his bandages and hurting his neck. Something had caught his attention but later he could never be sure if it had been a noise or just a sudden chill. Looking over his shoulder, he saw a shadow cross between him and the lighted living room window of his cottage. He scrambled to his feet. Victor, he thought, but then he wondered why Victor should be skulking around the back of his house.

Charlie stood up and reached for his revolver. It wasn't there. Then he remembered he had taken it out of his waistband and put it on the coffee table. Sometimes when he was sitting it dug into his ribs in a painful manner. The shadow had stopped by the window. Charlie squatted down and watched. No, the person was too thin to be Victor. Now the shadow began moving again. It was moving toward the dock. Was there enough light to be visible? Charlie thought. He was wearing a blue shirt and dark slacks. Maybe the shirt was visible. The bandages, the white bandages would be visible. The shadow moved closer. It was a man wearing a stocking cap. Charlie stood up.

"Virgil, we can talk."

The man moved more quickly. He was carrying some kind of stick. No, it's not a stick, thought Charlie, it's a shotgun. The man had almost reached the dock.

"Virgil!"

As the man raised the shotgun, Charlie flung himself backward. Even before hitting the water, he heard the explosion. Charlie splashed onto his back and the cold took his breath. His glasses were knocked off and disappeared in the dark. Kicking loose his shoes, Charlie took a deep breath and dived under, trying to swim along the bottom. In the pool, he could swim forty yards without taking a breath, but there he wasn't encumbered with clothes. Charlie worked his way out of his pants, sticking his wallet and keys in his underwear. The water was so cold that it hurt his head. He kept swimming until his lungs would take no more. Then he surfaced slowly.

He was about twenty yards out. A man was standing at the end of his dock, a man holding a shotgun. Charlie dove again and began swimming parallel to the shore. Without his glasses the few lights along the shore looked as dazzling as stars.

19

Leroy Skinner wore light-green pajamas under a blue terry-cloth bathrobe that was so ragged it looked like the victim of a territorial dispute. It was seven o'clock Saturday morning and he and Charlie were drinking coffee at a round oak table in the living room of Skinner's log cabin. Skinner drank his coffee with little sips that sounded like kisses. The coffee was steaming hot and Charlie blew on his so he wouldn't burn his mouth. Without his glasses the room looked blurry and he kept squinting, trying unsuccessfully to bring it into focus.

Charlie had called the retired insurance investigator the previous evening from a pay phone near a closed convenience store on Route 9P, about three quarters of a mile from his cottage. Standing in his sopping-wet shirt and underwear, Charlie had told Skinner that he needed his help. Skinner was the first person Charlie had called; he didn't feel like calling anyone else, not even Victor. Skinner lived about fifteen miles away. It had taken him twenty minutes to reach Charlie, who had been crouched down in the dark by the corner of the store so he wouldn't be seen. Skinner had also brought a towel. He drove a big 1980 Buick Riviera and the heater was on full blast.

"You take your swimming pretty seriously, Mr. Bradshaw."

Charlie hadn't said anything. He was too cold to speak. The bandages on his neck had come off in the water and one of the cuts was bleeding again. And he had hurt his feet walking barefoot across the stones. After he stopped shivering, Charlie had asked, "Can I spend the night at your place and borrow some clothes? Someone's trying to kill me."

"It would be an honor."

On the way back to Skinner's log cabin on the hill, Charlie had told him about Virgil Darcy's release from prison, then the threatening letter and the attempts on his life.

"Why didn't you call the police instead of me," Skinner had asked.

"I don't know, there's something about the whole business that I haven't worked out." Then Charlie had laughed. "Maybe I just didn't want Peterson to find me in my underwear."

Skinner had then asked about the Mulholland murder and Charlie told some of what he had learned, mostly possibilities that he had eliminated. He had begun to say something about his own clumsiness eighteen years earlier, but he didn't know how to address it and he didn't want to complain about himself. It didn't seem to Charlie that he was speaking clearly; the whole business felt like a confusion, but perhaps what felt confusing was that Virgil Darcy was trying to kill him. It seemed wrong somehow. But also Charlie was tired and his body hurt and without his glasses everything looked fuzzy. When they had reached the log cabin, Skinner's wife had put a fresh bandage on Charlie's neck. He drank a cup of hot cocoa and shortly after that he had gone to bed to a short night of bad dreams: red-eyed creatures jumping out at him from behind rocks while he tried to run away across muddy fields, oh, so slowly.

Charlie had woken early to hear the noise of plates rattling in the kitchen and to the smell of freshly brewed coffee. A brown bathrobe was draped over a chair by the bed and Charlie put it on. His neck felt better but he was stiff. He touched his toes ten times, then went into the kitchen.

"Sorry if we disturbed you," Skinner said apologetically. "We get up early around here."

Sitting at the round table, Charlie had eaten two bowls of hot oatmeal and several pieces of toast. He felt as if he hadn't eaten for several days. Now he was having a second cup of coffee as he and Skinner watched the sun come up over the distant hills. The fields were misty and the rising sun dyed them red.

"I've been thinking," said Leroy Skinner in his slow way, "are you absolutely sure that the third threatening note came from Virgil Darcy?"

Charlie was surprised. "I'm sure my friend Victor didn't send it."

"No, but maybe it was written by some other person."

"Why?"

"So he could kill you and have suspicion thrown on Darcy."

"But who'd want to do that?" Even though he asked the question, Charlie knew the answer. He just wanted to hear somebody else say it.

"The man who killed Grace Mulholland," said Skinner. He passed a hand over his bald head, scratching his scalp. "Remember that note which Grace supposedly sent from Mexico? It must have been her murderer who sent it or had it sent. What's to say he wouldn't send another fake letter? When something works once, people like to do it again."

"But how would he know about Darcy?"

"From what you say, your friend Victor isn't particularly reticent. He might have told lots of people about his joke."

Charlie leaned back in his chair. The big living room of the log cabin had a cathedral ceiling and suspended from it were about twenty model planes, one with a wingspan of at least eight feet. Charlie squinted at them. The planes made all the air colorful. "No," said Charlie, "Victor's not good at keeping his mouth shut."

"Whoever killed Grace Mulholland must be feeling pretty anxious," said Skinner. "Certainly you've talked to him, and the more people you eliminate, the more pressure he must feel. He's tried to kill you twice and he'll probably try again. I'll bet he even messed with your brakes. And this Virgil Darcy's position isn't particularly secure either. The murderer can't afford to have him talking to the police."

"Darcy told some people he was going to look for a job down in Albany," said Charlie. "Peterson thought it was an excuse to throw the police off his trail. But probably that's just where he is, somewhere down in Albany."

"If you were killed and then Darcy was killed in a way that looked like suicide, then Grace Mulholland's murderer would feel pretty safe."

"Would he really do that?"

"What's his alternative? Giving himself up?"

Charlie finished his coffee. "Would you mind driving me over to my place so I can get some clothes and another pair of glasses? I think I better get busy."

"Just let me get dressed first," said Skinner. He stood up and walked slowly toward the bedroom, a big clumsy sack of a man whose passion was the graceful constructions of paper and balsa wood that dangled above him.

By eight o'clock Skinner's baby-blue Buick Riviera was pulling into Charlie's driveway. There was no one else in sight. "Not much of a yard," said Skinner, looking around him. He parked next to Charlie's Mazda 323, which was half the length of his own car.

"I've got the lake." Charlie and Skinner got out of the car. Charlie kept squinting in order to see better. He wondered what his chances were of finding his glasses in the lake. It was a cool sunny morning and sunlight sparkled on the water. Charlie felt troubled but he blamed it on his inability to see clearly, rather than on any fear that someone might be lurking nearby. He wore old clothes of Skinner's: baggy pants, baggy shirt and shoes two sizes too big. It made him feel like a clown. Unlocking the front door, he stood back to let Skinner enter.

The files with Charlie's old notes were still on the coffee table but they weren't as Charlie had left them and some had fallen to the floor. He went to the bedroom to get an old pair of glasses, then looked over the files see if any were missing. None were. The glasses were not as strong as he needed. Even though Charlie could see better, objects were still a little fuzzy. Something was wrong, something else was missing. Then Charlie realized what it was. He looked under the papers and among the cushions on the chair. He looked on the floor. His .38 was gone.

"Something the matter?" asked Skinner.

"Whoever was here took my revolver," said Charlie.

"Do you have another?"

"No. I mean, I hardly ever need it."

"At least your friend won't have to chase you with his shotgun." There was a note of disapproval in Skinner's voice. Then he reached under his coat. "Here, you can borrow this. I brought it along just in case."

It was a long-barreled revolver, a chrome-plated .45. To Charlie it looked like a cannon. He started to say that he wouldn't need it, but then thought that was foolish. "Thanks," he said, taking the revolver. It seemed to weigh five pounds. He wasn't sure that he could even carry it in his belt.

"Never had to fire it," said Skinner, "although I showed it a couple of times. It's like having a big dog with a big bark."

"Let me get dressed and I'll give you a cup of coffee."

"Nah, I got to get back. I'll just wait for my clothes."

Charlie went into the bedroom to change. He carried the big revolver and it reminded him of the big .45s that Bob Ford liked to carry. They hadn't protected him. He too had met a killer with a shotgun. Charlie sat on the bed to tie his shoes. He had had little sleep the previous night and he could almost feel his bed calling to him. Then he shook himself and returned to the living room. Skinner was standing with his hands behind his back, staring out at the lake.

"The water would be nice," he said, "but I couldn't fly my planes here."

Charlie handed him the clothes. "Thanks for everything."

"My pleasure. Let me know what happens."

As Charlie watched Skinner walk back to his car, the phone started ringing. He went to answer it, thinking it might be Victor. It was a nurse from Forest Gardens. Maximum Tubbs's condition had gotten worse.

Maximum Tubbs died that Saturday morning. When Charlie reached Forest Gardens shortly before nine, he found his friend barely conscious. Charlie took his hand, which felt like twigs wrapped in cool wax paper.

"It's okay, Charlie," Tubbs whispered. "I'm sick of hanging around."

Charlie couldn't think of anything to say. He was afraid of weeping, then didn't understand why he should be afraid. "I'll miss you," he said at last.

"Give me a good party. Let even strangers come, I don't care. Let them have fun."

"Pete Mendecino said he had a trumpet player lined up: Joey Lucetti." He continued to hold Tubbs's hand.

"He's the best. And Charlie, I want the casket open. I don't care that I look like shit. I want to be there."

Charlie realized he would have to hire a hall. He wanted to get the Canfield Casino in Congress Park. At the end of the nineteenth century it had been the most famous gambling hall in Saratoga. It seemed the right place to hold a wake for an old-time gambler.

"And Charlie," said Maximum Tubbs, even more faintly, "you got to relax more. I worry about you."

Charlie tried to smile. Skinner's big .45 was giving him a pain in his side and he guessed it was that which made him look troubled. Or maybe it was grief. Charlie straightened Maximum Tubbs's pillows and then telephoned Victor. The phone rang and rang. Considering that Victor had a cellular phone, Charlie couldn't understand why he wasn't answering. Charlie hung up, then drew up a chair to the side of the bed. Tubbs had shut his eyes. Charlie watched him breathe, his thin chest slowly rising and falling. It seemed that only the finest thread linked him from life to non-life. It was such a tenuous connection that Charlie had the sense he was keeping Tubbs alive with only his intense desire that he would not die. And in that moment Charlie let him go, as if accepting the certainty of his friend's death for the first time. It was like setting aside a heavy weight. Charlie leaned back in his chair. He too began to think of the wake, Maximum Tubbs's farewell party. And it would be more than just a wake for the man, but a wake for part of the life of Saratoga that no longer existed: gambling halls and touts and bookies and fast bets. Charlie felt sleepy and tried to make himself more comfortable in his chair. He wondered about the trumpet player Joey Lucetti and if he could play "St. James Infirmary." Charlie tried to think of the lyrics: "Put a twenty-dollar gold piece on my watch chain so my pals will know I died standing pat."

When Charlie woke up, he saw that Maximum Tubbs was dead. Charlie felt a moment of panic that Tubbs had gone without Charlie being able to speak or act or save him, as if he had snuck away without wanting Charlie to know anything about it. And then Charlie worried that Tubbs might have needed something from him but he had been asleep. The room felt empty and Charlie felt alone. He tried to remember what Maximum Tubbs's last words had been, something about Tubbs worrying about him. It occurred to Charlie then that he should have brought a video camera and recorded Tubbs over these past few weeks just so he could keep something of him: some last advice or words of encouragement. Now it was too late.

Charlie stood up and removed the oxygen tubes from Tubbs's nose. Then he pushed the buzzer for the nurse. Tubbs's eyes were nearly shut with just a whisper of space between the lids as if Tubbs were secretly looking at him. The corpse didn't resemble much of anybody. It seemed as vacant as an empty suit of clothes. Charlie took Tubbs's hand—already it was cooler. He wanted to weep but was unable to weep. Charlie gently put the hand back on the blanket. Going to the phone, he again called Victor but there was still no answer. Then he dialed Janey Burris. It was just ten o'clock in the morning.

Charlie met Janey an hour later outside the Canfield Casino: a square, three-story red-brick building with a large hall attached to the back. Ostensibly he had called to ask her advice about the wake, but actually he wanted to hear her voice and hear how she spoke to him. Couples were strolling in the park and two boys were tossing a football. Charlie watched Janey park her rusty Ford, then walk toward him. She wore a long blue coat and had a very businesslike walk, very erect and determined. The breeze fluttered her short dark hair. Charlie looked at her small hands with their blunt nails and thought how much he liked them. They seemed both delicate and efficient.

"I'm sorry about Maximum," she said, letting Charlie kiss her cheek.

"He wanted a large wake," said Charlie. "I'm trying to get the Casino. I may have to pull some strings, ask my cousins to apply some pressure. Maybe even ask Peterson."

Janey glanced at Charlie without speaking. He thought how pretty she looked. And he thought he had to keep talking, otherwise he would lose it. Lose what? he thought. Control, seriousness, bravery, dignity. Then he gave it up.

"I'm sorry I can't be the person you want me to be, Janey," he said. "But I love you more than I can say."

She continued to look serious. Then she took his hand. "I love you too, Charlie. I'm just afraid you'll get hurt. You need people to help you."

"I've been trying to get Victor on the phone but he doesn't answer."

Her forehead wrinkled slightly. "I don't mean Victor."

"I've been talking to Peterson."

"It's a whole attitude. You don't believe in cooperation and people working together."

"I guess I don't trust it. It's too California."

"Charlie!" She smiled a little. "How's your neck, does it still hurt?"

"It feels a lot better." He turned away slightly and in his blurred vision it seemed he could see the outline of Maximum Tubbs's corpse in the sloping lines of the hill.

"Have the police found Virgil Darcy?"

"No. I don't think he's the one who shot at me anyway." He told her how someone had come to his cottage the previous night and how he had been forced to swim away. Janey looked at him with increasing concern, even though he tried to make it seem less than it was. He spoke of losing his glasses and having to telephone in his underwear. He tried to make a joke out of it, but Janey didn't laugh.

"Anyway Skinner suggested it might be the guy who killed Grace Mulholland and not Darcy at all."

"But how would he know enough to send the letter?"

"That's what I want to talk to Victor about."

Janey took Charlie's sleeve. "Charlie, I want you to go away for a while. Tell Peterson everything you know and then leave. I'll even go with you. We can go to Miami for a week or so. We'll have a good time, a wonderful time."

Charlie stepped back. "It's not Peterson's case. It's my case."

"But he can handle it."

"I want to see it through."

Janey stepped forward and pushed Charlie with both hands, making him stumble. "You are the most exasperating man! If you get yourself killed, I won't even come to your funeral! How can you protect yourself?"

Charlie wanted to show Janey the huge .45 that Leroy Skinner had lent him, but there were people nearby. He looked at her face, full of distress and irritation. He didn't see how he could ever be the person she wanted. Reaching out, he touched her cheek very gently with his right hand. "I do all right," he said. "And I try to do better."

20

It was not quite dark when Charlie entered the Hotel Bentley that Saturday afternoon, although it was dark within the hotel and Charlie needed the flashlight. The gray cat met him in the lobby and Charlie thought the cat seemed nervous, but maybe it was the wind or maybe the cat was just hungry, or maybe, thought Charlie, it's me that's nervous. Charlie adjusted Skinner's .45 so it was stuck in the front of his belt. The barrel chaffed his leg, so he took it out altogether and carried it loosely in his left hand. The revolver was so big that Charlie imagined pulling it behind him in a little wagon. The wind had picked up again and Charlie wanted to check a loose window on the third floor. He stood for a moment in the lobby and looked up into the darkness of the main staircase. The gray cat rubbed against his legs and purred. Charlie's memory kept presenting him with brief images of Maximum Tubbs lying dead, covered with a thin blue blanket, and Charlie kept shaking his head in order to clear it. The fact of Tubbs's death kept striking him again and again and each time it felt like a surprise.

After leaving Janey in the park that morning, Charlie had spoken to the gamblers Solly Hurlwitz, Pete Mendecino and Rodger the Beagle, who promised to notify Tubbs's friends and fellow gamblers and tell them about the wake, which would be on Tuesday in the Canfield Casino. Charlie would contact the people on the list that Tubbs had given him. Solly Hurlwitz swore that cardplayers would fly in from all over the country. ''Hucksters, dicemen, three-card monte, you name it,'' he had said excitedly. ''All the good guys!'' The funeral would be Wednesday morning. Pete Mendecino said he had the band. Rodger the Beagle promised a roulette wheel. Hurlwitz was in charge of the girls and the booze. Chief Peterson said he would stay out of it unless there was any shooting. Charlie talked to Peterson several times during the day, mostly to see if he had gotten a line on Virgil Darcy. He hadn't, although he had learned that Darcy was driving an old Chevrolet. Charlie hadn't mentioned the trouble out at the lake or his belief that Darcy was innocent, but he told Peterson to go easy on Darcy if he found him, that they had no real proof that Darcy had done the shooting. For that matter Charlie doubted that Peterson could find much of anything, or at least not quickly.

During the afternoon Charlie had driven up to Glens Falls to talk to Darcy's friend Russ Montgomery, who lived in Darcy's rooming house and who had originally known him in prison. Montgomery wasn't home but by pestering various people Charlie was able to track him down to a bar near the Crandell Library where Montgomery was watching college football and drinking beer and shots. He was a skinny man about Charlie's age who in his youth had had a passion for mail fraud. Now he was a janitor, or ''custodian,'' as he preferred to be called.

''You know how many people have been bothering me about him?''

''You mean other than the police?'' Charlie had said. He asked the bartender to bring him a Rolling Rock and a bag of chips, then he canceled the chips. He hadn't been swimming enough to be eating chips.

''Some were cops, some weren't. I couldn't keep track.'' Montgomery described one of his visitors as an older man with frizzy gray hair, who Charlie realized was Victor. Montgomery also grudgingly gave Charlie the names of two men in Albany. ''Virgil might have seen some of these guys or he might not. Right now they're probably watching football. Personally I think Ohio State is the most overrated team in the country."

Charlie had driven back to Saratoga around three-thirty and once more tried unsuccessfully to find Victor. Then he went over to Vince Reardon's restaurant: Mother McDougle's. Reardon wasn't there. A waiter said he was probably at home watching football. Reardon had a house over on Jumel Place near the barns where the horse auctions were held in August. It was a large yellow house with a wraparound front porch. Charlie rang the bell and hammered on the door but there was no answer. Through the front window he could see an impeccably neat living room with a lot of overstuffed furniture covered with light fabrics.

Charlie had returned to his office and called the Santa Fe detective, Ben Howard. "I been trying to reach you," Howard said in his drawling voice. "Mary Rose Reynolds had to go up to Espanola. She's supposed to be back tonight. If you can't get her tonight or tomorrow morning, give me another call. Say, Bradshaw, where should I send my bill?"

Charlie thought about this bill as he climbed the stairs of the Bentley. And he thought about the cost of the wake being planned for Maximum Tubbs and how it could easily exceed the fifteen thousand dollars that Tubbs had given him. But the money didn't matter, or not really. He could talk to someone at the Adirondack Trust on Monday and take out a loan. Still, it was another burden and it might mean that he would have to work for his mother that summer as hotel detective. But first Charlie needed to find Virgil Darcy and make sure he was all right, even warn him to leave the area for a day or two. Then he had to find Grace Mulholland's killer. He had little doubt now as to who it was.

There was a noise downstairs, somewhere in the back, like a door slamming. Charlie jumped and the light from the flashlight skittered across the walls. Then he turned off the light and hurried back to the stairs. He was up on the third floor, which had one long hall running between the two staircases. Charlie thought he heard something down below but the wind created so many little noises that he couldn't be sure. He backed up until he reached the middle of the hall, then he stopped and listened. The old building creaked and groaned. The cat kept meowing and rubbing against his legs. Charlie tried to push it away, but it kept coming back as if it thought he was being playful.

Charlie heard a thump from the stairway. He knelt down. He thought of how his .38 had been stolen from his cottage and how humiliating it would be to be shot with his own revolver. Again there was a noise like the scraping of a shoe. If the person coming up the stairs still had the shotgun, he could spray the whole hall. Charlie lay down on his belly and held Skinner's big .45 out in front of him. The gray cat brushed against his face, pushed its jaw along the knuckles of Charlie's right hand. There was another noise from the stairs, a creaking and something bumping against the wall. Someone was definitely climbing toward the third floor. Hurriedly, Charlie shoved the cat away. He didn't want to hurt it or be rough with it. He could hear it purring right by his ear. The cat climbed onto his back and began kneading its paws against the fabric of his sport coat. Charlie rolled over, forcing the cat to jump off. Then he stretched out the revolver, holding it with both hands. Slowly he drew back the hammer. Another bump and scraping noise from the stairs. The person had almost reached the landing. The cat again began to climb onto his back. Trying to ignore it, Charlie pointed the revolver at the place where the person's head would appear. There was a flickering light as if from a match or a lighter. Charlie tried to jerk his shoulders to dislodge the cat but he was afraid of accidentally discharging the revolver before he was ready. He held the butt of the revolver against the floor and sighted down the barrel. He tightened his finger slightly on the trigger as he heard another noise.

"Charlie, are you up there?"

It was Victor. Charlie rolled over. There was a yowl from the cat. Slowly he took the revolver off half-cock. He began to sweat. He felt he had nearly killed his best friend.

"Here," he said, flicking on the flashlight.

"What the fuck you doing playing with a cat up here in the dark? Pretty kinky, Charlie."

"I was getting ready to kill you."

"Ahhh," said Victor.

"I thought you were someone else." This is what fear gets you, thought Charlie: mistakes and embarrassment.

"No," said Victor, "I ain't nobody but myself. Maybe we should go downstairs and have a drink. I got some stuff to tell you."

"Maximum Tubbs is dead." Charlie stood up.

"I know. I was over there. Were you with him?"

"Sort of. I mean I'd fallen asleep. But we'd talked a little earlier. I got the Canfield Casino for his wake."

"I hope you're ready for about five hundred people."

"At least."

As they went downstairs, followed by the cat, Victor said, "You seem a little jumpy. Were you really going to shoot me?"

"Someone tried to kill me again. This time out at the lake."

"I guess that would do it."

Charlie got the key for the cupboard behind the bar and took out a bottle of Jack Daniel's.

"Jack Daniel's, if you please," sang Victor quietly. A candle in a brass candlestick stood on the bar and he lit it. "That's a pretty big firearm you're carrying, Charlie."

"How come you don't answer your phone?"

"I dropped it. Then I accidentally kicked it. It rings all the time but when I answer I can't hear anything, not even anyone breathing."

Charlie gave Victor a glass of whiskey.

"You got any maraschino cherries?"

"Forget it."

"I found Darcy, he's down in Albany. Seems perfectly innocent. He's got a job in a gas station and he's staying over near Tivoli Park." Victor sipped his whiskey. The candle flame flickered in the mirror behind the bar.

"How many people knew about this little joke of yours with the threatening letters?"

"Ah, Charlie, do we have to talk about that?"

"We do."

"Well, I was talking about it with some people over at The Parting Glass, then over at the Firehouse, then a couple of other places. And when Eddie calls me on the phone we usually talk about it some. It was a hot topic."

"So how many people knew of it?"

"Oh, I don't know. No more than fifty."

"Let's go down to Albany."

"I'm driving?"

"And make it fast. Darcy may be in danger."

Victor set his empty glass down on the bar. "How come we always use my car when there's trouble?"

"You got the Mercedes, Victor. I'm driving the Mazda 323."

"Charlie, you know I like to be called Vic."

"Sure, Vic."

It was six-thirty by the time they reached Albany. On the way down, Charlie talked about Maximum Tubbs and how he would miss him. It was not something he had intended to talk about but he couldn't get it off his mind. And then he mentioned Janey Burris and their quarrel: her accusation that he liked to spend too much time by himself. By the dash lights Charlie could see Victor nodding his head.

"Maybe you should join some clubs like that Mulholland woman," said Victor. "Book clubs and travel clubs and cooking clubs. You could be a real charmer if you loosened up. I know a guy who wants to start a transvestite club. I'll give him your name and the two of you can sit around in tutus: two tutus."

"Be serious, Victor."

"I find seriousness an overrated commodity. It makes the smile muscles go all puffy, it fucks up your chances for a hot social life and it makes you sad. Anyway, some people are chummy and some aren't. You're a thoughtful sort of guy even if you're brooding about lunch. If Janey wants someone who plays bridge or acts in amateur theatricals, then she should look elsewhere.''

''I don't want her to look elsewhere,'' said Charlie.

''Then loosen up a little. Have you considered dyeing your hair?''

Charlie didn't bother to answer.

''Don't knock it, Charlie. Since I've been adding color to the old gray mop, my love life's taken on an additional color of its own. Women like a young look. Youth's where it's at.''

Victor parked in front of a brick building near Tivoli Park. ''Darcy's got a small studio apartment,'' said Victor, ''moved in last week according to the landlord. Semifurnished and cheap.''

They got out and Victor locked the doors. The air had gotten colder and Charlie couldn't see any stars. They hurried up the front walk. Nobody was on the sidewalk and there were no cars on the street. Charlie still had the .45 in his belt and it kept poking him uncomfortably. The front door was off the latch and Charlie pushed it open.

''He's up on the third floor,'' said Victor.

It was a run-down building but clean and the brass door plates shone. They climbed the stairs to the third floor. At each landing there were different cooking smells.

''Makes me wish I'd brought a sandwich,'' said Victor. ''I get moody when I hear my stomach growl. We're looking for 317.''

Charlie stopped in front of the door. He thought of what Virgil had looked like twenty years earlier and what he probably looked like now. Charlie felt a certain anxiety about seeing him. He felt bad about Virgil and didn't want to face his anger. He wondered if he was right that Virgil might be in danger. Most likely he was exaggerating. No, he thought, I'm not exaggerating.

''What're you waiting for?'' said Victor. ''Christmas?''

Charlie knocked three times and they waited. He knocked again.

''It seems that everybody I look for is never there,'' said Charlie.

''Try again.''

Charlie knocked again and waited. Then he suddenly dropped

down to his knees and started sniffing. Victor stared at him as if Charlie had gone crazy.

''I smell gas,'' said Charlie.

Victor knelt down as well. ''Should I get the super?''

''No time.'' Charlie backed across the hall and ran at the door, hitting it with his shoulder. The door refused to budge and Charlie was afraid he might have broken something in his arm. Then Victor ran at the door. There was a splintering of wood and the door flew open. A smell of gas seemed to embrace them.

''Open the windows!'' shouted Charlie. He ran toward the kitchen and pushed open the swinging door. A man who Charlie guessed was Virgil Darcy was lying with his head on the open door of the oven. Charlie turned off the knobs, then dragged Darcy back into the living room. Victor had the windows open and a cool breeze was blowing through to the hall. Darcy was still warm but Charlie couldn't find a pulse. ''Call an ambulance,'' Charlie told Victor. Half a dozen people had gathered at the door of the apartment. Their eyes looked wide and uncertain.

Charlie had taken CPR training many years before and for the next ten minutes before the ambulance arrived he blew into Virgil's mouth, then pushed down on his chest, two to one, two to one. Virgil remained unconscious. When one of the ambulance crew took over, Charlie sat back on the floor. The room seemed to be swirling around him and his arms ached. After a moment, he got a glass of water. Then he and Victor followed the ambulance over to Albany Memorial Hospital.

''I'm glad you did that and not me,'' said Victor. ''It's too intimate.''

''So you'd let him die?''

''I guess it's one of those big questions,'' said Victor. ''Maybe I could do it for a friend. Nah, I couldn't even do it for you. Janey, I'd do it for Janey Burris. She's got nice lips.''

''It's not a romantic occasion,'' said Charlie.

''I guess I got a wider view of romance.''

They waited outside the hospital emergency room until nearly ten o'clock. Every so often ambulances would pull up and stretchers were rushed past them. The waiting room was full of the anxious and bored. Victor went off to get sandwiches but Charlie wasn't hungry. He kept thinking of Virgil as he had originally known him, as a twelve-year-old candy thief with pale blond hair. It seemed terrible to think that he had attempted suicide. At last a doctor approached Charlie. He looked so serious that at first Charlie thought that Virgil had died.

"Your friend's going to be okay," said the doctor, "but he barely made it. He says someone slugged him. I've called the police. You can say hello if you want, but make it short."

Virgil was in a room with green walls in a bed with green sheets. When Charlie had been giving him CPR, he had hardly noticed that Virgil was nearly bald. It occurred to Charlie that Virgil looked older than he did: thin face, bad teeth, big wrinkles around the eyes and mouth. Seeing him in the hospital bed made Charlie think of Maximum Tubbs. Victor stood behind Charlie picking his teeth. He hated hospitals and was only waiting to get out.

"I guess I'm supposed to thank you for being alive," said Virgil quietly. He lay on his back and stared at Charlie.

"You don't have to. The doctor said somebody slugged you, can you tell me anything about that?"

"I didn't see anyone. I came in sometime after six o'clock. There was someone in my apartment. I heard him behind me, began to turn and pow! The next thing I knew I was puking into a pan here in the hospital."

"So you didn't even get a glimpse?"

"I couldn't tell you if it was a man or a woman."

"The cops think you've been trying to shoot me," said Charlie. "I'd got a couple of threatening letters with your name at the bottom."

Behind him Charlie could feel Victor cringe.

"I don't wish you well, Charlie," said Virgil, "but I wouldn't shoot you. Maybe if I was standing at the top of a flight of stairs and you were on the step beneath me and there was nobody nearby and you were looking the other way, well, maybe I'd give you a push. But shooting, it's too messy and anyway I don't want to go back to the slammer."

"I appreciate that," said Charlie.

"I'm giving you nothing and I want nothing from you. Not even my life." Virgil said this without expression, but he kept staring at Charlie, as if Virgil too was struck by the passage of time, that they were both twenty years older.

"I wanted to ask you something else," said Charlie. "Those guys you were involved with: Joey Damasco and Frank Bonita. Didn't Bonita come from someplace up north?"

"Yeah, Wevertown," said Virgil. "That's where they found the car."

"What car?"

"The car we used in the holdup, a big Fairlane. They dropped me off in Saratoga, then drove up to Wevertown. This was in the spring. In the fall a couple of hunters found the car in the woods. The cops figured they'd dumped the car and taken another. That's why they were never picked up."

"And there's still no trace of them?"

"Not as far as I know."

"Were they friends, those guys?"

"Sort of, but they kept arguing all the time. It got on my nerves."

There were some voices in the hall and two men in suits entered the room. Even though he didn't recognize them, Charlie knew they were cops. It was something about the eyes: no surprises anymore, nothing nice in their stockings.

21

When they got back to Saratoga around eleven-thirty that night, Victor drove over to Vince Reardon's house on Jumel Place. The house was dark and there was no car in the driveway.

"What kind of car does he drive?" asked Charlie, staring up at the house. He could make out pale curtains in the windows.

"A Toyota Celica, a green one. You really think he's guilty because he's got a baseball team?" asked Victor, continuing a conversation that had occupied them for some minutes.

"It's not just that he supports the baseball team," said Charlie. "It was this remark by Bob Ford just before he got shot: 'Charity covereth a multitude of sins.' It just got me thinking about Reardon in a slightly different way."

"And who's Bob Ford again?"

"Victor, he's the guy who killed Jesse James." Charlie couldn't understand how Victor could sometimes be so dense.

"Ah, that clarifies everything." Victor backed out of the driveway. In the glow from the dash lights his nose looked green. The night had gotten colder and snow flurries blew across the hood of the Mercedes.

"But also I liked Reardon," said Charlie. "All those other people eighteen years ago, I didn't have much use for."

"Let's see if I've got this straight," said Victor. "Everybody you dislike are basically the good guys because you can't stand them and everybody you like are basically the bad guys because you think they're great. Is that how it works?"

"Well, I had no real suspicions about him and I was suspicious of nearly everyone else." Even Charlie had to admit that it didn't sound logical.

"Charlie, if Sherlock Holmes had said this kind of stuff, then Arthur Conan Doyle would have gone broke."

"There's more," said Charlie. "Reardon told me that Mulholland claimed to know Spanish and there was no evidence that she'd ever studied Spanish. In my notes I quoted him as saying, 'She said that she hadn't been anywhere yet but that she knew some Spanish.' Really it was the word 'yet' that got me thinking about him because it suggested that she wanted to go someplace and no one else had ever said anything like that."

Victor cut over toward Lake Avenue and turned left toward Broadway. There was little traffic. On a cold Saturday night in November Saratoga looked like any other small town. Little whirlwinds of snow blew across the pavement.

"So all that was the extent of your great analytical ability?" asked Victor.

"Not quite. I also managed to call Reardon's ex-wife from the hospital in Albany. She'd just got home from someplace. I asked if Reardon could have saved the money for Mother McDougle's working as a waiter and she said she didn't know, that she had no idea where the money had come from. Maybe Reardon had saved it and maybe not. So I asked why they'd gotten divorced and she said that living with him was like living with a zombie. She never knew what he was thinking or feeling. In the restaurant he was all charm, but at home it was as if a switch had been turned off. So I asked if she thought he could have killed Grace Mulholland and she said she didn't know. Fifteen years she lives with the guy and she doesn't even know whether he could commit a murder? Don't you think that's suspicious?"

"Vaguely."

"So I asked if Reardon knew anything about cars. Like would he know how to disengage the push rod in a brake cylinder? And she said he used to work for a garage before he became a waiter."

"And this is your proof?" asked Victor.

"It's not proof," said Charlie. "None of it's proof. It's just one more piece of damaging information."

Lights were on in police headquarters. Victor turned left on Putnam by the offices of the *Saratogian,* which were dark.

"Reardon could have easily heard about those threatening letters I wrote," said Victor. "Like it was a joke and I told a lotta people. I drop by his restaurant now and then. He's got a good lunch special with homemade minestrone. The same thing about Virgil Darcy being in Glens Falls—either I mentioned it in Mother McDougle's or somebody else could have told him. Eddie Gillespie calls me and we talk. But what I don't see is why we don't just take this stuff to Peterson."

"Because we don't really have anything," said Charlie. "No hard facts. Reardon can just deny it. Nobody saw him in Albany, nobody saw him in Virgil Darcy's apartment building."

"But he had to talk to Darcy's buddy up in Glens Falls," said Victor. "And he must have talked to somebody in Albany. They could build a case. You just want to do it on your own, don't you? Same old Charlie. You didn't even tell anything to those Albany cops."

Charlie looked out at the street and didn't say anything. The cuts on his neck were almost healed but he could still feel them if he turned his head sharply. Victor made a left onto Caroline Street. Most of the bars seemed closed or empty. Mother McDougle's was up on the left just past the Turf Bar. The restaurant also seemed dark but then Charlie saw a light in back. Charlie again wondered how many of his smart ideas were just rationalizations, how many of his big decisions were spurred on by no more than an appetite for excitement.

"There's his car," said Victor. He pulled up to the curb behind the Toyota Celica and he and Charlie got out. Tucked in his belt, Skinner's big .45 jabbed Charlie in the ribs. They shut their car doors quietly.

"So how we going to do this?" asked Victor.

"You go up to the front and I'll try the back."

"And he's got a gun?"

"A shotgun and a revolver, my revolver."

"And all I got is a broken Motorola Flip Phone," said Victor. "Maybe I can shy it at him."

Charlie left Victor standing on the sidewalk and began making his way around the back along the black-topped driveway which led to the restaurant parking lot. Most of the windows were dark, just a glow from the bar area. There was no light over the driveway and Charlie had to move slowly. He kept thinking that this was the sort of behavior that Janey Burris disliked: his decision to go after Reardon alone instead of notifying the police. But maybe it was because of moments like this that he ever did anything at all: an adrenaline rush that left the daily world far behind, pounding heart, rubbery knees, emotional turbo drive. This is childish, thought Charlie. But even though he believed it was childish, he didn't go back and telephone Peterson. Hard grains of snow blew against Charlie's face. Over his sport coat he wore a dark-green raincoat, but he hadn't put in the winter lining yet and the wind blew through it.

There were no cars in the parking lot. A back porch was attached to the rear of the restaurant with two doors, one to the kitchen and one to a hall which led to the bar. There were also two windows which were covered with grates. Charlie stumbled on the steps and barely kept himself from falling. The only light came from a distant streetlight and a faint glow through the window of the door leading to the hall. The door to the kitchen was locked. The door to the hall was open. Charlie considered the unlikely possibility that it had been left open by accident, then he slowly turned the knob. The hall was warm and smelled of grease and spilled beer. He shut the door behind him and listened. From up ahead he could hear the muttering of voices. Charlie moved slowly down the hall, keeping his left hand on the wall and his right on the butt of the .45 stuck in his belt.

Charlie was tiptoeing about as quietly as he thought it was possible for a person to move, but about ten feet from the end of the hall, Victor called to him. "Hey, Charlie, Reardon's got a gun pointed at my head. He says if you don't come in here nicely with your hands up, he'll shoot me."

Charlie sighed. Slowly he raised his hands and moved forward. Maybe Janey was right after all, maybe he should consult with the police more often. Charlie stepped into the bar, which was lit by a single brass lamp with a green glass shade standing on the counter near the beer taps. The room was medium-sized with half a dozen tables. Reproductions of French Impressionist paintings hung in elaborate frames on the walls. Victor stood near the bar with Reardon right behind him. Reardon held Charlie's small .38 and had the barrel pushed up under Victor's jaw, making Victor raise his head at a sharp angle.

"Keep your hands up, Charlie, and turn around. You," he said to Victor, "move over against the wall."

Charlie felt Reardon move up behind him. The barrel of the .38 was pressed against his back as Reardon patted him down for a weapon. He withdrew the .45 from Charlie's belt and dropped it on the rug, where it fell with a thud. "Quite a six-gun, cowboy," said Reardon. Then he shoved Charlie violently toward Victor. "What'd you have to fuck with me for?" he shouted.

"He grabbed me right away, Charlie," said Victor.

"Shut up," said Reardon. His blue bowtie was untied and the strands hung down the front of his white shirt.

Charlie took his place next to Victor. Reardon stood about eight feet away. Skinner's .45 lay on the floor between them. No one else was in the restaurant.

"You made a real mess, Charlie," said Reardon. "You really got yourself a problem." Reardon was so mad that the words spat from his mouth. His face looked compressed somehow, pinched with anger. Charlie wondered how he had ever thought him handsome.

"If you give yourself up," said Charlie trying to speak calmly, "we'll forget this business with the revolver. You won't get charged with it. Otherwise you go to jail for a long time."

"Maybe I won't go to jail at all," said Reardon. "Maybe they won't find your bodies."

"That's an unpleasant thing to say," said Victor, wrinkling his nose.

"Shut up!"

"Other people will guess you killed Grace Mulholland," said Charlie. "You won't get away with anything." He took a step away from Victor to the right.

"Maybe not, but at least I'll have the pleasure of killing you." Again Reardon sputtered the words. The revolver shook in his hand. "You interfering little twerp, it's going to be nice to see your blood!"

Charlie considered Reardon's cordiality in the past week and how false it had obviously been. Then he tried to imagine his own obituary in the *Saratogian.* It wouldn't say anything nice. Furthermore Janey would be miserable and his mother would have to fly back from southern France. And then there was the wake for Maximum Tubbs. Charlie couldn't possibly allow himself to get killed. He didn't have time for it.

"You killed a woman," said Charlie.

Reardon pushed a hand through his blond hair. "She was stupid. She wanted too much."

"You got her to steal money."

"She was the one who told me about it, who said how easy it'd be. She'd have done anything for me. You think I wanted to be a waiter for the rest of my life?"

Charlie took another step away from Victor along the wall. A table and some chairs were a few feet to his right. "It was clever of you to make her like you. How long did it take?"

"Not long, a couple of weeks." Reardon seemed to calm down a little. "One night I went over to her house and refused to leave. I had some stuff I'd been writing in a journal about how much I liked her. It was really graphic. I told her I wanted her to see it. She kept telling me to leave but then she gave in. She broke down completely. We had sex that night. She was terrified and she loved it. I had a hard time not laughing."

"Why'd you kill her?" Charlie tried to keep his voice conversational, as if he found nothing uncommon about having a gun pointed at him. Reardon had lowered the revolver a little. My revolver, thought Charlie with irritation.

"She figured out I didn't want to run away with her and said she was going to the police. I hit her with something, a log from the fireplace. I was sick to death of her. She was too clingy and kept calling me up. I was sure my wife would find out."

Charlie took another step to the right. "How'd you know to put her in the cellar at Jacko's?"

"It was nearby. I mean, I hadn't really been planning to kill her but she started yelling that I didn't love her. I couldn't stand her noise."

"Was it hard to keep lying to me at the time?" asked Charlie. "You stayed pretty cool."

"You were a jerk. I only had to feed you a story and you swallowed it. I could have told you anything." A brandy snifter with some amber fluid stood on the bar. Reardon began to reach for it, then changed his mind.

"How'd you arrange that letter from Mexico?" asked Charlie. "That really tricked us." He moved a little more to the right. He didn't mind calling himself a jerk but he disliked other people doing it.

"I had friends down there. Don't move any more, Charlie! D'you think I'm stupid, that I can't see you? I'm sick of this talk!" Reardon took a step back and raised the pistol.

At that moment Victor's telephone began to ring: an insistent buzzing noise. Before Reardon could respond, Victor took the telephone from his pocket and flipped it open. "Hello?" He paused. Then he smiled and held out the phone to Reardon. "It's for you."

Reardon lowered the revolver and took a step forward. "What the—"

Reaching to his right Charlie grabbed a wooden chair and flung it at Reardon. In the same instant he dove for the revolver on the floor. He landed hard on his belly with his hands around the grip, then rolled over on his back with the revolver above him. Reardon had stumbled when the chair hit him. He recovered his balance and fired twice. Charlie felt a burning sensation in his left arm. Then he fired once, aiming back over his head at Reardon, who stood about ten feet away. The .45 made a huge noise, much louder than the smaller revolver. Reardon fell back against the wall, dropping the revolver and holding his belly. Blood poured from between his fingers. Charlie scrambled to his feet. He kicked the .38 away from Reardon, who was sliding down the wall, still holding on to his belly.

"Call the police and get an ambulance," Charlie told Victor.

Reardon was curled up on the floor. His face looked like crumpled paper and he made a wheezing noise. Charlie tried to tell himself that he felt bad about shooting him, then he began to worry that he didn't care. He didn't care if Reardon lived or died. Charlie could hear Victor talking excitedly on the phone. "Make it snappy," he kept saying, "make it snappy!" Charlie's arm was bleeding but the wound didn't seem serious. His stomach hurt from his swan dive onto the floor and he rubbed it.

Victor hung up. "They'll be here right away."

"Tell me," said Charlie, "was that call really for Reardon?"

Victor picked up his cellular phone from where he had dropped it. "I told you, Charlie. My phone's busted. It was just Eddie Gillespie trying to get through one more time."

22

Eddie Gillespie wiped fake maple syrup from his mouth and leaned back in the booth. He wore a clean white shirt with a hand-painted tie showing flamingos, palm trees and golf carts on a black silk ground. His tousled black hair sparkled with gel which made the curls resemble waves stalled at the moment of breaking. ''So what Charlie told me was he had some really exciting work and I said, 'How exciting?' I mean I'd been in bed for four days and I saw no reason to get out, ever. Irene was bringing me treats. I had her feeling so bad that she was talking about getting a waitressing job so she could start giving me money. Even the baby was being quiet.''

It was eight forty-five Tuesday morning and Eddie Gillespie and Victor were having breakfast at the Spa City Diner on Broadway on the south side of Saratoga. Victor wore a dove-gray suit, a dove-gray shirt and a dove-gray tie. In his lapel was a red carnation. He was nibbling at a bowl of hot oat bran, trying to be nice to his cholesterol because he planned to be bad to it later on.

''Charlie was gone all day Sunday, someplace up north,'' said Victor.

''Yeah, Wevertown, a pokey little place.'' When Eddie talked, he curled back his lips, showing his large white teeth. ''Well, I asked him what kind of excitement and he asked if I'd ever read *Tom Sawyer.* I didn't know what the fuck he was talking about. A book? I should read a bunch of lies written by some guy who couldn't get a real job? 'Caves,' Charlie said in a hushed voice. To tell the truth, I should have said no right there, but I don't know squat about caves, so I thought, Why not? And of course there was the hundred smackers lying right in front of me on my grandmother's holiday quilt and there was Charlie with his arm in a sling. I felt sorry for him. And Irene, I could see she already had that hundred bucks spent. So yeah, to make a long story short, I said yeah.''

''And he had some other guy?'' asked Victor, patting his lips with a napkin.

''That's right, a spelunker. I thought it was a communicable disease, but it turns out to be a guy who explores caves for a hobby. That's a new one, I thought. But then, after I visited one of those caves, I figured it was a disease after all. I mean, the guy loves crawling miles underground through gooey piles of bat shit. Tell me if that's not sick. And he was a nerdy little guy. Not enough sex is what I decided. Anyway, we drive up there.''

''Up where?''

''Wevertown, like I said, the three of us crowded into Charlie's little Mazda. It's like riding inside a sewing machine.'' Eddie took another bite of his pancakes and glanced out the window. It was snowing lightly and several cars on Broadway had their lights on.

''Anyway, Charlie's got this survey map and the spelunker's marked four places: caves. And there's another X, which was where some car was discovered in the woods a long time ago. So Charlie points to the X closest to where the car was found and says, 'We'll try that one first.'

''We get there and I'm glad I got my work clothes because it's cold and snowing and we have to walk about two miles through the woods. Charlie and the spelunker are both carrying big flashlights and that should have told me something about what lay ahead: no lights, no electricity. I was carrying a pick and shovel and that should have told me something too. In no time my feet are freezing but Charlie keeps saying how grateful he is that I came along and how much he owes me. You know how he can be: like honey on toast. So I keep my trap buttoned, which is not to say that a complaint doesn't pop out now and then, but nothin major.

"After a long time we reach a pile of rocks, a sort of hillside and the spelunker gets excited like a hound on the trail. He's got all this nerdy equipment like nylon ropes and all his clothes are Gore-Tex and he's got a miner's hardhat with a little light. It made me gag to see him but he was a harmless kind of guy. No sex, like I say. No sex, no drugs, no rock and roll. Anyway, he locates this rabbit hole and says proudly, 'Here's the entrance.' You know, Vic, maybe I'm slow on the uptake but I thought caves were bigger or at least their doorways were bigger but this seemed smaller than a manhole. And it's muddy. And it's dark. And it smells. Charlie is smiling and complimenting the spelunker and I'm wondering if he'd get mad if I snuck away. But where'd I go? Back to the car and wait? Well, while I'm thinking this, the spelunker dives down just like a rabbit and disappears into the hole. Then Charlie looks at me in such a way as to make me figure that he wants me to go next: nodding and smiling and trying to make me feel good."

"I usually like going with Charlie," said Victor, "but I'm glad he passed me up yesterday." He had a finger in his mouth checking out a filling that had worked loose.

"It was no treat." Gillespie shook his head and the glossy dark curls shimmied. A waitress refilled their coffee cups. The restaurant was crowded and there was the constant sound of plates banging together, conversation and laughter.

"So we crawl into this hole," continued Eddie, "and we go on our bellies for a while and we go on our knees for a while and there are some side tunnels and we explore those as well and some of the stones are dripping and soon my knees are pretty wet. And I ask Charlie, 'What're we looking for?' and he says, 'Rocks,' just like he might've said, 'Sugar candy.' Well, it seemed to me that we'd found nothing *but* rocks but they weren't the right ones, and after we'd spent an hour in that nasty hole, we climb back out and trudge another two miles through the woods to another hole, this one a little bigger. I complain and Charlie gives me a ham sandwich from his backpack and a slug of whiskey from his flask. We stand around yammering for a while and it turns out the spelunker is also a dentist. 'I'm into cavities,' he says. Believe me, it took an hour to realize he was making a joke.

"Well, the spelunker crawls into this cave and I follow him and again there are side tunnels and wells going down and chimneys going up and the rock in some places was a little loose so we have to be careful otherwise the whole thing would come down on top of us. Vic, I tell you, I hated it. Charlie says, 'I thought you wanted excitement.' And I say that being terrified is the wrong kind of excitement, because excitement is also supposed to be fun, which means basically not life-threatening. At that point we're in a side tunnel not far from the main entrance and the spelunker discovers still another side tunnel but after a few feet we find it's blocked with rocks.

"Both Charlie and the spelunker get excited and the spelunker starts digging with the pick. He'd done some digging before but it hadn't amounted to anything. This time, however, he's really eager and stones are flying every which way. I ask Charlie what's going on and he says the ceiling had fallen, which doesn't sound so great, although Charlie and the spelunker obviously think it is. Anyway the spelunker digs, then Charlie digs but has to quit because his arm starts bleeding again and so I start to dig and Charlie holds the light. And I feel about as low as I can feel but then I feel a lot worse because I'm the lucky guy who finds what Charlie's looking for and it scares the bejesus out of me."

"Find what?" asked Victor. The waitress paused to offer them more coffee, but neither Eddie nor Victor was interested.

"A hand or maybe just the skeleton of a hand with some meat attached and a couple of rings. Like that's what I'm good at these days, finding dead things. Believe me, it's a talent I could do without. Anyway, I jump and hit my head on the ceiling. The spelunker starts digging and discovers that the hand is attached to a wrist and the wrist is attached to an arm. Then he finds a pistol, a big .45 automatic. 'That's enough,' says Charlie, 'let's get the cops.' So we crawl back out although I'm almost in a panic with the thought of that dead guy behind me, like he might come creeping after me. We hurry back to the car and drive into Wevertown. Charlie lets me drink more whiskey and I start feeling better. 'Still excited?' he asks, being funny, you know. Charlie knows jokes like King Kong knew how to type. Then Charlie calls the state cops and the FBI. It's around eleven-thirty and by two o'clock we've got all the company you could ask for and they head back into the woods, but not me, I stay right there in Wevertown where it's warm and they got beer and I'm right too because Charlie and the others don't get back until about nine o'clock that night. Charlie looks dead on his feet but he's also about as happy as I've ever seen him, because he's found not just one dead guy but two."

"And who were these dead guys?" asked Victor.

"Frank Bonita and Joey Damasco, the guys that robbed the Marine Midland in Albany with Virgil Darcy. Charlie figured they'd never gone anyplace at all. They'd been buried just like Grace Mulholland had been buried, except these guys buried themselves. And when Charlie first went up to Wevertown he was looking for abandoned buildings but then he found out there were a bunch of caves. It looked like Bonita and Damasco had gone to one of these caves to hide out because they had food and candles and suitcases. But then they must have quarreled, so either Bonita shot Damasco or Damasco shot Bonita with that big .45 and it brought down the roof. They were both in there and the money was in there as well, over two hundred grand. The cops were tickled pink and Charlie got a lotta compliments of the tough-guy sort, like, Not bad, Bradshaw, and Good work, Bradshaw."

"He must have liked that," said Victor, grinning. Then he turned and looked around the restaurant. "He should be here any moment. It's after nine o'clock."

"Yeah, he wanted to talk to someone at Marine Midland about the reward money. And the wake starts at ten. I don't like getting shit-faced before noon. I start getting melancholy around four o'clock and have bad thoughts about myself. Maybe I should drink some olive oil to coat my stomach.''

''You don't need to get drunk.''

''I feel I owe it to Maximum Tubbs. Drunk and disorderly. And there're really going to be girls?''

''That's what Charlie says, and a roulette wheel.''

''Too bad old Tubbs couldn't have died once a month.''

Victor was considering this possibility when he saw Charlie and Janey Burris come through the front door of the diner. Charlie paused to shake the snow out of his hair. Then he noticed Eddie and Victor and waved. Janey took Charlie's arm as they approached the booth. Charlie was wearing a suit and tie, Janey had on a blue dress.

''So,'' said Victor, moving over to give them room in the booth, ''are you ten grand richer? I got a deck of cards.''

''Five grand,'' said Charlie, grinning, ''half goes to Virgil Darcy. After all, he told me about Wevertown.''

''And the other five will probably go to pay for all the extra people he invited to the wake,'' said Janey, shaking her head, then laughing. They had continued to stand. Charlie was resting his arm on Janey's shoulder.

Victor was struck by how happy they looked. ''And how's Vince Reardon?'' he asked.

''He'll live,'' said Charlie. ''Peterson's already talked to him. But that big gun sure put a hole in him.''

''You going to eat something?'' asked Victor.

''Not me,'' said Charlie. ''We've got to get over to the Canfield Casino. We have about fourteen hours of drinking and carousing ahead of us.''

''My kind of excitement,'' said Eddie Gillespie, licking his lips. ''Just don't tell my wife.'' He scrambled out of the booth. Victor got out more slowly and covered the check with a ten-dollar bill.

''Your wife's probably already there,'' said Janey. ''Charlie paid for a sitter.''

FOR THE BEST IN MYSTERY, LOOK FOR THE 

☐ THE PENGUIN COMPLETE FATHER BROWN
G.K. Chesterton

Here, in one volume, are forty-nine sensational cases investigated by the high priest of detective fiction, Father Brown, whose cherubic face and unworldly simplicity disguise an uncanny understanding of the criminal mind.
718 pages *ISBN: 0-14-009766-X*

☐ BRIARPATCH
Ross Thomas

This Edgar Award-winning thriller is the story of Benjamin Dill, who returns to the Sunbelt city of his youth to attend his sister's funeral—and find her killer.
384 pages *ISBN: 0-14-010581-6*

☐ APPLEBY AND THE OSPREYS
Michael Innes

When Lord Osprey is murdered in Clusters, his ancestral home, with an Oriental dagger, it falls to Sir John Appleby and Lord Osprey's faithful butler, Bagot, to pick out the clever killer from an assortment of the lord's eccentric house guests. *184 pages* *ISBN: 0-14-011092-5*

☐ GOLD BY GEMINI
Jonathan Gash

Lovejoy, the antiques dealer whom the *Chicago Sun-Times* calls "one of the most likable rogues in mystery history," searches for Roman gold coins and greedy bird-killers on the Isle of Man.
224 pages *ISBN: 0-451-82185-8*

☐ REILLY: ACE OF SPIES
Robin Bruce Lockhart

This is the incredible true story of superspy Sidney Reilly, said to be the inspiration for James Bond. Robin Bruce Lockhart's book tells the thrilling story of the British Secret Service agent's shadowy Russian past and near-legendary exploits in espionage and in love.
192 pages *ISBN: 0-14-006895-3*

☐ STRANGERS ON A TRAIN
Patricia Highsmith

Almost against his will, Guy Haines is trapped in a nightmare of shared guilt when he agrees to kill the father of the man who will kill Guy's wife. The basis for the unforgettable Hitchcock thriller.
256 pages *ISBN: 0-14-003796-9*

☐ THE THIN WOMAN
Dorothy Cannell

An interior designer who is also a passionate eater, her rented companion who writes trashy novels, and a rich dead uncle with a conditional will are the principals in this delicious thriller. *242 pages* *ISBN: 0-14-007947-5*